ALONE ON PASTURE RIDGE

ALONE ON PASTURE RIDGE

J. R. HIGHTOWER

ALONE ON PASTURE RIDGE

This is a work of fiction. All of the characters, names, incidents, organizations, and dialogue in this novel are either the products of the author's imagination or are used fictitiously.

iUniverse books may be ordered through booksellers or by contacting:

iUniverse
1663 Liberty Drive
Bloomington, IN 47403
www.iuniverse.com
1-800-Authors (1-800-288-4677)

ISBN: 978-1-5320-4048-1 (sc)
ISBN: 978-1-5320-4050-4 (hc)
ISBN: 978-1-5320-4049-8 (e)

Library of Congress Control Number: 2018903145

Print information available on the last page.

iUniverse rev. date: 06/22/2018

This story takes place in southern New Mexico in the late 1870s. The landscape and the landmarks are real, but the story and characters are fictional and are not related to any person living or dead.

To my grandson Gabe, for his patience and company,
and to my daughter and son-in-law, Suzette and Gene,
for providing the environment for this story to grow.

CHARACTERS

Robert "Rob" Wilson: Our hero and lead character
Dr. Simms: The East Texas doctor
Jessie Hatfield: Rob Wilson's sidekick, friend, and partner
John Wilson: Rob Wilson's uncle, the lawyer
The Duke of Dog Canyon: The coyote that adopts Rob
Juan Mórales: Paco's cousin in La Luz
Mr. Masterson: Operator of the La Luz gringo cantina
Paul Stephenson: Owner of the La Luz store
Paco Mórales: The Mexican cook
Turner Sutton: The rancher with the artesian well
Bill: McHenry: Tuner Sutton's friend and foreman
Wise Elk: The old Indian chief
Little Deer: The young Indian brave with Wise Elk
Jim Healy: The bully in Tularosa
Pepe Herrera: The twelve-year-old orphan from Tularosa
Emily Hernández: The beautiful girl from Tularosa
Ignacio Hernández: Emily's father
José the vaquero: Ignacio Hernández's foreman
Julio Rodriguez: The oldest brother from Tularosa
Marco Rodriguez: Julio's younger brother
Samuel Bloomberg: The El Paso banker
Mr. Dell: The El Paso cantina operator
Juanita Rodríguez: Emily's friend and Julio and Marco's sister
Mama Garcia: The boardinghouse proprietor
Jedidiah Dell: The trading post operator
Levi Stephenson: The El Paso storekeeper and Paul's twin brother
Martha Stephenson: Levi's wife
John Henry Adams: The barber in El Paso
Art: The newspaperman in El Paso
Mrs. John Henry Adams: John Henry's wife
Jimmy Lee Jackson: The young rustler
Father Ryan: The La Luz padre
Dr. Esteban Chávez: The doctor from Tularosa
Dr. Paul Peterson: The new La Luz doctor

CONTENTS

Chapter 1

THE END AND A NEW BEGINNING

Rob had been sure his little sister, would get better. Sally had rallied and appeared to have improved … until that morning when Rob found Sally dead in her bloody bed. The glazed, unseeing look in her open eyes told him she was gone.

Six weeks before, Rob's daddy returned from buying cattle in Del Rio. A week after he got home, he came down sick. Rob's mama and sister had nursed his daddy, and in just over a week, both of them got sick. His daddy died three weeks after he returned home. Rob's mama died two weeks after his daddy. And now Sally was gone.

Before Dr. Simms left for the last time, he turned, put his hand on Rob's shoulder, and said, "Robert, typhoid fever is caused by tiny things called germs. You must burn the clothes, bedding, towels, rags, and anything else soft your family touched. Those things are contaminated. Anything you want to save, you must wash with whiskey and then heat as hot as it will stand. When this is over, you must burn the house to the ground, burn the outhouse to the ground, cover the outhouse hole with lime, and fill it with dirt. Robert, do you understand?"

"Yes, Doctor … I understand … I promise."

The next morning, Rob got up early, had coffee, and picked at his breakfast. He was in front of the house, searching for anything else he could do. He had a small fire to boil water and a bigger one to burn the contaminated items. He was trying not to breathe in the smoke. Rob walked inside to look for other items he needed to burn. He was devastated. After looking around inside, he ran outside, stood in the front yard, shook his fist up at God, and screamed, "Why, Lord? Why them and not me?" He collapsed, crying like a baby. That's how his closest friend found him. Jessie Hatfield rode up, stepped off his horse, and put his hand on Rob's shoulder until he stopped sobbing.

Before this, Rob had been a teenage boy laughing and getting into mischief. He followed his daddy's orders close enough to stay out of the woodshed but had lots of fun. Jessie was two years older than Rob. He and Rob became friends while they were on those long rides behind the cattle and going to town to pick up supplies for Rob's mama. The boys talked of what they intended to do with their lives. They talked of the girls they wanted to court and the huge ranches they intended to build. They bragged about the fast horses they would breed and race at the Fourth of July celebrations and the county fairs.

But now Jessie Hatfield was on the hill behind the house, digging another grave. Rob wrapped his little sister in a clean quilt and carried her to Jessie's side. They had placed her grave next to her mama and daddy's. When it was ready, they lowered her into it. Rob was vaguely aware of Jessie reading from the family Bible.

After a few minutes of silence, Jessie touched him on the shoulder and said, "Let's get it done, Rob."

"Gimme that Bible." Rob threw the Bible in the grave with his little sister, and they covered it and her with dirt. Rob covered the grave with river rocks while Jessie fashioned a white cross with pickets from the yard fence. Jessie handed the cross to Rob, and he placed it on the grave. Then they shored it up with more river rocks.

Rob looked around as they walked back to the house. The Wilson ranch was a nice place. It had a creek running through it, good grass, a good remuda, and a big herd of cattle. Besides the cattle his daddy bought in Del Rio, there was the herd they owned before the trip. Rob looked at the barn with the large, round, horse-high, bull-strong corral. There were horses, mules, two milk cows, hand tools, saddles and tack, a wagon, and a buckboard. The ranch had a plow, a hay rake, and other farm implements and tools. There was enough tack and harness to run a ranch with a good hay field and a big garden.

"Jessie, come on. Let's go find out what I have left." In the house, Rob looked in the cupboard and opened the Mason jar where they kept coffee. He had eighty-two cents. He dumped the coins in a pan and poured whiskey over them.

"Daddy took all our cash money to go buy cattle." Rob realized he had to grow up and take control of his life. Everywhere he looked, something reminded him of the pain.

"I can't try to replace Daddy on this place. Everything I look at reminds me of Mama … or Daddy … or Sally." Rob knew he could not stay there any longer. He said, "Will you help me gather my stuff from the house and take it to the bunkhouse? Jessie, go in the kitchen and pack what tools and things we need to camp, cook, and eat."

In his room, Rob changed into a clean pale blue store-bought button-up shirt. The bought off-the-shelf shirts came in one sleeve length: long. Rob put on his sleeve garters to hold up his sleeves. He put on clean pants. They were a nondescript, common variety. Rob pulled up his leather suspenders, put on clean socks, smoothed his pant legs, and folded his pant legs over to fit inside his boots. He pulled on his high-heeled boots, stood up, and stomped his feet. His scuffed boots were still serviceable and very comfortable. He put on his leather vest and strapped on plain steel spurs with small, tinkling rowels.

Rob was a handsome young man of nineteen. He was six feet tall, and his chestnut-brown hair was cut short. His blue eyes varied from the deep blue of the western sky when he was happy to icy steel blue when he was upset.

Rob walked into his mama and daddy's room and picked up his daddy's gun rig. He took it to the kitchen, washed it with whiskey, and put on the gun belt. The gun rig for the short gun was a polished brown leather belt with bullet loops all the way around his narrow waist. A matching holster cradled a gleaming blue-black Colt .45 and hung from the belt on his right hip. His daddy's short gun rig was one of the few family items Rob kept.

Rob returned to his room; took shirts, socks, long johns, and his other pair of clean pants; stuffed them in a flour sack; and tied it shut with a string. He put on his dark gray felt hat with the black leather hatband, which ended in thongs that dropped through holes in the wide brim. The tied thongs streamed down over his shirt collar in back. If the wind threatened to blow his hat off, they could be flipped under his chin and pulled tight with the silver slide his mama had given him for Christmas. He draped his coat over the arm that held the sack, picked up his saddle gun, and walked out to the porch. He took his flour sack, rifle, and coat to the bunkhouse. Jessie followed along, carrying another pair of sacks filled with the coffeepot, a Dutch oven, an iron skillet, cups, plates, and flatware. Jessie had carefully washed the items with whiskey. He filled the Dutch oven and the skillet with supplies and staples and then tied the bags shut with twine.

Jessie was not as tall as Rob and was heavier. He had black hair and gray eyes. His clothes were much like Rob's, but his light gray felt hat was well broken in. As he walked to the bunkhouse, his spurs with the big Mexican rowels made a pleasant little jingle. Jessie's short gun rode on his left hip in a black holster and belt with bullet loops around his waist.

After stashing the sacks in the bunkhouse, Rob sloshed coal oil on the big house and fired it. He took the rest of the coal oil, poured it on the outhouse, and set it ablaze.

Rob and Jessie stood back and guarded the surroundings while the buildings burned. Rob remembered the good times with his family. He turned around, retched, and lost his breakfast.

After Rob regained control, he drew a bucket of water from the cistern, rinsed out his mouth, washed his face, and said, "I'm going to sell this place. Let's go talk to my uncle John, the lawyer. I'll make arrangements to sell the ranch with the stock and everything we can't carry away."

That surprised Jessie. He said, "Rob, do you realize you will have to start over from scratch? At least here you have a fully outfitted ranch with a bunkhouse, a good barn, and a corral."

"Yes, but if I sell it and go somewhere else, I can get away from the pain. I just don't want to hurt anymore."

Jessie's parents had died, and he considered telling Rob the hurt would not go away but fade with time. Jessie realized he could say nothing to soften the immediate hurt. If that was what his friend wanted to do, he would try to help him do it.

They rode to town to talk to Rob's uncle. When they reached the uncle's house, Rob said, "I found Sally dead in her bed this morning." He collapsed and cried. After he regained control of himself, he and the family went through hugs and commiserations. He told the story of burying Sally and of burning the house and the outhouse.

When things settled down, Rob took his uncle outside and said, "Uncle John, I can't stand it anymore. I want to sell the ranch, including all the stock—except for my horse and a packhorse—and go someplace and find a new start."

John Wilson had lost his brother when Rob's daddy died, so he was familiar with the pain Rob was experiencing. After trying to talk Rob out of selling the ranch, John gave up and agreed to help.

It took only two days to find a fair-price buyer for the ranch. Uncle John drew up the papers and rode to the courthouse to talk to the judge. He wanted Rob to sign the deed and bill of sale to clarify that selling the ranch was what Rob wanted to do. He needed approval for Rob, a minor, to sign the deed and a bill of sale.

When Uncle John got back from the judge's office, he said, "The judge approved of you signing the papers. But only if I cosign them as executor of your mama and daddy's estate."

Rob showed unusual wisdom for his age when he said, "Give me five hundred dollars in gold, and put the rest of the money in the bank for me. I will draw on it when I find my new start."

Jessie and Rob talked for hours about the possible location of the "new start." Rob talked to his uncle, the banker, and others. Sadly, all that talking was no help. Everybody thought they should go in a different direction. Only Jessie was thinking the same direction as Rob.

Chapter 2

THE NEW START

Rob and Jessie agreed they should go to New Mexico. A Mexican wrangler from New Mexico worked on the Wilson Ranch. When they finished the chores in the evening, the boys practiced their fast draw, bragged about the bandits they would track down, and listened to the wrangler talk about New Mexico. The New Mexico desert landscape differed from the woods and valleys of East Texas. The culture was unlike what they were familiar with, the people were different, and they didn't know a soul in New Mexico.

After traveling over two weeks and riding into southern New Mexico from East Texas, Rob and Jessie were looking out over the Tularosa Basin. They were at the top of what they would learn was the Otero Mesa rim.

Rob said, "What a beautiful place."

Jessie looked at the Great White Sands and said, "Yep, it sure is, but what's all that white stuff? That looks like a snow-covered desert that goes on for miles."

"I don't know. It's too warm to be snow, but it sure is pretty."

They worked their way down about five hundred feet on the west face of the rim into the desert and turned north. They came to an almost flat alluvial fan below the mouth of a huge canyon that was more than four miles wide.

"Jessie, this is a good ranch location ... if there's water."

"That's what I was thinking. Trees would be nice."

They rode on north. By midday, they passed the mouth of a triple box canyon.

Rob pointed at the canyons. "There's a good place to secure a herd. There's plenty of room, and there's enough grass on the north slopes to keep a herd for a while."

"All you need is water."

They rode up to the edge of a big arroyo. The arroyo was twelve to fifteen feet deep and ranged in width from one hundred to two hundred feet. The sides were almost vertical walls. They sat and studied it.

Rob said, "We could build two sides and have a corral, the other two are already here."

"Yeah, but what'd we build 'em out of? There ain't no trees."

Rob said, "There was mesquite, growing in the red sand dunes a ways back. The south faces of the foothills have ocotillo we could use for a barrier fence."

"Yeah, we could build a corral there in the narrows with a lot less work, but there ain't no trees."

Rob said, "Trees are not everything. I remember some of the mesquite was of fair size. I'm sure they are big enough for fence posts."

Riding on north to the mouth of a long, narrow, deep canyon, they looked for water.

Rob said, "Along the west face of these mountains, there must be creeks or streams—or at least springs. There has to be water in this canyon, in that big triple-box canyon, and in that first huge canyon. There should be a spring under some of the overhangs, but they are up high and hard to reach."

"Rob, if a spring is there, it can't spring much or water would be running down the mountain under the overhang."

Rob said, "You are right, Jessie. I was just thinking about where there should be water."

They were at the base of a beautiful, long, narrow, canyon. Rob looked around and noticed how many deer tracks there were. "We need meat. If you'll gather firewood and make camp, I'll see about finding us something to eat. I wonder if those are tracks of immense whitetail deer or from some of the big Rocky Mountain mule deer we heard about back in Texas? I'm going to see."

Rob rode south and then turned east along the edge of the big arroyo that had originated in the box canyon south of their camp. He rode east so the sun would be at his back. He had gone less than two hundred yards when three deer stood up at what Rob judged to be about seventy-five yards. All were bucks with antlers in velvet. They had been bedded down in the shade under the south edge of the arroyo. Rob shucked his saddle gun and shot the younger buck.

Rob was proud of his saddle gun. With part of the proceeds of the sale of the family property in Texas, he had purchased a brace of the new Winchester '73 model carbines. He had presented one to Jessie, who had been overwhelmed. Jessie had never owned anything that fine.

Rob sat and observed the downed deer for a full minute to make sure it stayed down. Once satisfied, he rode toward it. As he approached the deer, he realized the distance was well over one hundred yards. When he got to it, it was huge by East Texas standards. That yearling buck must have weighed two hundred pounds after Rob field dressed it. By the time he had the deer loaded on his horse and walked back to camp, Jessie had camp set up, a fire going, and coffee made.

Jessie heard Rob and his horse walking into camp. Without looking up, he said, "I've been wondering where we will get more water."

When he looked up, he said, "Gawd damn. That's the biggest deer I ever saw."

Rob said, "We don't have a shelter where we can hang the meat. I'll go cut some of those big agave stalks from that group of plants that bloomed last year. We can tie six or seven of those fifteen-footers in a teepee shape with a piece of rope and hang the deer from the apex."

Jessie said, "I'll get a piece of tarp from the packhorse outfit and cover the stalks to shade the deer. I'll wrap it around the stalks and tie it on with string. That'll keep the sun off and still let air circulate 'tween the deer and tarp. I think it will keep okay." It was late spring, and the boys knew from their cattle-driving experiences that the desert nights got cool—sometimes even cold—and the deer would cool out and keep in the shade of the tarp.

They got the deer hung in the agave stalk teepee. Rob said, "I cut off the hind legs at the knee so the critters can't reach the deer. How hungry are you. Can you get by if I cut six or eight pounds of venison round steak for dinner and still leave enough leftovers for breakfast?" He laughed.

Jessie snorted. He had whipped up a batch of sourdough biscuits using the starter he kept in an oilcloth pouch inside his shirt. His mama gave him a part of her starter back in Texas. He guarded that starter with his life, being sure to feed it every time he took a start and added a few drops of water before it got dry.

They broiled the venison over the fire and cooked the biscuits in a Dutch oven. What a feed they had. They hadn't eaten since coffee and leftover biscuits at breakfast.

The aroma from their cooking did not go unnoticed. Rob looked up to see a big he-dog coyote looking at them from the top of the arroyo. The coyote did not seem to be afraid. He just stood there watching them. Jessie talked to the coyote. Rob trimmed off a few scraps from the deer carcass and tossed them toward the coyote. The coyote was too timid to get the meat, but he didn't run either.

Rob said, "How strange. He's not afraid of anything. He acts like he owns this area. I will call him the duke of our canyon."

While they ate, Rob looked up and admired the mountains. He realized how big they were. They were not like the little hilly mountains back in Texas. These were the southeast corner of the great Rocky Mountains.

Rob said, "Look … the vegetation changes halfway up the mountain face to more brush. Higher up, there's piñon and juniper trees. On the top ridge, above the head of the canyon, tall long-leaf pines grow."

Jessie had his mouth full but looked up and nodded

Rob said, "How high do you think those mountains are? I've seen nothing like these mountains."

"Me neither." Jessie wiped his mouth with the back of his hand.

They tried to estimate how high the mountains were. After a lengthy discussion they agreed the mountaintops must be half a mile higher than the camp. Rob and Jessie had no experience to draw on to estimate the altitude differential. They only got it half right because the tops of the Sacramento Mountains were a full mile higher than the basin.

While they ate supper, Rob found an arrowhead on the ground under his feet. "Look at this. The last rain exposed it." He pointed the arrowhead out to Jessie. They both looked around, realizing they might be in country inhabited by hostile Indians. That got their attention and made them uncomfortable.

After sundown, in the dark before the moon came up, Rob said, "I see light or fire reflecting from the clouds in the north." He marked the direction of the light on the cloud with a dried ocotillo stick. "You notice that light out in the middle of the basin … just south of the white stuff?"

"Yeah, I did. You think they're friendlies?"

"I hope so, 'cause if we can see them, they can see us. We better check on it."

Rob and Jessie bedded down after supper. Before long, Duke slipped in to eat. After eating the meat, he trotted back up the arroyo. He drank from a small water-filled pothole and curled up to sleep.

As the sky over the mountains began turning gray, Rob woke up. Jessie had already stoked up the fire and had the coffee on to boil. They munched on leftover biscuits and venison and washed it down with hot coffee as the sun flooded the eastern sky in a blaze of yellow, orange, and gold.

As they ate, they looked out over the basin. They were in the shadow of the Sacramento Mountains. They watched as the sunlight touched the top of the San Andreas and Organ Mountains on the western horizon. As the sun rose over the mountains in the east, the sunlight rolled down the face of the western mountains, walked across the desert, and hit the brilliance of the sparkling white sand.

After the sun came up, Rob said, "The ocotillo stick I set last night points due north, along the western edge of the mountains."

Rob noticed the coyote standing on the edge of his arroyo. He trimmed off more scraps of the venison and tossed them in the coyote's direction.

The coyote knew what had happened. He also knew he could not wait until dark to go get his prize. The other desert creatures would have it before sundown. He was happy when Rob and Jessie saddled up, gathered their belongings, mounted up, and rode north.

Duke found the scraps but seemed aggravated that they had pulled the deer up so high on the century plant stalks. He couldn't reach it, but he thought they might come back and stayed. Duke picked up one of the lower hind legs that Rob had cut off at the knee. He ambled over to the shade under a greasewood and gnawed on the bones.

Traveling was difficult because of the arroyos coming from the mountain canyons.

Rob said, "This may look like a desert, but it rains here—and sometimes it rains a lot. When it rains, the water has to come roaring out of these mountains to cut these canyons and huge arroyos."

"You're right … and look at those giant boulders it pushed down the canyons. We better be careful where we locate our headquarters. We don't want one of those giants rolling into our kitchen."

Rob laughed and said, "You're just scared your dinner might be late."

Jessie looked at Rob and puffed up. After he thought about it, he relaxed and grinned.

About an hour and a half north of the camp, they came to a huge canyon with a permanent stream flowing from it. Rob said, "Look how the erosion formed this giant alluvial fan at the canyon's mouth and kept it flowing two miles out into the desert."

When they reached the top of the big alluvial fan, they could see six or seven miles north.

Jessie said, "Look. There's a settlement with lots of big trees and a good deal of vegetation."

Rob said, "That must be where the light came from that illuminated the clouds last night."

An hour later, they rode up to a village. The canyon above the village had a good permanent stream, judging from the big cottonwood and willow trees.

Jessie said, "The residents have dug irrigation ditches to channel water into the village for their own use. Look at the big bushes and trees they have."

Rob said, "Yeah, I see fruit trees, pecan trees, fig bushes, grapevines, and vegetable gardens."

"Yes, sir—and smell those mouthwatering aromas coming from the kitchens already."

At the village edge, they came upon an old Mexican man tending a herd of goats. Jessie asked, "Sir, what's the name of this town?"

The old man said, "The village is called La Luz, and there is a cantina that serves bacon and eggs." He pointed north.

"I didn't ask about bacon and eggs, but that is an idea."

They thanked the old man, tipped their hats, rode into the village, and walked into the cantina. They sat down and ordered frijoles with bacon, eggs dirty on both sides (over easy), tortillas, and hot coffee.

After they had eaten, Rob said to the innkeeper, "We're new here. My name is Robert Wilson, and this is Jessie Hatfield. We're looking to start a new ranch. Is there any ranch land available around here?"

The innkeeper put out his hand and said, "Hello, Mr. Wilson and Mr. Hatfield. My name's Masterson." After they all shook hands, he said, "Hummm ... well, ya had the courtesy ta ask rather an' just squattin' on a place, so I'm a goin' a tell ya, but let me get us a beer first."

When Masterson got back with three mugs of beer, Rob said, "We appreciate this, Mr. Masterson."

As they drank their cold beer, Masterson said, "Most all the range 'round here's spoken fer. The water's been claimed, an' even though 'tis open range, all the range ' round water is took up. If ya try ta claim land here, ya fer sure gonna have trouble with the ranchers and farmers 'at come afore ya."

Rob sipped his beer and said, "What about down south of here? We saw nobody ranching down there. If we could find water, the grass looks good."

"Aye ... that it is. If ya go south of Alamo Canyon, that's the big canyon with the big cottonwoods and the grapevines and the creek, 'bout five miles south o' here, I don't know of nobody ranchin' 'tween there and the old rock pi'tures in the Jarilla Mountains. Maybe to the Texas line."

Masterson took a pull of his beer, scratched his chin, and said, "As fer water, there's perm'nent water in Alamo Canyon. Alamo is cottonwood in Spanish, an' there's a few springs along the mountain, but the next year-round water is Dog Canyon, 'bout ten miles south of there." He looked the two young men over and added, "The tricky part is a gonna be that ya got 'a be tough 'nough to hold on to the water rights, the range 'round the water goes with 'em."

Rob said, "We saw the canyon with the big cottonwoods coming here, Alamo Canyon you say. We are camped on a spring about ten miles south of it,"

Jessie asked, "What about Indians there? Are they hostile? We found this arrowhead?"

Looking at the arrowhead, Masterson said, "'At'll be Dog Canyon. 'Iss arrowhead might be from las' week or a thousan' year' ago. Flint don't show its age. 'Em Indians been there way over a thousan' year'." After a pause and a drink of beer, he continued, "Ya might have some trouble with a few, but mostly they'll treat ya like ya treat them. Share the water an' treat 'em with respect, and ya'll not have much trouble. Once't in a while, some Mescalero 'Paches may come by an' some young buck may take afence ta yer presence. Try not to start a blood feud with 'em. Don't look weak jus' peaceable."

They were respectful to their host, using the manners that their daddies had hammered into them when they were younger. The host and his family thought they were very pleasant ... for gringos. Rob thanked Masterson for the information, complimented the cooking, and they tipped their hats to the women. Jessie left a few extra coins on the table for the server and the cook. The young men made a positive impression that would serve them well.

They found a general store, stepped down and walked in. The storekeeper greeted them with a friendly smile and a nod. "I'm Paul Stephenson. What can I do for you?"

Rob said, "It's good to meet you, sir. My name is Rob Wilson, and this is Jessie Hatfield."

Rob bought coffee, bacon, and pinto beans, which were also known as frijoles. Jessie splurged and bought two pounds of sugar and some dried apples.

Back at Dog Canyon, Duke had a good breakfast and another drink. He was lazing in the sun and trying to figure out how to get at that deer. He had chased off the fox and herded it up the canyon, being careful not to get too close because he did not feel like fighting. Duke carefully guided the skunk family up the canyon toward the spring. He sure didn't want a skunk fight.

Duke investigated the scents around the camp. He did not like smelling the coffee grounds or the stink of fire, but the ground where his man had slept smelled good. He noticed the riders far off to the north and slunk back into the bushes to watch. From across the arroyo, he watched a golden eagle, which had been circling, land on top of the teepee. That deer meat smelled good, and the eagle was trying to get to the meat under the tarp.

As Rob and Jessie rode up, the golden eagle flew away. Duke was back in the bushes on the arroyo rim.

Jessie pointed out the tracks on the ground and said, "Your coyote had lots of company today."

Rob scanned the ground and said, "Mr. Fox and a skunk family came visiting. I sure am glad that coyote didn't attack the skunks. A covey of quail passed right through our camp, too."

They inspected the teepee.

Jessie said, "That damned eagle that flew away when we rode up was on top of the teepee and left two sizable deposits running down the tarp."

Jessie had put a pot of beans to soak before they left that morning. He rinsed the beans in fresh water, seasoned them, and hung the covered pot over the fire. "There's several hours left before sundown. Let's go exploring."

They rode around the base of the mountain and into the mouth of the canyon toward trees and lush vegetation. The canyon was a virtual rock box with only the bottom end open to the west. Its alluvial fan stretched over a mile into the desert. The fan sloped up about two hundred feet higher than the desert floor. About fifty feet above the alluvial fan and one hundred yards into the mouth of the canyon was the source of the lush vegetation: a spring. Below it was a sizable pool. Coyotes, birds, and other critters had been drinking there. The water ran down the canyon and disappeared into the desert.

Rob and Jessie worked to clean out the spring and the pool. Rob said, "Look how the storm water pours down the canyon a few yards north."

"Yeah, it has dug another arroyo that runs off into the desert to the northwest and disappears."

They rode a wide circle but got back to their camp in time for Jessie to stir up more sourdough biscuits and add water to the beans.

They did not understand that camping at an altitude of 4,500 feet meant that water boiled at a lower temperature. Jessie said, "It sure takes beans a lot longer to cook here than back home."

Before long, the bread began to brown in the Dutch oven. The simmering beans smelled wonderful. It amazed Rob how Jessie had salt, pepper, chili powder, cumin, garlic, and other spices somewhere on their packhorse where he kept coffee, bacon, beans and flour.

They cut the thighbone off the deer and set it on the edge of the fireplace. Before sundown, they had beans, biscuits, and venison.

Jessie said, "I'll crack open this bone, and we will have an extra treat—marrow butter for our biscuits."

After they ate, they drank coffee and watched the magnificent New Mexico sunset, while looking for any sign of life out in the basin. They saw no movement, but as the daylight faded, Rob said, "There's that one light or campfire—same place as last night." Rob marked the direction of that light with his ocotillo stick.

On the south side of the arroyo, Duke spoke to the stars. Rob cut off more deer meat and tossed it toward where the coyote had been.

Rob poured more coffee for them both and sat down on his saddle. "We need to ride out to the west and find that camp or ranch … or possibly an Indian camp, whatever it is. It's only about ten miles."

Jessie nodded, sipped his coffee, and picked his teeth.

As they finished scrubbing their plates with sand and wiping them clean with a flour sack, there was a ruckus south of the arroyo. Duke and Mr. Fox were at it, growling, snarling, and fighting. After a bit more rustling in the bushes, it went quiet.

The two cowboys laughed at the squabble, rolled out their bedrolls, and bedded down for the night.

"Night, Rob."

"Good night, Jessie."

Chapter 3

A New Friendship

In the morning, Rob quietly walked south. He saw where Duke chased the fox and then patrolled the area where Rob had thrown the meat. He did not know how much meat the fox ate but decided it wasn't much. Duke had claimed the area and established ownership.

After coffee, leftover biscuits, and venison, Rob and Jessie saddled up and inspected the area around the camp. About midday, Rob noticed dust far off in the south. They continued to ride, admiring the spring grass, the green ocotillo leaves and blooms, and the beauty of the other cactus flowers.

Rob saw that the dust kept getting closer and said, "I'm going up on the hill to see if I can figure out who's coming."

"Okay. While you're gone, I'll straighten up camp and see if I can find somethin' for supper to go with that venison."

Rob climbed the first foothill. It was a steep but easy climb, and when he reached the top, he looked around the canyon. He saw a trail going up past the first foothill. It weaved its way up all the way to the bottom of the giant cliff that enclosed the canyon. Then the trail followed the bottom of the cliff around the canyon to the smaller canyon on the north side and disappeared into the trees.

Rob sat on the first foothill, watching the dust. After half an hour, he saw a wagon with horses following. After a while longer, Rob made out, it was only one horse following the wagon. It was nothing to worry about. He worked his way back down, mounted his horse, and rode back to camp.

Jessie found tubers in the red sand under the long blades of thin dark green shoots and a bunch of wild onions. He didn't recognize the tubers, but they looked and tasted good. He saw where one of the creatures of the desert dug up one and ate most of it so he knew they were not poisonous.

When Rob got back to camp, he said, "Mount up and let's go see whose coming."

Rob knew a wagon could not travel north and south close to the mountain because of the deep arroyos. It had to go farther west, out in the basin, to get on passable ground. Rob and Jessie rode a mile or so west, found the trail, and waited. Shortly, they watched an old but well-kept chuck wagon pulled by four mules and trailed by one horse. An old Mexican man wearing a white cotton shirt and pants was driving. He adjusted the red sash or scarf he wore in place of a belt and pushed up the front of his big straw sombrero. The old man looked like any Northern Mexican except, when he stuck out his foot to mash the brake, in place of leather sandals, he wore boots with medium-high heels. He pulled up and sat still and quiet.

Rob said, "Howdy. I'm Robert Wilson. This here is Jessie Hatfield."

The old man nodded at Jessie and said, "Señor Wilson, my name is Paco Mórales"

"Well, Mr. Mórales, what brings you to this basin?"

"Señor Wilson, I was the cook for a big trail herd going to Santa Fe from East Texas. The trail boss decided to go on west and go up the Rio Grande Valley so we would have fresh water all the way. It does not rain much until the Indians dance for rain after the summer solstice."

Jessie said, "Why are you here by yourself now?"

Paco said, "We were crossing West Texas and eight nights ago in the middle of the night, we had a terrible thunderstorm with mucho lightning. It stampeded the cattle and the remuda too. I was lucky. They ran the other direction and did not trample the chuck wagon and Paco."

Rob said, "Sorry to hear that, Mr. Mórales. Where are the others?"

"Señor, the stampede killed the trail boss, the foreman, and two drovers. The drive broke up because the cattle and horses scattered all over. Most of the drovers were shiftless no accounts, and after the last dozen wandered off, I buried the boss and the others. Then, I decided I would ride to La Luz and see my cousin. My cousin's name is Juan Mórales. I am on my way there now."

"Wow! It must have been a big herd to have so many drovers."

"Si, señor. It was more than three thousand head of cattle. Señor Wilson, what are you doing here at Canyon d Perro?"

Rob said, "Canyon d Perro? I didn't know that was the name of our canyon."

"Si, señor. It is named after the giant prairie dog town. You must ride with care west of here so your horse does not step in a prairie dog hole and break the leg."

Rob said, "We rode to La Luz yesterday. What is your cousin's name again?"

Paco got excited and said, "His name is Juan Mórales. Did you meet him?"

"No. I don't think so. We only met the innkeeper, Mr. Masterson, at the cantina and the storekeeper." Rob said.

Paco said, "That must have been Señor Paul Stephenson's store."

Rob said, "Yes, that was his name. What will you do after you visit with your cousin, Mr. Mórales?"

"Señor Wilson, please call me Paco."

"Okay, Paco. You can call me Rob."

"And I'm Jessie."

"Bueno, Señor Rob and Señor Jessie. I'm looking for a new outfit to cook for. Do you know of any outfit that needs a cook?"

Rob liked the looks and feel of this Paco Morales. He was old but clean. The chuck wagon was well-maintained, clean, and his animals were well kept. "We need a cook and somebody to help around the camp now and around the house when it's built, but we don't even have a herd yet. We are looking to set up a ranch on this open range. Right now, we are only two—and my friend Duke, the coyote." Laughing, he waved off toward the arroyo.

Paco said, "A coyote is your friend?"

"Well, I throw out meat at night, and it's gone in the morning. I guess we are friends. I saw him clearly just once. He is a big he-dog. This morning, the meat I threw him before the fight was gone and his tracks are all around."

"What fight, señor?"

Rob told him about hearing the coyote and the fox fighting and about the fox, the skunks, and all the tracks.

Paco realized this gringo must be special. Coyotes did not take up with most men. Most gringos shoot coyotes and do not throw meat to them. The animals are well cared for, his horse is clean, and his tack is neat and well kept.

"Señor Rob, if you and Señor Jessie will have me, Paco will cook for you, keep your camp, and then keep your house when it is built."

Seeing the agreeable nod from Jessie, Rob said, "Okay, Paco. We can't pay much now, but you can be a part of our new venture."

Thus, they made the deal. Both sides based their feelings about the other on their observations, and both sides felt comfortable with the arrangement.

"Señors, we need to move a little closer to the mouth of the canyon. There is always water there."

Rob asked, "How do you know, Paco?"

"Señor, it is known that for hundreds of years, Canyon d Perro or Dog Canyon, as it is known by the gringos, has been a pathway from the desert floor to the high-up mountains. First the old ones, then the Apaches, both Mescalero and Chiricahua, then the cavalry chase the Apaches up the eyebrow trail then back down the canyon. It has served as a stopover place for generations. From the canyon mouth, you can see far into the basin, so nobody can sneak up on you. If they come down the canyon, you can hear the horses. If a man on foot comes down the eyebrow trail, loose rocks will fall down—and you can hear them fall."

Jessie said, "Paco, you are a wealth of information. Let's pack up and move camp to the spring in the canyon mouth. Lead the way, Paco."

"No, Señor Jessie. We must camp a little away from the spring so that Duke the coyote and his friends have a place to drink. In the very dry times, even the mule deer must drink there."

Paco and Jessie were setting up camp a little way from the spring. Jessie gave Paco the wild onions, the tubers, the sugar, and the dried apples.

Paco was thrilled and said, "Tonight, we will have a feast: roasted venison, frijoles con onions, baked tubers, biscuits, and a special treat."

Paco rehydrated the dried apples and added butter, sugar, cinnamon, and a pinch of salt. He lined the Dutch oven with a piecrust of flour, lard, water, and salt. He put the apple mixture in the crust, covered it with another layer of crust, and crimped the edge all the way around. With a small knife, he cut six small slits about two inches from the center and placed the cover on the Dutch oven. He lovingly placed the Dutch oven with the pie and another with the biscuits in the coals of the fire and put more live coals on top.

Rob rode around the canyon and saw that a good bit of piñon and juniper firewood had washed down the canyon in flash floods. He also looked at the ocotillo and cholla wood. Rob knew the dry, hard skeleton of ocotillo and cholla made a very hot, smokeless, fast-burning fire and would make a good cook fire. He looked out over the red sand dunes and knew they had mesquite growing in them. Rob remembered how gathering mesquite wood was very hard work, but it made strong, long-lasting fence posts and was great firewood that required little or no curing. When Rob turned back west, he saw a flash of an animal in the arroyo. The Duke of Dog Canyon maybe?

When he got back to camp, the horses and mules were munching on grain. Rob asked, "Where did you get the oats, Paco? My daddy always said a scoop of oats every day not only makes a horse long-winded, it makes him easy to catch up every morning."

"Señor Rob, I had them in the wagon for the trail boss's horses when I drove off to get away from the stampede."

Rob said, "Well, someday we can pay him back."

"Oh, no, Señor Rob. He is muerto … dead."

"Oh, yeah. I'm sorry. I forgot. Well, we will use the grain now and pay somebody else sometime. We will pay it ahead." Rob stared into the sky.

"That will be a good thing, Señor Rob."

"Paco, do you know where we could buy any cattle or horses?"

"No, Señor Rob. I have been gone a long time."

Paco cooked the frijoles with the wild onions and roasted the tubers on the edge of the fire. He rubbed salt, pepper, and garlic on thick venison steaks and broiled them over the fire. He uncovered the sourdough biscuits in the Dutch oven. The food was wonderful, and he had the big chuck wagon coffeepot with all the coffee they could drink. After supper, Paco dug out the other Dutch oven, and with huge wedges of apple pie for dessert, they lounged on their bedrolls, sipped hot coffee, and picked their teeth. They listened to Duke talking to the stars.

That night, Jessie said, "Paco, look at that light in the middle of the basin. See it? You know who that is, Paco?"

"No, Señor Jessie. Maybe Apache, but mostly they don't build a fire you can see in the night. They build a fire in the arroyo that you cannot see. That must be a gringo. If it has been in the same place two nights in a row, it is definitely a gringo. But, I do not know of anybody that stays out in the middle of the basin."

After dark, Jessie studied the fire out in the west and said, "Because that light is so even in its brightness, it must be a lantern. A fire tends to flare up and flicker. Only a lantern burns like that."

Paco said, "I will go to La Luz and ask my cousin if he knows of anyone homesteading out in the basin. In the moonlight, you can see that the light is close to the white sand." He took a plate of leftover frijoles and venison, walked to the arroyo, set down the plate, and said into the darkness, "Duke, take good care of this gringo."

The next morning, they decided all three of them would go into La Luz.

Paco said, "Señiors, Tularosa is just nine or ten miles north-northwest of La Luz. It is a much bigger settlement, and both places have a creeks in the canyon above the towns. You could see if there are any horses or cattle for sale there."

After breakfast, Paco took a plate of food to the arroyo and called out to Duke, "We will be back. Do not bother my mules."

Before noon, they were in La Luz. Paco found his cousin. To Rob and Jessie's surprise, Juan Mórales was the goat herder they had gotten directions from on their last trip. Juan and Paco had a discussion in Spanish that went too fast for Rob and Jessie to understand much.

Paco came over and said, "Señor Rob, you and Señor Jessie can go to Mr. Masterson's cantina, but they do not allow Mexicans. Juan and I will go to the Mexican cantina. I will ask around about the light in the west."

Rob said, "No! We're all part of the Dog Canyon outfit. We will all go together."

"That is very kind, Señor Rob, but you go eat with the gringos. We will go eat with the Mexicans, and we will both learn more information. We can meet back here at the time of the siesta."

Jessie said, "Paco, you are a man of uncommon brains. Okay, we will see you back here in a couple of hours."

Rob and Jessie walked into the Masterson cantina, sat down at a table, and ordered food and beer. Even though it was only April, it was warm. The cold beer tasted good.

Jessie said, "Where in the world did you get that wonderful cold beer?"

Masterson said, "The freighter 'at runs from El Paso ta the mines at White Oaks stops and sells it ta me. I've a dugout behind the cantina. I store it deep in the ground so it's always fifty-five degrees, 'corden to my therma-meter."

The food was good, and the coffee was hot. While they ate, two men walked in, bellied up to the bar, and ordered whiskey. Rob would not have paid much attention except that both had on recently cleaned, shiny six-shooters and full cartridge belts. Otherwise, they were typical looking. Both wore long-sleeved cotton shirts, and the taller one's arms were long enough to not need sleeve garters. He wore leather chaps over his blue denim pants. The other man wore brown pants with suspenders over his shoulders. He wore a sombrero even though he was a gringo.

After they had eaten, Rob said, "Mr. Masterson, do you know of anybody homesteading out in the basin just south of the white sand?"

The men at the bar overheard, and the taller one said, "I have a ranch near the white sand."

Rob stood and said, "My name is Robert Wilson. This is my friend Jessie Hatfield. We're new here and are trying to start a ranch at the base of the mountains. At night, we noticed a light out in the basin south of the white sand." Rob offered his hand.

Taking Rob's hand and shaking it, the man said, "I'm Turner Sutton. This here is my friend and foreman Bill McHenry. That must be your light we see at the mouth of Dog Canyon."

Rob admitted that it was.

Turner Sutton said, "We looked there first, but I found an artesian well out by the white sand that springs hot but sweet water. If you let it cool, it's right tasty."

Rob said, "I saw no green vegetation out there or any trees or other evidence of an artesian well. How did you find it?"

"It was the damnedest thing," Sutton said, relaxing and pushing up the front of his wide-brimmed light gray felt hat. "I was riding to Las Cruces and skirting the sand on the south. Of a sudden, my horse stepped in a hole and broke his leg. When I got to my feet, I saw that the hole was full of water. I had to shoot the horse. Bill worried when he heard the gunshot, and he came to see what the matter was. After he saw I was okay and what happened, he doubled back and brought back another horse. The water kept running out of the hole. We rode on to Las Cruces, and Bill bought a shovel."

After a sip of his drink, Sutton said, "The next day, on the way back, the hole was still full of water. Bill took the shovel and dug around the dead horse's leg. We managed with both our horses to drag away the dead one. We were amazed at how fast the little pool filled. All you had to do was have the pool below the level of the water in the well hole.

By the time the pool was full of water, the water had cooled. Our horses meandered over to drink. Afraid they might be drinking bad water. I walked over and tasted it myself and it was sweet and good. So, we rode back to Las Cruces and filed a claim. There's good grass on the flat and apparently water a plenty. Hot work, all this talkin'." He downed the rest of his drink. Then he said, "Bill, let's eat. I'm starvin'."

Rob asked, "Mr. Sutton, do you know of any stock for sale? We have a little money. We sold everything back in Texas and came west."

Sutton answered, "Hell, call me Turner. No I don't know of any available stock, but I'm trying to organize a trail drive to get a herd driven up from El Paso. How many cattle you thinking about?"

Rob said, "Well, three or four hundred head ... depends on the price."

Turner whistled and said, "That's a pretty big start. I'll keep you in mind. If you're going to stay there in Canyon d Perro, you better file a claim. Since the war, many more people are coming west, looking for a place to light. This is in Doña Ana County, so you must go to the land office in Las Cruces to file the claim. You'll ride right by us. Stop by the Artesian Well Ranch on the way, and I'll ride with you."

Rob said, "Thanks. I'll do that. Mr. Su ... ah Turner, you and Bill are welcome at Dog Canyon anytime. Come on, Jessie. We better get our outfit together. Duke will eat all that venison before we get back."

They stopped at the store and bought more supplies, including a good supply of sugar and dried apples. "Do you have any other fruit?" Jessie asked.

The storekeeper said, "It's too early in the year for fresh fruit, but I have some dried figs and raisins from the grapes of last year's crop."

Jessie said, "I like raisins. I don't think much of figs, but Paco might do good with 'em." And he bought a bag of raisins and two pounds of dried figs.

They found Paco. He had brought along one pack mule to haul back the supplies, and they loaded the supplies on the mule. They headed south for Dog Canyon. After they passed Alamo Canyon with the little creek and the big cottonwoods, they looked west. Even with the afternoon sun in their eyes, they could see the slight dust of Turner Sutton and Bill McHenry approaching the artesian well out in the basin, by the south point of white sands.

When they got to the Dog Canyon camp and stepped down, Paco said, "Señor Rob, your coyote guarded the camp today."

Rob looked around at the coyote tracks. They were everywhere, but Duke had bothered nothing.

Paco served a supper they enjoyed very much, and they settled down with coffee and leftover apple pie. They enjoyed the beautiful sunset of vivid pinks on the clouds drifting over the velvet blue New Mexico sky.

Over coffee, Rob said, "Paco, did you learn anything from your cousin about stock for sale by anyone in the basin?"

"Juan told me a man named Señor Sutton had filed homestead papers on the place just south of the white sand. He also told me there are horses for sale in Tularosa, but they are very dear. He didn't know of any cattle for sale."

Later Jessie said, "Paco, can you find the place where those cattle stampeded?"

"Si, Señor Jessie. Why?"

Jessie sat up and put down his coffee. "I was thinking we could take some of our cash, go to Tularosa, and buy some horses. If we could hire cowpokes, we could go south and gather stampeded cattle. They are wild cattle now. If we gather 'em up, bring 'em here, and brand 'em, they would belong to us. Then, we could go buy more horses, and we'd still have cash left. If someone already gathered the stampeded cattle, we'll have lost nothin' 'cept a little time 'cause we'd of had to buy the horses for the ranch anyhow."

Rob said, "What a great idea. We might be able to get twice the start we planned. Jessie, you never told me anything about this idea of yours."

Jessie said, "I just been studying on it. What do y'all think?"

Rob said, "I don't see that we've got anything to lose. Let's see if Turner Sutton and Bill McHenry will throw in with us. We might gather up enough cattle for both our outfits."

Paco added, "We should start in the morning before somebody else has this idea."

Chapter 4

Preparing to Hunt for Cattle

*O*ver their sunrise coffee, Paco asked, "Señor Rob, how many years do you have?"

Rob said, "Twenty years. Why?"

After more conversation, Jessie admitted he was almost twenty-three.

Paco said, "Señor Jessie will have to file the claim until Señor Rob is twenty-one."

Rob and Jessie thought about that.

The evening before, Paco had taken his double-barrel shotgun and brought in a mess of quail.

After a hearty breakfast of fried quail, sourdough biscuits, gravy, and the big coffee pot of coffee, Jessie said, "I could take the packhorse go to Turner's ranch and offer Turner and Bill the opportunity to join us. Then, with or without the Artesian Well Ranch people, I could ride to Las Cruces to file the claim on Dog Canyon Ranch. After that, I—or we, if they join us—could meet you back here."

Paco said, "It would not take so much time if you ride south down the Rio Grande after you file the claim. Stay on the west side of the Organ and Franklin Mountains and east of the Rio Grande until you reach El Paso to meet Rob and Paco at the de Leon Ranch corrals. The de Leon corrals are on the land that serves as the downtown plaza. It will be easy to find."

Rob said, "Paco and I could go to Tularosa, buy extra horses and try to hire more cowpunchers. On the way back, we could stop in La Luz for more supplies. Paco could visit with his cousin Juan and check for more news. Then we will head south."

Paco said, "We can go down the basin on the east side of the Jarilla Mountains and the Franklin Mountains to El Paso to meet Jessie and hopefully the others at the downtown plaza."

They all agreed with the plan to save time.

Rob cut off the last haunch of the deer, dropped it in a clean flour sack, and put it in the wagon. Not knowing Paco had fed Duke the last of their other meat, Rob took the rest of the deer carcass to the arroyo and set it out for Duke.

Rob shouted, "Take care of the camp while we're gone!" and laughed.

Rob and Jessie saddled up while Paco hitched up the wagon. Paco packed his saddle and tack in the wagon and tied his horse to the back of it. They all said their so-longs and rode away.

Jessie approached Turner's ranch and stopped to holler out a warning, "Hello the camp?"

Bill answered, "Come on in, Jessie. I've been watching you over a quarter hour."

Jessie rode on in, and Turner said, "It's good to see you, Jessie. Will you have coffee?"

Jessie nodded and said, "Thanks. I will."

Turner and Bill had finished breakfast and were excited about the prospect of riding with Jessie to Las Cruces.

Jessie drank his coffee while they were getting their gear together to ride to Las Cruces. Then he told them about Paco's story of the stampede and his idea to go find the stampede area, gather the stampeded stock, and drive the stock back to the Tularosa Basin. He gave them time to think about what he told them. "We want to offer you guys the chance to join us. Rob and Paco are on their way to Tularosa to buy horses and recruit cowpokes. Then they will meet me—or us—in El Paso at the de Leon Ranch corrals downtown."

After almost no discussion, Turner and Bill excitedly agreed to go. They gathered their bedrolls and other possibles for a longer trip.

While Turner and Bill saddled up, Jessie and his horses sampled the artesian well water in the pool. Jessie decided it was good water and filled his canteen.

Within a quarter hour, the three of them were riding southwest toward the San Augustine Pass, the gap in the Organ Mountains, which was the easiest mountain crossing to Las Cruces.

Paco said, "Señor Rob, we go more fast if we go more in the desert to avoid arroyos with the wagon."

They headed west and crossed the tracks of two northbound unshod horses. They were alert as they hurried north to cover the twenty-plus miles to Tularosa.

In just a few minutes, they came upon two Mescalero Apache. One of them was an old man with an injured leg. The other was a young brave whom they understood was the old man's grandson. A bright red headband held back the young brave's long black hair. He wore a fine quality but undecorated doeskin shirt, doeskin leggings, and a breechclout. He had a bow and a quiver of arrows on his back and a knife belted on his side. Their ponies were spent, and they could not run from Rob and Paco. The Indians resigned themselves to whatever devilry the white men had planned.

The Apache spoke Spanish, and Paco easily communicated with them. They were down on their luck and trying to get back to Mescalero when the old man's horse shied from a rattlesnake and threw him. He landed wrong and broke his lower leg. The old man was wearing doeskin pants and a matching long tail shirt with a touch of turquoise beadwork across the yoke. His leather belt held a large antler-handled hunting knife.

Both men wore elk rawhide-soled, knee-high doeskin moccasins. The young brave's moccasins were undecorated, but the old man's were decorated with white and turquoise beads on the tops of each foot.

"I can set the leg if you will help me, Señor Rob."

Rob agreed and said, "Ask the Indians what they are doing down by Dog Canyon."

Paco complied, and the old man reluctantly told him they needed flint. There was good flint in the big triple box canyon. Not only was it of high quality but it also had good medicine.

Paco told the old man, "I am going to help your leg, but it will be painful." He built a fire and put water on to boil. He sat the old man on a keg in the shade of the wagon while Rob went searching for suitable mesquite sticks for splints and a crutch.

The old Indian said, "Why he do this? White mans not help Mescalero."

Paco said, "This gringo is unusual and made of better stuff than most." Then Paco told him about the coyote.

The old Indian sat quiet in deep thought.

Rob came back with a mesquite wood crutch and the splints.

Paco cleaned the leg by washing it with hot water. He inspected the leg and said, "Señor Rob, hold his knee still while I set the broken bone. Only one of the lower leg bones is broken."

It amazed Rob that the Indian didn't even flinch. He just sat there.

When Paco was through, the old Indian tried to stand.

Rob said, "No. You can't ride. Get in the wagon with Paco."

Paco translated.

As they were helping the old man onto the wagon, Rob said, "Paco, tell the young brave to tie the old man's horse to the wagon and ride his own horse."

The young brave protested. He told the old Indian the white men would steal his horse. The old Indian talked at length to the boy in Apache. The young brave looked inquisitively at Rob and tied the horse to the back of the wagon.

They started toward Tularosa. Rob hadn't thought about what he would do with the Indians, but he couldn't leave them in the desert with a broken leg.

By early afternoon, the little group rode into Tularosa. Rob was aware of the strange looks they got from the local people. They stopped at a water trough in front of the general store.

While Paco watered the stock, Rob entered the store and said to the storekeeper, "Is there anybody in Tularosa with horses for sale?"

The storekeeper said, "Why, yes. Ignacio Hernández, just west of town, raises good horses." He gave Rob directions to the Hernández place.

Rob thanked the storekeeper and left. When he got outside, he found two cowboys bullying the old Mexican and the two Indians. Rob had trouble containing himself, but he did not want to get in a set-to with the local people. He took two deep breaths and said, "Sir, my name is Robert Wilson. This is my cook, Paco Mórales. We found these two Indians in need on the trail."

The bigger of the two cowboys blurted out, "Well, my name is Jim Healy, and I don't like Indians or meskins."

Like a regular cowboy, Healy had on a wide-brim felt hat with a leather hatband with long thongs coming down through the brim and tied. That enabled the hat to be pushed back and worn hanging on his back as it was now, He wore a sweat-stained light brown shirt and faded denim pants. He had a big six-gun holstered on his belt with just a hint of neglect on it. When he got close to Rob, he reeked of whiskey.

Rob said, "I'm sorry you feel that way, Mr. Healy. If you give us a minute, we will leave your town."

Healy roared back. "Well, whatever your name is, I'm going to take care of these Indians right now so they won't be of any more bother to us."

Before Healy could close his mouth and reach for his gun, Rob had drawn his six-gun and had it pointed at Healy's nose.

Rob said softly, "If you touch any of my people, it will be the last thing you ever do."

Healy's sidekick took one step forward in time to look up the barrels of Paco's double-barrel shotgun. The holes in barrels of the shotgun looked as big as silver dollars. He froze as Paco shook his head in the negative and grinned.

Rob said, "Mr. Healy, if you and your friend will step back, we will be on our way and be no more trouble to anybody."

Healy realized his pistol had not even cleared leather when Rob's forty-five was in his face. Few people were watching, so he backed down.

Rob mounted his horse and tipped his hat, and the little party rode off toward the west.

The storekeeper had been observing the proceedings and said to the little orphan boy, Pepe Herrera, "Pepe, go as fast as you can and tell Mr. Hernández what has happened here and that he should expect visitors. I will give you this penny if you beat the strangers to the Hernández place."

Pepe took off at a dead run.

Rob found the Hernández place with no trouble. As they rode into the yard, the most beautiful girl he had ever seen stepped off the porch and greeted them with a smile. She was a few inches over five feet tall, slim, lithe, and toned. Her lovely head sat atop a long neck with a beautiful throat. It rose from her well-formed shoulders that were just peeking out of her snow-white peasant's style blouse. It was obvious the blouse had been washed and ironed before she put it on. Her skirt was long, full, blue, and white gingham that had also been laundered. She had brown leather sandals buckled around her dainty little feet. She said, "Hello. My name is Emily Hernández. May I help you?"

Rob was so stunned he could not talk. He tipped his hat and opened his mouth, but he couldn't make a sound.

Paco realized what had happened, smiled and said, "Señorita Hernández, we are here to see Señor Ignacio Hernández about buying some horses. This is Señor Rob Wilson. He is the boss of our outfit. My name is Paco Mórales. Is Señor Hernández here?"

"Yes, sir. He is in the barn. I'll get him." Emily walked toward the barn. Her long, raven-black hair shined iridescently in the sunlight.

With his unique sense of humor, Paco whispered, "When it is important, you talk pretty well."

Rob was strawberry red.

Ignacio Hernández walked up to the yard and said, "Welcome to my rancho. Please step down." Hernández was a tall man, taller than Rob. He was lean, but with the obvious strength of a hardworking man. His brown buckskin pants with slits up the outside bottoms of his legs and small silver conchos closing the slits. His shirt was white cotton of the Mexican style with full puffy sleeves. His short buckskin vest was, open at the front with short leather laces tied over small conchos that could close it. He wore pointed-toe Mexican boots with long rowel spurs and tiny silver conchos on the leather strap that fastened them on. His black Spanish-style felt hat had a wide, flat brim. It had a diamondback rattlesnake skin hatband with another small silver concho fastening it on the right side just in front of the three-inch rattles.

When Rob stepped off his horse, Hernández held out his hand and said, "I'm Ignacio Hernández. How may I help you?"

Hernández observed the Indians, the Mexican and this young cowboy. He thought about what Pepe had just told him about what had happened in town.

Rob took his hand and shook it. "It's good to meet you, sir. My name is Robert Wilson."

Hernández turned around and said, "Emily, will you put on some fresh coffee please?" Looking at Rob, he said, "How may I be of service?"

Rob said, "Mr. Hernández, we need horses and mules. And do you have any advice about what to do with these Indians?"

Hernández said, "The Indians may be a problem. The Mescalero Apache have a reservation over by Fort Stanton that President Grant established a few years ago. The problem is many of them still live thirty miles away, between Bent, New Mexico, and Sierra Blanca Mountain. Some of the Mescalero have gone raiding down in Mexico. Those left are in bad shape. They call this time of year the 'hungry time.' It's too early for crops, berries, or fruit, and the wildlife is poor and scarce. The Indian agent is supposed to provide food and supplies to the tribal members, but the food and supplies always seem to be late. If you send them back now with a broken leg, they will have a hard time. I can help you with the horses and mules though. How many do you need? Do you need cow ponies, draft horses, or pack animals?"

Rob said, "We need ten cow ponies and four more mules for the wagon if you have 'em. What's the going price?"

Hernández said, "Let's go look at them—then you can choose."

"That sounds good. Come on, Paco. Let's go look at the stock. One more thing, Mr. Hernández, do you have water I could give my Indian friends? We had to leave town in a hurry, and they didn't get a drink."

Mr. Hernández turned to one of his vaqueros. "José, agua por indios, por favor."

"Mr. Wilson, I have appaloosas I sell to the ranchers and mustangs I sell to the army. I can fix you up with a good team of mules. The appaloosas will cost you twenty dollars each, the mustangs are fifteen dollars, and the mules are twelve-fifty. Do you need saddles and tack?"

Rob said, "Whew! I heard your horses were very dear. We could use four saddles, a packsaddle, and tack for five horses—if it is not too expensive."

"Mr. Wilson, the saddles and tack will be my gift to you for taking Jim Healy down a few notches."

Rob said, "How did you hear about that?"

"Little goes on in Tularosa that I don't know about."

Rob and Paco looked over the animals. They were impressed. They picked their animals and struck a deal with Mr. Hernández. Rob paid a surprised Hernández in gold with no haggling.

Rob turned to the young Indian and said, "I'm sorry. I don't know your name."

Paco translated, and the young Indian told Rob his name was Little Deer. Grandfather was Wise Elk.

Rob said, "It will be hard for you if you go to the reservation now. If you will do whatever you can to help, you are welcome to go with us to Texas and back with a herd of cattle. I will pay you cowboy wages. After your leg is healed, you can decide what you want to do. Think about it while I finish with Mr. Hernández."

Rob said, "Mr. Hernández, I need more trail hands. Do you know of anybody who needs work?"

Hernández stared into the distance for a few seconds. "Yes, maybe. The Rodriguez brothers need work. They are young but good vaqueros. I will send Pepe to inquire about their interest."

Emily Hernández came out with cups all around and coffee. Rob could not help but stare at the beautiful girl as she poured his coffee. She boldly looked him in the eyes. Her big green eyes and exquisite lashes took Rob's breath away. She was so beautiful it made Rob's heart hurt. He sipped the coffee and it was superb coffee. She was as pretty as she had seemed the first time he had seen her. He fumbled with his hat, and drank the coffee without saying a word. Paco almost fell off the porch from the need to laugh.

Rob tipped his hat to Emily and said, "Thanks ... for the coffee, ma'am." He turned to the Mescalero and asked, "Have you decided what you want to do?"

Paco translated. "Yes. They want to go to Texas."

Within a few minutes, Julio and Marco Rodriguez trotted up with their bedrolls. They wore white cotton shirts, pants, straw sombreros, and leather sandals. They belted their pants with a piece of braided heavy twine. One of them had a short gun in a holster on a gun belt slung over his shoulder. He had only eight shells in the belt, but the gun was clean.

Rob walked up to them and said, "My name is Rob Wilson. This is Paco Mórales, Wise Elk, and Little Deer. We are going to Texas to gather a herd and trail it back to Dog Canyon. Mr. Hernández speaks well of you, and I will take his word if you are interested in work."

The young men looked at each other, grinned, and nodded enthusiastically. "Yes, Señor Wilson. We want to go to Texas."

Rob said, "All right. Put your bedrolls in the wagon, pick a horse, saddle up, and get ready."

Ignacio Hernández stepped forward and said, "No, you boys each pick out one of my horses. You can bring me back a horse someday."

Rob said, "Will you help herd the horses and mules, Little Deer?"

Little Deer looked at Paco who translated. Then he grinned and nodded with enthusiasm.

Rob thanked the Mexican cowboy for the water for the Indians, turned to Ignacio Hernández, and said, "Thank you for everything, Mr. Hernández."

The men shook hands.

Rob mounted his horse, tipped his hat to Emily, and said, "Ma'am."

With that, the expedition turned south and rode away.

Emily said, "Papa, Doña Ana County has some fine new citizens. I hope they stay here."

Ignacio Hernández stared thoughtfully and nodded as the group rode away.

The Dog Canyon outfit made good time and arrived back in La Luz before dark. They set up camp just outside the village.

Wise Elk was in pain from the wagon ride.

Paco said, "Little Deer, build a fire and put water on to boil." He found his cousin and said, "Juan, do you have any painkiller?"

Juan told Paco that he had willow bark (aspirin) and a peyote bud (mescaline). He gave some of each to Paco.

Paco cut off a small piece of the peyote bud and gave it to Wise Elk. Wise Elk, recognizing the hallucinogen, put it in his mouth to chew.

Paco joined Little Deer at the fire, made willow bark tea, and gave it to the grateful old Mescalero.

Paco and Rob went to Stephenson's store and bought all manner of grub and supplies for the trail drive.

Little Deer had killed two rabbits with his bow and arrows. With steaks from the deer haunch, fried rabbit, frijoles, and sourdough biscuits, they had a good supper.

Rob wondered how Duke was doing, but he figured that that coyote had been by himself for a long time and would be okay.

Rob and Paco doctored Wise Elk's leg. They checked the bandages to make sure they were not too tight. The leg looked okay. It was not very discolored or swollen. After supper, Paco made more willow bark tea and gave it to Wise Elk. He cut several more slices of peyote and gave them to Wise Elk. Paco was surprised that Wise Elk didn't become nauseous like most people who chewed the peyote buttons.

While Paco plundered in the wagon and inventoried the supplies, he heard a sound and saw a small movement under a tarp. He thought it was a rat, but when he raised his club to kill it, he discovered the rat was Pepe Herrera. Pepe had quietly stowed away in the wagon and made the bouncing hot ride under the tarp.

Everyone was looking up at the commotion in the wagon.

Paco held Pepe by the scruff of the neck and said, "Señor Rob, you better come over here. We have a rat."

Pepe said, "I can go to Texas. I am an orphan, but I told Señorita Emily that I was going so she would not worry about me. She is the only one who cares about me." Pepe wore the white cotton Mexican peon clothes and sandals much like the Rodriguez brothers except that he had an old felt sombrero rather than a straw one.

Rob said, "You're Pepe from the Hernandez place, right?"

Pepe nodded.

"If he wants to go bad enough to stowaway, maybe you can do something with him, Paco. I don't want to take the time to take him back to Tularosa."

"I can do something with him."

Rob gave Pepe a stern lecture about telling the whole truth and not hiding things from Paco and his elders.

Rob said, "Paco, better get Pepe some supper and something to drink. I bet he's thirsty after that ride."

Pepe ate like a harvest hand.

Paco said, "Ay, Chihuahua, another one."

At sunup, they coffeed-up, ate breakfast and broke camp. They loaded the wagon, gathered the stock, and started south.

The trip south was uneventful. On the third afternoon, they rode into El Paso. Jessie, Bill, and Turner were waiting in the plaza.

Jessie said, "It's good to see you. I was getting worried. We looked everywhere and could not find any cowboys who appeared reliable."

Rob said, "We found two young Mexican cowpokes and a Mescalero brave who is good with the animals. We also have an old Mescalero to help Paco."

After a round of introductions and handshakes, Rob turned to Turner, Jessie, and Bill. "I'm sorry to report that we only have ten extra horses plus Jessie's packhorse."

Turner said, "Well, I guess one fresh horse a day will have to do."

Rob found a gunsmith and bought five used Henry saddle guns with scabbards and four .44-caliber Colt-conversion short guns with gun belts. Julio had one of his own. The gunsmith furnished a box of shells with each weapon, but after thinking about it more, Rob bought another thousand rounds of ammunition. He passed saddle guns to Marco, Julio, and Little Deer and gave Paco the rest of the weapons and ammunition to pack in the wagon.

Rob said, "Listen up. I bought Henry 44 caliber rifles and I paid the extra three dollars for the conversion of the Colt 44 caliber cap and ball six guns to cartridge guns so you can use the same ammunition in both of your weapons. That way, you will only have to carry one caliber cartridge and you won't have to worry about mixing them up. Remember not to carry those Henry's with a shell in the chamber. They don't have a safety, and the firing pin will be resting on the rim of the bullet. Leave the chamber empty. If you need to use them remember to jack a shell into the chamber. Got that?"

Paco translated for Little Deer, and they all said, "Yes, sir."

Rob said, "Another thing, you must carry those short guns with the hammer resting on an empty chamber so you won't shoot off your toes—or worse. Even if we get in a hot gun battle, leave those Colt conversions loaded with five cartridges and the hammer resting on the empty chamber. Okay?"

The boys all said, "Yes, sir."

Jessie, Turner, and Bill were impressed with the supplies, the stock, and the new hands.

They ate a great dinner at a cantina. The cantina had a mariachi band and a pretty Spanish dancer. The young gentlemen were amazed and thrilled with the entertainment. They applauded until their hands were sore.

After window shopping and looking around downtown, they bedded down. They were all too excited to sleep. They would head for the Llano Estacado in the morning.

Chapter 5

GOING TO THE
LLANO ESTACADO

The next morning, everybody was up before daylight. They were more comfortable with each other, and Rob and Paco had gained respect for the Rodriguez brothers and Little Deer. Despite their limited conversation, the boys had done a good job of handling their remuda when they drove it away from home. Rob looked at Jessie and grinned. Their confidence was growing.

After breakfast at the cantina—a first for all the young gentlemen and for Wise Elk—they finished loading and packing the gear.

While Rob and Jessie went to the bank, Pepe said, "Señor Paco, what is the Llano Estacado?"

Paco thought about that while they started packing up the camp, then he answered the question. "Pepe, The Llano Estacado is a huge area from the Canadian River in the north end of the Texas panhandle all the way south to where the Pecos River turns east before it runs into the Rio Grande. It is bordered on the west by the Pecos River and stretches over two hundred miles east. It is about three hundred miles north to south and almost flat. There are no mountains or buttes to use as landmarks. When Francisco Vasquez de Coronado led the conquistadors exploring back in the 1500s, they became lost because there was nothing to guide them in the Llano. When they did find their way back to where they started into the Llano, they drove stakes into the ground to mark where they had traveled so they could find their way back. It became known as the staked plain or Llano Estacado. Coronado traveled on through to what is now the Oklahoma Indian Territory and north into Kansas, looking for the lost cities of gold before turning back west. It remains dangerous to travel the Llano. Many men have entered the Llano Estacado and never returned. They say it is not unusual to find human skeletons in the Llano Estacado of men that perished from hunger or thirst."

When Rob and Jessie entered the bank Rob introduced Jessie and himself to the banker. The banker said, "My name is Samuel Bloomberg. Welcome to El Paso's finest bank. How may I help you?"

Rob said, "I have a substantial amount of money on deposit in a bank in East Texas. I'd like to have it moved here to your bank."

Bloomberg's eyes lit up like lanterns. "No problem at all, Mr. Wilson. If you will give me the name and address of the bank, I can take care of that for you."

"Well, my lawyer has taken care of that part. His name is John Wilson of Nacogdoches, Texas. Lawyer Wilson, can give you the name of the bank."

"I can do that for you Mr. Wilson."

"Mr. Bloomberg, we are going to recover a lost herd of cattle and will be gone several weeks. When we get back, we want to draw out five hundred dollars. Occasionally, Jessie may come to do our business. We are partners in the ranching operation."

Sam Bloomberg said, "Mr. Wilson and Mr. Hatfield, I assure you that I will have everything in order. Upon your return, you can pick up your money in gold."

When Rob and Jessie got back to camp, the cowboys had saddled the new horses and mounted up to try them out. Ignacio Hernández's horses were well broken but spirited. After a short rodeo, they headed slightly south of due east to skirt the Guadalupe Mountains on the south.

A loose protocol was set with Rob, Jessie, Turner, and Bill in the front, Paco, Wise Elk, and Pepe in the wagon, and Little Deer, Marco, and Julio trailing with their remuda. Little Deer possessed a special way with the horses and mules. He touched them, stroked them, and talked to them in Apache. Before they stopped to camp for the night, the horses and mules in the remuda had relaxed and settled into an easy rhythm.

Over another of Paco's tasty suppers, Turner said, "You did a good job of gathering the horses, mules, and young cowboys."

Rob said, "Thank you, Turner. I'm glad you feel that way."

Paco said, "After two hard days, we can camp on the Pecos." He sipped his coffee. "Even though it is springtime and rain is unlikely, if the river is not high, we should cross the river before we stop. Sometimes it rains in the night far upstream, and the river fills up."

It was a peaceful night. An owl was asking his question of the dark, and the coyote called out the stars.

The next morning, Pepe sought out Rob and Jessie. "I can ride, and I am too young to be stuck in the wagon with the old men. I must get away from them and ride a horse. You have plenty of horses."

Rob was reluctant and scratching his head said, "Well, I don't know."

Jessie said, "How old were you when you started riding?"

Rob said, "Okay, go pick out a saddle and some tack."

Pepe's face lit up like a full moon on a summer night and he ran to the back of the wagon.

Rob playfully punched Jessie on the arm and said, "Okay, smarty. Go pick him out a horse."

Jessie came back with one of the appaloosas, which he knew to be well broken. Pepe came dragging a saddle with Paco close behind carrying a saddle blanket, bridle, and a saddle gun.

Rob motioned Paco to the side and asked, "What are you doing with that Henry?"

"Señor, do you want Pepe to be a man or a boy?"

Rob walked off, grumbling to himself.

Jessie put a hand to his mouth, feigned a cough to hide his laughter, and smiled at Paco who grinned back.

They mounted up and started off. Pepe joined Little Deer and the Rodriguez boys.

The next two days passed without incident. After they passed south of the Guadalupe Mountains, they turned more north. After two o'clock on the third afternoon, they topped a rise and looked down on the Pecos River.

The Pecos River ran in a wide draw it cut out of the Pecos Valley over thousands of years. Its flood stages had washed out the draw over a mile wide, and rimrock sandstone ledges ran along most of both sides. At that time of year, the Pecos River was less than twenty yards across as it meandered through the Pecos Valley. No wagon trail existed off the rimrock down to the river at their location.

Rob said, "if you and Bill ride upstream, I'll go downstream. The first one finding a wagon passage down will fire two shots. The rest of us will follow."

Rob looked at Paco and Paco nodded. He had not gone far when he heard two shots to the north. He was relieved and turned around. He passed the wagon and remuda and found Bill looking down at a wagon trail. Turner was at the bottom by the river.

The thirsty horses and mules scented the water, and the boys had their hands full holding them back.

They found the reason for the wagon trail: A good gravel bottom crossing in the river. They crossed over, letting all the stock drink their fill.

Rob said, "We will make an early camp here today. Stake out the extra horses and mules so they can graze, but keep the riding stock tethered close to camp. After supper, switch the tethered stock for the animals that have been grazing."

Turner said, "That Rob Wilson has a head on his shoulders. He always tries to think ahead and be prepared."

Bill nodded.

That night, they had a feast. Jessie had killed a pronghorn antelope.

Paco put it on a spit and made the boys all take turns turning it over the fire. He said, "That way, the meat will be cooked in addition to being smoked. It will keep better."

They ate barbequed antelope, beans, and biscuits with real butter that Paco had bought from the cantina in El Paso. They had big wedges of apple pie Paco baked in the Dutch ovens and washed it down with hot coffee. They were all so full they could hardly walk.

Rob said, "Go switch out the stock, boys, but leave the saddle cinches loose on the fresh horses. I will take the first shift and will wake Jessie for the next shift. Turner, if you and Bill agree, you can split the third watch. East of the Pecos is Comanche country. I don't want those horse thieves to get any ideas."

Paco said, "Pepe, I will wash the pots and pans while you go down to the river and wash the plates, cups, and flatware. Pepe, be mindful of the water moccasins by the river. They mostly hunt in the night."

Everybody tended to their personal needs and checked their gear. They were all so full that things quieted down in a hurry. The boys finished with the stock. Pepe and Paco wrapped up the kitchen duties while Wise Elk mended a saddle. Shortly, all was quiet. A 'coon chattered down by the water, and the bats squeaked as they helped control the flying insects.

Rob cinched up his fresh horse. He had picked out one of the new appaloosas to try it out. He rode in big circles around the camp and remuda. On the third round, Rob was thinking about the beautiful girl in Tularosa. Her beauty was timeless. He couldn't decide whether she was seventeen or twenty-two. He ran the mental pictures through his mind of her stepping off the porch with a big smile and saying, "Hello. My name is Emily Hernández. May I help you?"

When he got into the salt cedar trees by the river, the young spotted rump horse pricked his ears forward and stared into the darkness. Rob stopped, drew his six-gun, and waited. He and the horse were both still and silent. In a short time, he heard light splashing crossing the river and then silence. The rest of his first shift as nighthawk was quiet.

After Rob came in and called Jessie, he crawled into his bedroll. A coyote bayed at the moon. Paco opened his eyes and smiled before going back to sleep.

The next morning, the whole outfit was full of piss and vinegar. They were all loaded and ready to roll in no time. Rob walked over to where he had heard the splashes the night before and found tracks in the sand. He could not tell if they were canine or feline. In the dry sand, the claws did not show. The river water had lapped up and washed away the tracks in the wet sand.

Rob said, "Be on the lookout. That animal last night could have been a wolf, a coyote, a bobcat, or a lynx. I don't think the tracks were big enough to have been a mountain lion."

Paco started to say something, appeared hesitant, then said, "We should turn a little more north now." And they headed off a bit more to the left of the sun.

They nooned on a little creek that flowed back toward the Pecos and enjoyed more of the leftover antelope, biscuits, and coffee. They made good time that afternoon. After an uneventful evening, they were rolling again at sunup.

A few hours later, Paco called a halt and motioned for them all to come to the wagon. He said, "That line of trees ahead is the small creek the cattle drive stopped on the night of the stampede. The drive camped on the small rise just to the north. The stampeding herd, when I saw them last, was running south along that creek." And he pointed to the right.

Turner said, "I suggest we spread out a little and work our way south to see if we can find the herd's tracks. They should still be visible. When we locate tracks, we can decide where to make camp. We can spread out from a central point and look for the scattered stock."

Everybody agreed it was a good plan, and they set off south with Paco and Wise Elk following the creek. The boys with the remuda were close at hand. Rob and Jessie were on the east side of the creek, and Turner and Bill spread out on the west side.

It was a beautiful spring day, and the warm sun was shining. There was a slight breeze out of the west, and waves of wispy cirrus clouds lazed through the dark blue sky.

The whole outfit nooned on a little bend in the creek and ate the last of the antelope, leftover biscuits, and hot coffee. They had all seen tracks that indicated the herd was still moving and still together. They decided to press on south and see if they could find where the herd slowed down and began to break up.

Paco had prepared a supper of freshly killed whitetail deer and watercress with wild onion and dandelion salad. The salad was wilted with a warm vinaigrette of bacon drippings, garlic, salt, pepper, and apple cider vinegar. Paco had gotten the tangy vinegar from Mr. Stephenson in La Luz. Of course they had beans, fresh hot biscuits and gallons of coffee.

Turner said, "This is the best-fed trail drive I've ever been on or ever heard about."

The others agreed.

Paco beamed.

Rob, Jessie, Turner, Bill, and Paco discussed strategy and decided this was a good place to begin the hunt.

The next morning after breakfast, Rob, Jessie, Bill, Turner, Julio, Marco, and Pepe fanned out to the south. Rob had cautioned everybody to keep the closest cowpuncher on each side in sight.

They left Little Deer in charge of the remuda. Paco and Wise Elk spent the morning gathering firewood. With Wise Elk driving the wagon and Paco walking beside it, they also gathered dry buffalo chips, cow patties, horse apples, and whatever else they could find to burn. The salt cedar that grew along the Pecos and its tributaries smoked and stunk. Long before noon, they had filled a canvas belly bag stretched under the wagon.

About noon, Rob fired two shots and gathered the riders together. Jessie passed out biscuits Paco had given him, and they all drank from their canteens. They had found a lot of tracks. The herd had slowed down and had begun to breakup. They decided to all work east of the creek until mid-afternoon, then turn around and all work the west side back to camp.

Rob said, "Remember to stay within sight of each other in case anyone needs help."

They all agreed and rode off on their appointed course.

The Rodriguez brothers were the first to find the cows. Five were bedded down in the shade in a little cut by the creek. Bill found three more, and Turner came in with five. Pepe was excited. He found the four spare mules grazing in a little draw. They seemed to be glad to be found by a human and started braying and raising a ruckus. Jessie had a small bunch of cows, and Rob riding the outside, found part of the remuda and brought in fifteen horses.

They crossed the creek and turned around, increasing their herd all the way back. By the time they got back to camp, they had fifteen horses, four mules, and 137 head of cattle. It was a good start. The horses and mules were a bonus they had not expected.

Paco poured coffee for the riders, and Wise Elk handed it out as they came into camp.

Rob said, "Let's break the night into three shifts of four hours each. Julio and I will take Pepe with us until he is more experienced. Turner and Jessie can take a shift and round it out with Bill and Marco. If we rotate forward a shift every night, no one will have to work the same shift over and over. Little Deer can keep an eye on the remuda. When he gets tired, Pepe can spell him. We had a pretty good day. Does anybody have any other ideas?"

Turner said, "The cattle seem to be staying close to the water, so we will have to work the little runs further out. Does anybody have a thought on which direction would produce the most cattle?"

Bill said, "It seems there are more cattle the farther south we go. Perhaps we need to go a little farther south tomorrow."

Turner said, "In the morning, let's move our herd and the camp south to where we turned around today. We can fan out from there and see what that brings."

All agreed with the new plan, and Paco refilled the coffee cups. Rob, Julio, and Pepe were first in line to eat. After eating, they got fresh horses, saddled up, and rode out.

Turner said, "Jessie, what brought you and Rob to New Mexico?"

Jessie said, "I was working on Rob's family's ranch in East Texas. Rob and I became friends. The whole family got sick with typhoid fever and died. I rode into headquarters, and Rob was shaking his fist at God and asking why them and not me. He collapsed in a heap and sobbed. I got down and sat with him until he stopped crying. We buried his little sister. She was the last of them to die. Rob was set on selling the ranch and leaving. When I couldn't talk him out of it, I decided he was my best friend so I'd better try to help him—and here we are."

Everybody sat in silence for a while, then silently they all crawled in their bedrolls. Everybody was tired, and nobody had any trouble going to sleep that night—even with the coyote complaining to the moon and a white wing dove cooing his lonesome call.

They rolled out at sunup and eased the cattle and the remuda south down the creek. About noon, they reached the turnaround point from yesterday and stopped. Paco and Wise Elk, hobbling on his crutch, began to set up the new camp while the cowboys staked out the remuda and rounded the herd. Everybody gobbled down a quick lunch, and the cowboys started off leaving Pepe, Little Deer, Paco, and Wise Elk to oversee the stock and the camp.

After things settled down, Wise Elk got up on the wagon seat where he could see well in all directions and peeled potatoes while he watched. Pepe and Little Deer saddled fresh horses and rode out to circle the herd. Paco saddled his horse and went exploring. He found more watercress, cattails with nice tubers, wild onions, and fresh sage.

He found a damaged abandoned wagon. It had three good wheels, a good tongue, and half the box was intact. Paco looked around and discovered what appeared to be the belongings of a family. He found neither human remains nor the remains of any stock. The wagon had been partially burned. So he figured it had been attacked by Indians. Paco gathered up his newfound produce, and rode back to camp.

He told Wise Elk about the wagon and the condition of the belongings.

Wise Elk said, "Maybe Comancheros. They come this far north sometime. They take whites, sell as slaves in Mexico."

Paco said, "That would explain why there are no bodies, only belongings."

After a pause, Wise Elk said, "Today, I was high up on the wagon. Far in the east, I see dust, four maybe five horses. We need tell the white man."

Paco said in exasperation, "Wise Elk, you must refer to and call Señor Rob by his name, not as the white man!"

Wise Elk protested, "But he is *the* white man. He unlike any other."

"No, there are many good white men. I agree, he is special, but he is only a man."

Wise Elk said, "I will think on it."

"I'm going to tell the boys to keep a sharp eye out." Paco walked away in a huff, kicking the small rocks in anger.

The cow-hunting cowboys had again fanned out on the east side of the creek. Their plan was partly successful, and they were finding more cattle. When the sun was halfway down in the western sky, they crossed the creek, fanned out, and started back north. Their luck got better, and on a long branch of the creek, they gathered more than four hundred head of cattle. By the time they got back to camp, they had 562 head of cattle and one stray donkey.

As they drank the coffee, the camp crew handed them as they came in, Paco told Rob about the wagon and about Wise Elk seeing the dust in the east. That shook up the men. They had been so engrossed in hunting the cattle they had not been watching as carefully as they should have. They were embarrassed and uneasy.

Rob called everybody together and said, "Get your guns, clean 'em, check your ammunition, and be ready for trouble. Paco, break out the .44s I bought in El Paso and distribute them to those who are needful. Give the last of the saddle guns to Wise Elk and keep yours handy."

Jessie was watching Pepe and noticed his hesitation at handling the saddle gun. He said, "Pepe, do you know how to handle that Henry?"

Pepe sheepishly shook his head. "No, sir."

Jessie gathered up Rob, Turner, and Bill and told them what he had discovered.

"Damn," said Rob. "I hadn't even thought about them needing to shoot or even wondered if they knew how."

Turner said, "If they don't know how to shoot, we probably can't make marksmen of them. But if we get in a fight, it will help—even if they don't do more 'n just make smoke and noise."

Rob said, "Each one of you take one of the boys and instruct him in the handling and the use of the saddle guns and the pistols. I will take Little Deer. Paco can interpret. Paco, talk to Wise Elk and find out if he needs shooting school too."

Paco passed out the gun belts and Colts to Wise Elk and the young gentlemen.

Rob said, "Ride herd on the cattle after you have cleaned your guns and helped the boys with theirs. When the first group comes back to ride herd, take the others for instruction and shooting school."

Paco and Rob walked upstream so as not to stampede the herd again and set up a shooting range, using the far bank of the creek as a backstop. Rob showed Little Deer how to clean and load the guns.

Little Deer did well with the saddle gun, but he could not hit a barn with the pistol. Satisfied that they had done what they could do with him, they walked back to camp.

On the way back, Rob suddenly stopped and asked, "Paco, can you shoot?"

With a smile, Paco said, "Señor Rob, I shoot very well, but I'm glad you remembered to ask about Paco."

Jessie and Bill took Julio and Marco to the makeshift shooting range. Both the boys did well and made Jessie and Bill more confident about the situation. They told the two boys to keep practicing and walked back to camp to help ride herd while Turner and Pepe left for their turn on the range.

By the time Turner and Pepe got to the range, the Rodriguez boys were shooting the flowers off the cacti with the Henrys, but like Little Deer, they were not very good with the pistols.

Turner said, "Pepe, if you relax, your brain will take care of your body. All you have to do is look at the target and bring up the gun into the line of sight so that the sites line up with the target. If you practice that, the gun will come up aimed directly at the target. Okay? Now try it."

Pepe picked out a prickly pear ear, raised the rifle, and fired. The kick from the rifle knocked him flat on his back. Everybody laughed, helped him up, dusted him off, and let him try again.

Turner said, "Don't relax quite that much. Spread your feet and take a fighting stance."

That time Pepe hit the prickly pear ear, and it was all great fun after that. Pepe was a natural shot and even did well with the six-gun.

Over supper of whitetail deer venison, fried potatoes, wild onions, biscuits, and coffee, Paco passed out ammunition to those who needed it. He said, "Señor Rob, we have 699 head of cattle, eight extra mules, and one donkey in the remuda—in addition to the horses we started with and the mules on the wagon. We took one of the ten new Hernández horses for Pepe, but counting Jessie's packhorse, we still have ten we left El Paso with. With the fifteen new ones, we have a total of twenty-five extra horses."

Rob was impressed but exhausted. After a lengthy discussion with Wise Elk and Paco, he bedded down early. He had the second shift and needed the sleep.

Paco set aside a plate of supper to give to Rob when he got up to nighthawk. He took another plate, went out to the trees by the river, and put it down as he had been doing since they left Dog Canyon.

Turner woke Rob and said, "All is quiet, Rob."

Rob got up put on his hat and boots and went to relieve himself. Paco got up, poured coffee and handed Rob the cold supper and hot cup. Rob ate silently, woke Jessie, and they walked to their horses.

As they passed each other on the big circles they made in opposite directions around the camp and the herd, Jessie said, "We had a good day today cattle wise."

"Yes, we did. We had a good day at the shooting range too. Those boys did much better than I hoped."

The next time they crossed paths, Rob said, "I think anyone who attacks this outfit is in for a surprise."

"Yeah, our group of young gentlemen is much more formidable than it looks. They are not to be trifled with."

Rob said, "Things are looking up."

As their shift wore on, Rob's thoughts drifted back to the girl in Tularosa. How could a girl that young be so pretty? Rob had not met her mother, and he wondered if she had been as pretty as Emily. He had liked Ignacio Hernández from the start and respected him even more now that he had ridden Ignacio's horses. Rob was thinking about how Emily looked him in the eye as she poured his coffee when his horse pricked his ears and looked to the left. Rob drew his six-gun and followed the horse's stare with his own. The moon was shining brightly, and his night vision was excellent, but Rob could see nothing unusual.

Suddenly, he heard a growl and a snarl. Rob looked in time to see an Indian stand and draw his bow. Rob raised his six-gun and fired as he ducked. The arrow flew just over his head. He heard the man grunt, when he fired but he did not know where he had hit him. The little spotted rump horse, to his credit, fidgeted, but stood his ground.

Rob heard a horse retreating to the east as the camp came alive. Little Deer was the first one there, and after assuring himself that Rob was okay, Little Deer inspected the bushes in the direction Rob had indicated.

Turner and Bill were the next ones there followed by Jessie. Jessie had walked his horse around the herd so as not to spook the cattle. Rob tried to settle himself down as he told the others what had happened.

Little Deer came back to report, using a combination of his newfound English, their limited Spanish, and hand signals. He told them that one brave, probably Comanche, had been in the bushes for a long time, probably timing Rob and Jessie's circles so that Jessie would be on the opposite side. He showed them blood drops on his fingers but indicated that he did not know where the man was hit.

Little Deer said, "How Comanche missed? It only this many steps." He held up ten fingers.

Paco said, "It was Duke. I saw him before we reached El Paso. After that, I put out food every night. It would be gone in the morning."

Rob remembered the growl and snarl, and he stood silently in amazement.

Turner said, "I'll get Julio, and we'll start our shift early. It's almost time anyway."

Rob said, "I'm grateful, Turner. I am still a little rattled."

Rob, leading his horse, walked back to camp with Paco. The others followed along and talked to each other excitedly.

Bill said, "You mean to tell me that a wild coyote growled to warn a man of danger?"

Paco said, "Si, Señor Bill—or maybe he just does not like Comanche. I have known Señor Rob and Duke's relationship to be special, but I had no idea how special."

The men crawled into their bedrolls and thought about what had happened. There was not much more sleeping in the camp that night.

Chapter 6

Emily Goes to Town

*A*s usual, Ignacio and Emily Hernández attended Sunday Mass. After Mass, Juanita Rodriquez, one of Emily's girlfriends and Marco and Julio Rodriguez sister, sought her out and said, "Emily, let's meet in town on Wednesday and look at the new catalog at the general mercantile."

Emily looked up at her daddy inquiringly.

He nodded.

Emily said, "Oh Juanita, that sounds fun. Let's meet at Mama Garcia's boardinghouse for lunch. After lunch, we can admire the new dress styles in the catalog."

"Wonderful, Emily. Mama Garcia always has her green chili chicken enchiladas on Wednesdays. I'll meet you there at noon."

"Oh, I can't wait. Thanks, Juanita. I'll see you then."

On the way home, Emily said, "Thank you, Papa. I haven't been to meet the girls in town for a long time."

"That is one reason I think you should go. I also remember how your mother used to like to go look at the new dress styles. Now don't get carried away and spend too much on material."

Emily thought, *How can you spend too much on dress material?* "Papa, have you heard anything about the Rodriguez boys? Are they back yet?"

Ignacio Hernández said, "Why, No, I haven't. Why do you ask? You've never paid any attention to the Rodriguez brothers before."

"Oh, I was just wondering. Juanita asked if I had heard anything about her brothers."

Ignacio looked at Emily and wondered if she wanted to know about Rob Wilson. He had really lit up her face when he was here.

On Wednesday morning, Emily was up early working on her chores so she would be able to finish early and meet Juanita. When she finished her chores, she changed her dress, brushed her hair, put on her best hat, walked into the living room, and said, "How do I look?"

Ignacio looked up, and his chest tightened. Emily looked very much like her mother—even in her mannerisms as she looked at herself in the mirror. Ignacio was unable to speak. When Emily turned to look at him questioningly, he pulled himself together and said, "Oh, you look beautiful, my darling."

"Well, thank you Papa." she said as she turned around again and looked directly at him in surprise. "Thank you very much."

As he handed her some money, he said, "I had José hitch up the buckboard for you. It's already out front. A beautiful young lady shouldn't have to hitch up her own wagon. You girls have a good time."

"Thank you, Papa. I put your lunch on the table in the kitchen."

"Thank you, my darling. How about bringing me some of Señora Garcia's empanadas."

"Of course I will." She smiled at him.

Emily walked out the door and was helped onto the buckboard by José, the vaquero who had gotten water for Rob's Indians.

She drove into town and turned north onto Saint Francis, Tularosa's main street, toward the boardinghouse to meet Juanita.

Suddenly Jim Healy stepped off the porch of the saloon, grabbed her horse's halter, and said, "Whoa there, whoa."

Healy looked up at the startled girl and said, "What's your hurry there, little girl?"

Emily was startled but with the anger rising in her she said, "Mr. Healy, please release my horse."

Healy smiled and said, "Oh, come on. Where are you going in such a hurry that a few minutes talking to me will make any difference?"

"Mr. Healy, where I'm going is none of your business. Now please turn loose of my horse."

Healy was not accustomed to girls not welcoming his attentions and frowned. "I'll let go when I'm good 'n ready."

Emily not intimidated one bit, took the buggy whip and lashed out at Healy yelling, "Jim Healy, I said let go of my horse." And she lashed out at him again.

Apparently surprised and caught off guard, Healy jumped back to avoid the whip. When he stepped back, Emily's startled horse started up the street. Healy was almost run over by the buckboard wheels. She regained control of her horse and hurried on up the street.

Healy looked furious. The witnesses had disapproving looks on their faces. Healy picked up his hat, brushed it off, put it back on, and walked back into the saloon.

Emily was in tears but collected herself before she got to the boardinghouse. She stopped, tied her horse to the hitching rail, and entered Mama Garcia's. Luckily, the lunch crowd had not arrived yet

Señora Garcia said, "What happened to you, Emily? Why are you crying?"

"Oh, it's nothing, mama Garcia. I'm all right. I am to meet Juanita Rodriguez. Is she here yet?"

"Yes. She's waiting at your table, but let's go wash your face first." She directed Emily to the kitchen.

After Emily freshened her face, Señora Garcia directed her to the table.

Emily turned to Señora Garcia and whispered, "Please don't say anything to Papa, Okay?"

The boardinghouse keeper shook her head and walked to the kitchen without answering.

After a wonderful lunch when the girls got outside, as Emily had feared, the vaquero, José was standing next to the buckboard. He was wearing his pistol. He smiled at Emily and said, "¿Empanadas por patron?"

"Oh … Papa's empanadas." Emily ran back into the boardinghouse.

When she returned with a small bundle, José helped the girls onto the buckboard and escorted them to the store. When they reached the general store, he helped them down and opened the door. He returned to the street and waited by his horse.

Emily almost cried again from embarrassment. She had told Juanita what had happened but wanted no one else to know. As soon as she saw the vaquero, she knew someone had sent word to her daddy. She didn't want to cause any trouble.

The girls browsed the catalog and admired the dresses. They studied the lines and the way the fabric was cut and talked about how to sew the dresses themselves. The incident with Healy lingered in Emily's mind and dampened the pleasure somewhat.

When they finished looking at and talking about all the dresses in the catalog, they each bought three sticks of hard candy and enough fabric for a dress.

"Oh, look, Juanita. Here are some of those new paper dress patterns the Buttericks invented in 1863. I haven't seen any of them before. It has taken over ten years for them to get to Tularosa. I'm going to buy one for my dress. When I'm through, you are welcome to borrow it."

They walked outside, and Juanita hugged Emily. "Goodbye, Emily. I will look forward to trying out that new dress pattern when you finish. Now don't you worry about Jim Healy. He probably just drank too much. Everything will be all right."

Emily said, "I hope you're right. I'd rather Papa not get involved. I don't want to be the cause of any trouble."

"You won't be. Listen to what I say. Everything will be all right."

"Oh, I hope so. Let's do this again soon. Next time, I'll come into town from the north. Let me give you a ride home."

"It's only two blocks. I will enjoy the walk. Adios, Emily."

"Goodbye, Juanita."

The vaquero rode his horse and silently followed Emily home.

When she drove up into the yard, Ignacio Hernández was sitting in the shade on the east-facing porch. The vaquero helped Emily down from the buckboard.

She put her hand on his arm and said, "Gracias, José."

The vaquero nodded, touched the brim of his sombrero, and said, "De nada, señorita." He smiled at her and took the buckboard down to the barn.

Emily walked up the steps and onto the porch. "Hello, Papa. Here are your empanadas. Mama Garcia said to give you her best." She handed him the little bundle and sat down in the chair beside him.

"Thank you, my darling." He took the bundle, opened it, and began eating one of the empanadas.

Ignacio finished the first empanada and started on a second. He paused between bites, and said, "I heard you handled Jim Healey like a roadrunner handles a rattlesnake."

As the tears welled up, she said, "Oh, Papa, I'm sorry, but he made me so mad, I lost my temper."

"Just remember, baby, roadrunner can be bitten if she is not very careful with a rattlesnake. He is not like a garter snake you can toy with."

"Yes, Papa. I'll remember." She dried her eyes and hugged him.

Chapter 7

THE MOTHER LODE OF CATTLE

*A*t daybreak over breakfast, Rob said, "You other cowboys, go south and take up where we left off yesterday. I will go east and check out where the dust Wise Elks saw came from. After that, I'll help the camp crew move camp and the herd further south. We'll meet you for supper where we turned around yesterday. Check your guns and your ammunition and keep your eyes open. Good luck."

Rob and Paco inspected the bushes where the incident had occurred.

Paco said, "Here are your horse tracks."

Rob said, "I found where the Indian waited."

"Look, Señor Rob. Here are Duke's tracks. I see where he laid for some time. He was probably watching the Indian."

Rob was still unable to believe what had happened.

When they got back to camp, Rob poured himself the last of the coffee and shook his head in amazement.

With Paco interpreting, Wise Elk told them the Apache story about the coyote being the spirit of a loved one who had crossed over to the next life. "That is why they are so mystical, whimsical, and hard to see. That is why they know us so well and are so smart. You will do well to return the favor."

While they packed up the camp, Rob rode east, found the tracks, and looked them over, and rode back to camp. When he got back to camp he said, "It was five unshod ponies headed south."

It had been about two weeks since Paco had set Wise Elk's leg, and with the crutch they had made for him, he was getting around much better. Wise Elk said, "Maybe I ride now." He hung his crutch on a rawhide thong over his shoulder like a bow. Paco saddled Wise Elk's pony and boosted him aboard. The old Indian became another cowboy.

They hitched up the wagon and started the whole outfit south along the creek. When they got close, Paco showed Rob the abandoned wagon.

"Señor Rob, if we saw off the burnt part of the front of the wagon, we can use the good part for a travois on wheels. We could attach the tongue to the back of it, put a bolt through the other end of the tongue, and bolt it to the back of my wagon. We could fasten the other good wheel on top of the tongue, and it could be a spare front wheel for my wagon and a rack for firewood."

Rob said, "You have a good idea—if we had a saw."

"You are not the only one who likes to be prepared." Paco reached into his wagon and produced a saw, a brace and bit, and a long bolt with several big washers and a double nut on it.

They worked hard, but Paco had given it a good deal of thought. He knew exactly what he wanted to do. They took bolts from the burnt part of the wagon and used them to bolt the tongue to the back of the wagon trailer. In less than two hours, they were attaching their new trailer to Paco's wagon. The trailer was the rear half of the wagon box over the rear axle. They attached the front end of the tongue to the back of Paco's wagon and attached the spare wheel to the back end of the tongue and the front of the box to provide a place to stack extra firewood.

They started the outfit to the south again, and the contraption worked exceedingly well.

Paco said, "We can now haul two extra barrels of water and more firewood, when we can find it, so we will have it for the long dry stretches between water and firewood."

Rob was amazed.

They reached their destination and set up the new camp. Rob went into the bushes along the river and killed three javelinas. When he brought them back to camp, Paco was thrilled. They had not had pork for a long time. Paco scalded them, scraped off the hair, cleaned the little pigs, and prepared them for the spit.

Wise Elk hobbled over, sat down on his keg by the handle of the spit, and volunteered to turn it and tend the fire for the rest of the afternoon.

In the late afternoon, they noticed a large plume of dust rising in the south. Rob rode out to meet the cowboys. He was overwhelmed when they came up, driving more than a thousand head of cattle. There were more than twenty goats following noisily along.

After they had rounded the cattle into their other herd and settled them down, Turner and Bill came in to tell the story over their traditional end of the day coffee

Turner sipped his coffee and said, "We gathered a few cattle this morning, and a little after midday, we found the mother lode. One of the main bunches of the stampeded herd was still together grazing through the bottom of a little draw as if they owned it."

Bill said, "We found the goats and what appeared to be a murdered goat herder. It looked like Indians killed him and his dog, but they did not take time to gather the goats. We buried him in a shallow grave. The goats followed us, and here they are."

Turner said, "We saw about fifteen horses south of here, but we had too many cattle to go after them. Maybe we can go after them tomorrow."

That night, Paco outdid himself with roasted javelinas, the watercress, dandelion, and wild onion salad wilted with the wonderful vinaigrette, a big pot of frijoles, cattail tubers, potatoes with onions fried in pork fat, and gallons of coffee. He had five Dutch ovens buried around the big roasting fire: Three with deep-dish apple pie and two with sourdough biscuits.

At Paco's direction, Pepe continually shoveled hot coals onto the top of the Dutch ovens to evenly brown the bread and the pie. Paco hoped there would be enough left for lunch the next day but the way these cowboys eat, maybe not.

The cowboys had not stopped for a midday meal and were famished. The camp hands thought they were starving, but it was mostly because everything smelled so good.

Bill said, "I'm hungry 'nough to eat a saddle blanket."

Jessie said, "I'm so hungry I could eat a sow and six piglets an' chase the boar a half-a-mile."

Turner said, "I feel like a posthole 'at ain't been filled up."

Rob topped it with, "I'm hungry as a bitch wolf suckin' nine pups."

With that, Paco called them to supper.

The cowboys were impressed with the new wagon trailer. Paco and Wise Elk did a little fine-tuning on the trailer after supper and joined the cowboys for pie and coffee.

Rob, Jessie, Turner, and Bill held a powwow.

Turner said, "I know we agreed we would split the gather and the expenses fifty-fifty. Bill and I will still pay our 50 percent of the expenses, but because we have so many cattle, we better split them sixty-forty. The Artesian Well Ranch will take 40 percent. We only have two waterholes and the artesian well pool. We'll take eight horses, and you take the rest of the stock. I'm afraid we might not have enough water for more. We never imagined the gather would be so big."

Rob started to protest, but Turner said, "Look, Rob. You and Jessie have basically given me and Bill it all. You could have come by yourselves and done the same thing with no help from the Artesian Well Ranch."

Reluctantly, Rob and Jessie agreed.

They decided that if they got home with all this bounty, they would give the Rodriguez boys and Pepe each two horses of their own. The boys could take their horses home if they left, but they were going to offer them a home and a job at Dog Canyon Ranch. Additionally, Paco would have his choice of mules, horses, and cows. He would also receive double wages.

Later they asked Paco to help them decide what Wise Elk and Little Deer should have. Should it be money, stock, a job, and a home? They had no idea what would be appropriate and appreciated. They also told Paco they were thinking of giving the goats to his cousin Juan.

The next morning, Turner, Bill, Julio, and Marco rode out to gather the horses and cattle they had seen the day before. It turned out to be seventeen horses and thirty-seven more cattle. Jessie and Wise Elk tended the herd, and Rob wrangled the remuda while Paco, Pepe, and Little Deer gathered wood to fill the trailer. Finally, they turned the outfit west-southwest and started home. Paco drove the wagon, and the other nine were cowboys.

What had started out as two cowboys was now four gringo cowboys, three young Mexican cowboys, one Indian wrangler, one old Indian with a healing broken leg, and Paco the Mexican cook. They had their nine original riding horses, one packhorse, Paco's original four mules, forty-two new horses, eight new mules, one donkey, twenty-five goats, and 1,793 head of cattle.

Even as short as the drive had been—from the creek where they found him back to the main camp—it became obvious that an old brindle longhorn was the lead steer. Before they had gotten back to camp yesterday afternoon, the old steer had taken his place as the lead steer, and the rest of the herd fell in behind him. Jessie realized what he had discovered and happily rode along beside the lead steer— sometimes with his gloved hand resting on the steer's massive horn.

Their new traveling protocol was, Paco driving his wagon that was pulling its new trailer. Jessie riding with the lead steer leading the herd. Rob and Wise Elk were flanking the herd on one side, and Turner and Bill were on the other. Julio and Marco were riding drag. Little Deer and Pepe were herding the remuda including the mules and the donkey. The goats were happy to follow noisily along unassisted at the side of Paco's wagon.

From time to time, Rob or Turner would ride point to check the best route back to the Pecos. Every morning and every afternoon, Rob sent Little Deer out to ride point and circle the herd to see if he found any Indians sign. They had been gone from El Paso over two weeks but didn't expect to get back for at least three weeks with the herd.

The point rider marked a campsite with a cloth flag. Paco drove the wagon ahead of the herd, being careful not to get out of sight. Still, he outran the herd and stopped at the indicated campsite.

Paco faced the wagon into the sun so the chuck table and work area at the back were in the shade until sunset. It would be in the sunlight in the morning. He built a fire and rinsed the beans he had put to soak that morning in freshwater. Then hung them to cook over the fire. He made coffee and sometimes he roasted or boiled meat, and he hunted herbs and tubers for dinner.

They managed to camp on a stream or creek all but one night, and the stock was well watered. When they reached the Pecos, everybody breathed a sigh of relief at being out of Comanche country.

After they crossed the river, everybody and all the stock was exhausted. Rob decided that the outfit should rest up an extra day. The cattle had plenty of water and grass and were easy to tend.

Paco roasted and smoked five javelinas the cowboys had killed and Little Deer brought in a whitetail deer for the larder. Along the river, Paco gathered greens, herbs, and tubers, and they ate very well. As a special treat one night, Paco cracked a clutch of sage hen eggs into milk they got from one of the tamer goats. He added sugar, vanilla, and cinnamon, whipped it, and poured it over the leftover bread and biscuits he had saved up. Mixing in the raisins and figs Jessie bought back at Stevenson's, Paco made a bread pudding. He baked it in Dutch ovens, and it was the most wonderful bread pudding the cowboys had ever tasted.

The next morning, they had packed up and were leaving the river. They had a little trouble getting the wagon and trailer to the top of the rimrock. By hitching an extra team of mules to the wagon—and with four mounted cowboys pulling with their lariats—they managed to get the wagon to the top. Everybody was in high spirits as they headed for El Paso.

That night, Rob, Jessie, Turner, Bill, and Paco held a meeting over coffee.

Rob said, "When we were in El Paso, the owner of the cantina told me his brother runs a trading post just south of the Texas-New Mexico Territory line. He recommended going back that way. I have been thinking and I am wishful to turn north about a day after we pass the Guadalupe Mountains, right after we cross the dry salt lakes. Then go due north a day and a half to the trading post. Paco can buy grub and supplies at Dell's trading post. From there, we can head northwest three or four days to the edge of the mesa rim, just south of Dog Canyon. We could head for home directly cross-country rather than trying to take the herd all the way west through El Paso and turn north to Dog Canyon. If we go north over the mesa, water might be scarce, but it would cut about a hundred miles off the trip home."

It was the first time he had used the term *home* for the Dog Canyon country, and he liked the feel of it.

Paco said, "I have heard of the trading post, but I have never been there. We are running low on supplies. The plan to turn north after the salt lakes would mean it is only three or four more days to the trading post where we can stock up on food and supplies." After a moment's thought he said, "If it is two or three days closer than El Paso, maybe we will not run out of flour."

Everyone agreed that it was a good plan, but they were sorry about missing the food and excitement of the city.

Rob said, "I agree. I hate to miss El Paso. I dread telling the younger cowboys they will miss El Paso. However, when we get the herd home and settled, I will take everybody back to El Paso for some fun." He thought, *Besides we need to go back to the bank and draw out more money.*

Rob announced the plan to the whole camp and observed the expected reaction. For a minute, he thought Pepe would cry. Pepe had been looking forward to another store-bought breakfast of ham and eggs that were dirty on both sides and toast with butter and jelly. After a while Pepe said, "Well, it will just taste better when I come back."

The next morning as usual they were traveling before full daylight, and Rob turned them slightly south. He lined them up to skirt the south end of the Guadalupe Mountains. They made good time over the next two days. The ground was relatively flat, and the traveling was good. They skirted the mountains and crossed the dry salt lakes. Rob turned the outfit north after they crossed the salt lakes, and they headed for the trading post.

Little Deer found a nice waterhole in the bottom of a draw on one of his point riding expeditions. There was enough water for the entire herd and the other animals. They camped there that night, excited that they would be at the trading post before the next evening.

Chapter 8

THE JEDIDIAH DELL TRADING POST

The following morning, the whole outfit was up, coffeed, packed, and rolling long before daylight. By late afternoon, they saw the trading post.

Rob located their campsite more than a quarter mile from the trading post's main building. While the others rounded the herd and set up camp, Rob and Jessie rode over and walked into the trading post.

The man behind the counter said, "I'm Jedidiah Dell—just call me Jed." Jedidiah was a short man with a potbelly. He was dressed in a white shirt, dark pants, with a long white apron tied around his ample middle.

Rob said, "I'm Robert Wilson, and this is Jessie Hatfield. We are setting up a new ranch at Dog Canyon, on the other side of the mesa. When we were in El Paso a while back, we ate dinner and breakfast at your brother's cantina. We enjoyed it very much."

They all shook hands.

Rob said, "Since that time, we have gathered a herd of cattle the other side of the Pecos. The cattle and the remuda are camped a safe distance from your trading post. Your brother recommended turning north just west of the salt lakes and traveling north to your trading post. He recommended turning northwest and crossing the mesa to the rim of the Tularosa Basin south of Dog Canyon."

Jedidiah said, "Let me get us a beer." He left the table and came back with three mugs of beer. "I will have to thank my little brother for sending you here. It is shorter than going around through El Paso, but you will need good luck to cross the mesa safely from here. The Mescalero cross the mesa back and forth on their way to Mexico. You've got a big herd. You won't be able to hide it. If the Mescalero are around, they will be able to see your dust for miles."

Rob said, "We are needful of supplies and does your trading post serve hot food?"

Jedidiah said, "Oh, yes, we serve food here—good food too."

Rob said, "I'd like to get the boys fed before we pick up the supplies. If it's okay with you, we will eat in two shifts because we can't leave the herd alone. How long before the first shift can eat?"

Jedidiah said, "Give me three quarters of an hour so we can bake fresh bread. Cook's got it kneaded and rising already. When it's done, we'll be ready."

Rob said, "I'll go arrange the two shifts. I'll send in the first batch in about forty-five minutes."

Rob gathered the men and said, "Turner, Paco, Wise Elk, Jessie, and I will ride herd on the stock while you others go in and eat as the first shift. You young gentlemen follow Bill's orders and mind your manners."

Marco stepped up and said, "No, el jefe, you honored ones must eat first. It is only right. We will ride herd on the stock. You must be the first shift."

Rob protested, but Paco and Turner argued that Marco was right. After a short discussion, Rob folded and agreed. By the time the stock was cared for and they had finished setting up camp, the time had passed.

Rob led the group to the horse trough in front of the trading post. They washed up and dried with flour sack towels Paco had brought. Feeling more presentable, they filed into the trading post for dinner.

They sat at a long table with benches on either side and waited. No one came for a long time. Eventually, Jedidiah came to the table and announced in a voice louder than necessary, "This trading post does not serve Indians in the dining room."

Rob stood up and said, "If anybody in the Dog Canyon outfit is not welcome, everybody in the Dog Canyon outfit is not welcome." Taking a silver dollar from his vest pocket and flipping it to Jedidiah, Rob said, "This is for the beer."

The beer was only a nickel a mug, but he walked out, and the others followed.

Wise Elk said, "It okay. You go eat. Little Deer and Wise Elk eat out back."

Paco did not even translate, he said, "Pepe, help get the fire started—and prepare to cook."

Rob mounted his horse and rode out to cool off and circle the herd.

Jessie said, "Turner, will you stay in camp and help Paco while I ride out and tell the others?"

By sundown, they had butchered an old one-eyed cow. Paco was cooking biscuits, warming beans, and broiling beefsteak.

Jedidiah came to apologize and asked them to come back and eat.

Turner said, "Thank you for the apology, but our young friend who bosses this outfit may have some newfangled ideas 'bout things, but he'll do to ride the trail with. Our supper's almost ready now anyhow."

There was a great deal of discussion among the cowboys, and the older ones had to explain it to the younger ones. After that, they agreed that they were proud of their boss and that if he asked it of them, they would follow him anywhere he would lead them.

Rob, Jessie, Wise Elk, Turner, and Paco held a war council over supper.

Rob said, "Wise Elk, what about the Mescalero?"

Wise Elk through Paco's translations told them it was true the Mescalero came down from the high up mountains across Pasture Ridge, around Tabletop, and down the Langford Trail or the

Sacramento River. Those were the only trails down the west face of the mountain on the south end. He told them the Indians knew the location of all the waterholes and springs.

Wise Elk told Rob, through Paco, there was water for the cattle, but they are unlikely to be able to water all the cattle at the same place. They will have to split off groups of the herd and water them at different places. He had traveled this route many times as a young brave, and he remembered many of the locations of the waterholes but things may be different now.

Jessie said, "How hostile will the Indians be if we encounter 'em?"

Wise Elk answered, "I am not sure. Some might be very hostile, and some would want to steal some of the beef. Others would want to steal the horses. It will depend on how successful their raids into Mexico were and how much they have had to eat. They will be armed but most will only have knives, bows, and arrows. Only some will have horses—unless they were very lucky in Mexico."

Rob said, "Check and clean your guns, check your ammunition, and check and sharpen your knives. We must all keep a sharp eye for the rest of the trip. Split into the three night shifts and take care of cow business."

Paco said, "Señor Rob, I would like to have Pepe help me tomorrow. We are running low on flour, and we are out of potatoes. We will need to harvest yucca roots. The yucca roots can be fried or boiled as a starch or pounded and dried to make flour."

Rob agreed and rode over to see Little Deer. "Can you handle the remuda by yourself for part of tomorrow? Paco needs Pepe to help him."

Little Deer said, "Jefe, Little Deer be fine by self with remuda."

"Okay, call me if you need help."

Long before daylight, they were coffeed up, packed, and gone. Rob pointed them northwest when they were due east of the round mountain and said, "Keep a sharp eye out. We may run into trouble."

Jessie and his lead steer started for Dog Canyon. Wise Elk's advice and information about the water was correct. They pressed hard and made good time.

Paco explained to Pepe, "Look for the yuccas with the fine long leaves like pampas grass leaves—not the ones you call Spanish daggers with the leaves like agave leaves. Those are soap root yuccas—and Pepe, don't pull up all the plants in any one area. We must leave some for seed for the future."

Pepe said, "Si, señor."

That night, Pepe peeled and sliced the yucca roots to fry them with the last of their onions.

Paco said, "Listen everybody, do not eat the yucca roots raw, they are a little bit poison until they were cooked."

The cowboys were amazed at how delicious the yucca roots were.

Rob said, "Paco, stay closer to the herd—and do not take the wagon out in front very far. Stay where you can see the others and where we can see you."

That cramped Paco style. He was only able to serve fried or broiled steak since he could not drive on ahead and had no time for roasting or boiling beef. Paco put the beans to soak in the morning, and cooked them that night so they could be served the next day.

That night Paco took the chuck and the round from one side of old one eye and put it on to boil so they could have boiled beef the next night. The night after that, he took the remaining beef and the broth he had boiled it in, added wild onions, yucca roots, and yellow tubers to make beef stew.

Rob sent Little Deer out to ride point most of the time, and worked Little Deer's place in the remuda. Little Deer reported the tracks of several groups of unshod ponies and moccasins, but all the tracks were more than a few days old.

Little Deer and Wise Elk conferred a good while before Little Deer rode out the second time that day. Wise Elk had given Little Deer a few things to look for to find water. Little Deer came back shortly before noon and with Paco's help, told Rob, that he had found one respectable waterhole that might water all the stock. In addition, he had found two springs but recommended those only for camp water.

Paco, Rob, Jessie, and Turner had a conference.

Rob said, "Little Deer found a water hole to water the stock and two springs for camp water. The problem is they are not together. We will have to split up to go get the camp water. I am fearful of splitting the wagon away from the other cowboys and the herd."

Paco said, "I sure wish we had those other two barrels of water in the trailer. If we did, we wouldn't have to have water now. If chickens had more brains, they would not sit on the roost and let the fox get them."

Turner said, "While the herd is at the waterhole we can take our three best marksmen and escort Paco to the spring. The herd will not be hard to tend. They will stay at the water. That way, we could leave six cowboys with the herd and both groups would be formidable."

Rob said, "According to Little Deer, it's only about two miles between the spring and the waterhole. When we get to the waterhole if we press hard we can be back with the camp water in an hour or less. If the Mescalero are watching us, by the time they realize what we are doing, they won't have much time to gather their party and attack either group."

Rob called Wise Elk and Little Deer and said, "Do you know how far it is to the next water?"

Wise Elk spoke at length. Paco translated, "The camp water spring is Caballo Springs, and it runs almost all the time. In wet years, there would be other springs between here and the mesa rim but this has been a dry year, and there may not be any more water until we get over the rim and down to Culp Canyon in, two, maybe three days."

Jessie said, "Well, that settles it. We can't go that long without water for the camp. The stock won't like it, but if we water them good at the waterhole, they can survive a couple of days. And who knows, it might rain."

Everybody agreed it was the best plan they had. They decided that even though Jessie was a good shot, he was the most experienced cowboy, was the most familiar with the young cowboys, and should stay with the herd. Paco would drive the wagon, and Rob, Turner, and Bill would be outriders.

By two o'clock, they reached the waterhole.

Rob said, "Check your equipment and clean and check your guns and ammunition." As he hitched a fresh team of mules to the wagon and unhitched the trailer, he added, "You outriders, saddle fresh horses."

Rob sent Little Deer, Wise Elk, Jessie, and Bill to scout the four points of the compass for Mescalero. While they scouted, he saddled himself a fresh horse.

Paco rigged the wagon for high-speed, rough travel. He unloaded the bedrolls, extra saddles and tack, extra ammunition, and the kegs and barrels except for the water barrels. He went through the wagon and unloaded everything else.

When all the scouts had returned with negative contacts and no fresh sign of Indians, Rob looked at the cowboys that were staying with the herd; and said, "You all will have to stay alert." Then he added a little softer, "Nothing bad will happen. The camp water team will be back in no time."

Rob rechecked the directions to the spring with Little Deer, and they were off at a fast trot.

It was a tooth-rattling ride for Paco, the mesa looked smooth a horseback at a distance but it had little ditches hidden in the grass of the draws and more rocks than they could count. The outriders' heads were on swivels, but nobody saw anything. They arrived at the spring and started filling the barrels. Rob rode up to the highest point around, to keep watch.

While they were filling the last barrel, they heard the shots.

Paco slammed the lid on the barrel and shouted, "Take off. I will be right behind you."

The three outriders rode hell-bent back towards the herd. They only heard ten or twelve shots. That scared the cowboys because as well armed as the young gentlemen were, they should have been able to hold out longer if they followed Jessie's orders.

It only took five or six minutes for the outriders to get back to the herd. All three had their saddle guns drawn and rode up unable to understand what they were seeing.

The herd was only slightly scattered, and the remuda was grouped and milling around Little Deer. The herd cowboys had taken cover behind the tack, bedrolls, supplies, and wagon trailer. Julio was bleeding from a shoulder wound, and Jessie had an arrow stuck in his thigh but was still mounted.

Wise Elk was on his pony with his arms raised up high between the herd cowboys and a group of about fifty Indians. The Indians were about equally divided between men on foot and men a horseback. Wise Elk was addressing the Indians and had their complete attention. Several Indians were bleeding, and two were on the ground. There was discussion back and forth between Wise Elk and two of the older Indians as the camp water party outriders returned.

The camp water party prepared to defend Wise Elk if need be. The other Indians stopped talking, and Wise Elk made a long speech with many hand signs and gestures. He turned and touched Rob on the shoulder and continued his speech while the Indians stared back and forth between Rob and Wise Elk.

As if on cue, Duke howled from the top of the hill, you would not think one coyote could make that much noise and it had the desired effect, All the Indians were silent.

Paco rolled up in the wagon with his mules at a gallop. He pulled up, close to Turner and Bill who were standing behind Rob and Wise Elk. Paco got down and trotted over to Wise Elk where he was able to hear the discussion and interpreted for the gringos.

He related that Wise Elk was forbidding the Indians to harm this group of white men and explaining was that a man protected by the spirits of the coyote was a man to be left alone.

Duke howled again and trotted down the hill toward the group, He only came down the rise about halfway and never got within fifty yards, but it was enough to make his point and many of the Indians backed up.

Wise Elk raised his broken leg and showed the leaders of the Indians. He turned and touched Paco and talked more. He touched Rob again, showed them his crutch, and talked more.

Paco did not have much Apache and was having trouble following the talk. He was unable to interpret for the gringos. He respectfully requested Wise Elk speak Spanish and ask the others to speak Spanish so he could repeat their words to the man of the coyote spirit and the other gringos. Wise Elk spoke one more line in Apache and then changed to Spanish.

Wise Elk pointed to Rob, turned around to point at the coyote on the hill only to find Duke was gone. He dropped his arm, shrugged his shoulders, and said he hoped they had not offended Rob's coyote.

Paco continued to translate; Wise Elk asked why so many braves were afoot. The oldest Indian told him it had been a hard winter in Mexico, and they had not stolen many horses. He went on to say, they were on their way back to Mescalero because a runner had come to tell them the people were starving.

Rob suspected the Indians had not eaten very well either. He risked asking Paco if it would be a good idea to offer to feed these men. Rob also suggested a truce be called so each side could attend their wounded. Paco translated Rob's question and suggestion.

Wise Elk rather than ask the other Indians, told them that there would be a truce and to attend to the wounded. Then, told them that later they would all sit down together and eat.

The Indians turned around, picked up the two men who were down, and set up a camp. They performed rudimentary first aid on their wounded, gathered wood from down the draw, built small fires, and roasted the antelope haunches they carried.

Rob said, "Paco, will you attend to their wounded? Bill and Turner, will you butcher a steer as fast as possible?" Rob added with a grin, "Make sure it's not Jessie's lead steer." He told Marco, "Start a fire, heat water, find Pepe and try to put Paco's chuck wagon back together for him."

Rob then walked over to Jessie, to check on his wound.

Paco had cleaned and bandaged Julio's shoulder and announced it was not as bad as a gunshot wound to the shoulder could have been. The bullet had gone through the flesh and out the back. It had gone in above the armpit and not broken any bones.

Paco started working on Jessie and told Rob, "Removing the arrow will be painful."

Then he asked Wise Elk, "Do any of the Indians have any peyote or willow bark?"

A young brave handed Paco a whole peyote bud. He sliced off a piece and gave it to Jessie and told him to chew it. Another brave brought him a pouch of willow bark.

Paco said, "Jessie, this peyote will probably make you throw up. Don't worry about that. Wise Elk is the only person I ever saw who didn't get sick when he chewed peyote." He hung the cooked beans and all the boiled beef he had over the fire.

Bill volunteered, "I'll make biscuits Paco. You go doctor the wounded Indians."

Wise Elk accompanied Paco to make sure there was no misunderstanding.

After Paco had been to doctor the wounded Indians he came back, found Rob, and said, "One brave was serious. He was shot in the chest and it must have been a rifle bullet because it passed clean through. Marco brought hot water and bandages. We washed and cleaned the wound. It had barely missed the Indian's lung. I sewed up the openings in the brave's chest and the back wound as best I could then bandaged them tight and moved on to see about the other wounded Indians. The other Indian that had been down was lucky. A bullet grazed his head and knocked him out but he had come to. I cleaned the wound, sewed it up, and bandaged it; the other Indians were teasing that one about his funny headdress when we left to come back."

Rob and Paco got back to the gringo camp, and Rob asked what they should do.

Paco said, "Butchering the steer had been a good idea. Nothing will help our relations more than a good feed."

Paco told Pepe to get all the yucca roots they had gathered and get help peeling and slicing them. Paco asked Jessie if he could have a start from Jessie's starter for another batch of biscuits. It would take all their flour, but it would be a good investment. He filled the other two Dutch ovens, and all five were filled with biscuits.

Turner and Bill finished butchering the steer and distributed one side of beef to the Indians. They took the front quarter—except for the rib eye and round from the other side—and put it on a spit over the fire. Paco put the sirloin and the rib eye in the wagon to broil steaks the next night.

Wise Elk asked Paco if they were able to spare any salt. Paco handed him a bag with almost two pounds of salt in it. Paco asked Wise Elk if the meat had been a good idea and was assured that it had been. Wise Elk went on to say, he had told the Indians that the man of the spirit of the coyote sent the meat as a gift and that he would tell them the salt was a peace offering.

When things quieted down, Paco, Rob, Bill, and Turner gathered at Jessie's bedroll. Rob asked what had happened while they were gone to get the camp water.

Jessie said, "Everything was quiet. Then, of a sudden, all hell broke loose. We were attacked by 'bout fifty Indians. Only 'bout a dozen shots were fired before Wise Elk rode out on his pony with his arms raised high and ordered the Indians to stop shootin'. As soon as they stopped, we stopped shootin'. Boy, I'll tell you one thing: I wouldn't want to fight our crew. Pepe and the Rodriguez boys can shoot, and they are pure-t-devils in a fight. Pepe shot the young brave in the chest, and Marco hit the one in the head while he was ridin' by on a horse. Julio wounded two others. I don't think Little Deer got off a shot, but he managed to hold the remuda together. I was on the other side of the herd and just got back over here in time to get hit with this damned arrow.

"The real hero of this little fight was Wise Elk. He rode out in the middle of the shootin' with his hands raised high, callin' for a cease-fire. It was the most amazing thing I ever saw. I didn't know he was a chief. He didn't ask the Indians to cease-fire—he ordered them to cease-fire. There were bullets flyin' and arrows whizzin' by, but somehow he didn't get hit. The Indians recognized him and stopped shootin'."

Paco said, "I asked Little Deer if his grandfather was a chief, and he told me Wise Elk was the oldest chief on the council. He also told me that Wise Elk is not his grandfather; he was Little Deer's grandfather's father. The whole tribe affectionately calls him Grandfather. I need to get the arrow out of Jessie's leg before it festers. The peyote has done about all it's going to do."

Jessie heard Paco, and said, "Okay, let's do it." He grinned drunkenly and said, "Then when that damn coyote howled and scared the hell out of the Indians, I thought I was goin' to fall off my horse laughing."

They couldn't pull Jessie's pants off because of the arrow. So Paco took his scissors and cut the pant leg from the arrow all the way down and opened the split pant leg up passed the arrow.

Paco told Rob to hold Jessie's leg still. The arrow was on the outside of Jessie's thigh bone so Paco was not worried about cutting the big blood tube that went down the inside of his leg. Paco quickly forced the arrow through Jessie's leg and out the other side. Jessie passed out as Paco forced out the arrow, but he had stood up to the pain and not made a sound. Paco broke off the arrowhead and quickly withdrew the shaft from Jessie's leg. He poured whiskey in and on the wounds and sewed up the holes and bandaged them with clean flour sack strips. They were very proud of Jessie for not making a sound as they realized the Indians had been watching, and a few Indians nodded in approval.

Turner stayed with Jessie as Paco washed his hands and walked over to the chuck wagon.

Rob went to check on the herd, the remuda, his cowboys, and the camp.

Bill, Pepe, and Paco were cooking as fast as they could. They had all five Dutch ovens around the fire full of biscuits, and both coffeepots were full. The beans and boiled beef were over the fire. Bill was tending the fires, shoveling hot coals onto the Dutch ovens, and stirring things. Paco had started Pepe frying yucca roots and was broiling steaks they had left from ol' one eye.

During Rob's rounds, Wise Elk said, "Giving meat to Mescalero good idea. Them save face by add to dinner. After dinner, we have ceremony and smoke pipe. I no sure if Mescalero have tobacco. If not, will be shamed."

Rob said, "I will ask Turner if we can have some of his tobacco. If it will help, you can take it and privately give it to the Mescalero."

Wise Elk said, "That be good thing."

They parted, and Rob continued his rounds. He had not even noticed that Wise Elk, and he had communicated without Paco's aid. He checked on Julio's wound and went to see Little Deer.

Rob found Little Deer with the remuda and Little Deer said, "I asked cousins to help with cattles. I no ask you."

Rob said, "Little Deer, that was a good thing and a fine idea. Thank you. You did well today by keeping the remuda from stampeding and keeping it together. As soon as Paco can let Pepe go, I will send him to help you."

Little Deer said, "I have cousins. No need Pepe. He help Paco."

"Okay, Little Deer that's better for Paco. Thanks."

A little before sundown, they were ready. The food was cooked, and Rob told Wise Elk to gather everybody. Wise Elk indicated to the two chiefs that they should sit across the fire from Rob and the gringos. With Paco's direction, Pepe, Bill, Turner, and Marco passed out food to everybody. Pepe poured coffee for those who wanted it and had a cup or a gourd. Proudly, the Mescalero passed out their antelope and beef. The Indians loved Paco's biscuits, and it was a good thing they had made more than 150. Paco's beans were wonderful, the fried yucca roots were good, and everyone ate their fill.

When they were finished eating, the gringos sat in their assigned places.

Wise Elk stood and with Paco interpreting began to speak, "We were all very lucky. Because of the wisdom of the Mescalero chiefs and the wisdom of the gringos, we have been able to avoid a bloody battle. Even though the main battle was avoided, warriors on both sides have shown much bravery and strength. It is my wish that now you put down your weapons, join in friendship, and smoke the pipe together."

A young brave handed the packed pipe to Wise Elk and held a small burning stick from the fire to light it. Wise Elk raised the pipe, offered it to the four points of the compass, puffed on the pipe, and handed it to the oldest chiefs. That chief puffed on the pipe and handed it to the other chief. He puffed on it and handed it back to Wise Elk. Wise Elk handed the pipe to Rob. Rob puffed on the pipe and passed it on to Bill, then Turner, then Paco. Who after he puffed carried the pipe to Jessie for him to wake up and puff.

Rob stood up, took the pipe back, and handed the pipe to the first chief and motioned for Paco to translate. "My friends and I have been blessed with abundance, and the Mescalero are suffering a hard time. It is my wish that the Mescalero share in the abundance of the Rancho Canyon d Perro. It is the wish of the gringos that the Mescalero take ten horses and two hundred head of cattle to their lodges—not as a gift but as a sharing of abundance. When the Mescalero enjoy abundance, the gringos would be happy if the Mescalero shared their abundance with somebody in need." There was a dead silence as Rob sat down on the blanket.

After a few seconds there was much talk and noise around the camp. Paco raised his hands to quiet everybody and spoke. The gringos, not knowing what he was saying only listened as Paco told the Mescalero in Spanish, "The man of the coyote spirit needed grain, and he received it from a dead man who could not be paid back. The man of the coyote spirit told Paco, 'Someday we will pay somebody else and pay it forward.' I think this is that day. This gringo is a man of his word and will go out of his way to help others. We all would do well to follow his example."

Everybody sat in silence, thinking about what they had heard. The sun settled in the west, and the bright gold and yellows morphed into brilliant reds on the puffy clouds that were scattered over the deep blue sky.

While everybody was quiet, Duke greeted the rising moon. Everybody watched as Rob stood up and took a plate of food out into the darkness.

The next morning, Paco doctored the wounded from both sides. He put Wise Elk's herb poultices on Jessie's leg, Marco's shoulder, and the chest and back wounds of the young Mescalero. He gave instructions that the poultices should be removed at sundown and replaced with clean fresh bandages. The bandages should be replaced each day until the wounds stopped leaking.

Jessie was put out that he was going to have to ride in the wagon.

Paco said, "Think about how lucky you are to be able to increase your fund of knowledge from Paco's wisdom."

Jessie rolled his eyes and pulled his hat down over his face.

Little Deer and Pepe cut out ten horses from the remuda as Turner, Bill, and Rob cut out two hundred head of cattle for the Mescalero.

Paco said, "My cousin doesn't have enough grass for twenty-five more goats. Why don't you give the Indians ten of the goats? They can use the angora wool to make blankets."

Rob said, "You go tell the Indians, and I'll have the boys bring the goats." The goats were not happy about being separated, and it took longer to separate the goats than it did to separate the horses and cattle.

While Rob was taking care of business, the other members of the Dog Canyon outfit and the Artesian Well outfit talked over coffee. They agreed that Rob had performed a masterstroke, and they had more cows and horses than they needed, and it was a great investment.

Turner said, "I think this might do a lot to improve the bad feelings between the white men and the Indians in southern New Mexico. I'm proud of my friend for thinking of it."

The sun was well up in the sky when everybody had said their goodbyes. The Mescalero took their gifts and started north, and the cattle drive headed northwest.

Jessie rode in the front with Paco until he tired of Paco's constant chatter and crawled into the back. Paco shut up and grinned.

The next two days were uneventful except for being out of flour and beans. Paco made do with yucca roots and added the sweet base of the agave plants for dessert. Turner killed two antelope, and they ate well. By the time they got off the mesa and down the rim into the Tularosa Basin, the animals were beginning to suffer from the lack of water. Everybody breathed a sigh of relief when the stock was drinking their fill from Culp Tank. They had gotten back with thirty-two new horses, eight new mules, one donkey, fifteen goats, and 1,591 head of cattle.

And what a good time it had been.

Chapter 9

BACK IN THE TULAROSA BASIN

The next morning, Rob asked, "Jessie, have you thought about a brand for us? We have to have a brand registered before we can brand our cattle. I sold the place in Texas with the stock and the brand."

"Yeah, I've thought about it a little. What do you think of the RJ brand?"

"That sounds fine to me except let's make it the JR brand. That has a better sound to it, and your name is on the homestead papers."

"Okay, Rob. That's fine with me."

"You start building a corral and move some of these cattle north to Dog Canyon and I'll go visit Ignacio Hernández and ask about a good blacksmith that can make us some branding irons. When I get back with the branding irons, we will have to go to the brand registration office and register the brand."

Jessie said, "Let's go find Turner and talk about splitting up the herd."

They found Turner and Rob said, "Turner, we have to have a branding iron made up and go register our brand. You already have your branding irons. Let's build a corral, start branding your cattle, and move them to the Artesian Well Ranch before they drink up all the water."

"That sounds logical, but if you are going to headquarter at Dog Canyon, we should build the corral closer to Dog Canyon. When it's built, we can move some of the cattle there and spread the water load here out some." Turner hesitated but continued, "Rob, do you know you need to go check the availability of your brand before you can register it and before you have your branding irons made up? Most good blacksmiths, if they don't know you, won't make you a branding iron unless you have the brand registration paper."

"Jesus, I didn't know about that. Where do we have to go to do that?"

"You can go to Santa Fe or you could just go to the El Paso office and do it there. New Mexico Territory and the State of Texas have an agreement to honor each other's registered brands. They will put a copy of it on the stage to Santa Fe and another to Austin to take care of notifying the New Mexico Territory offices and the state of Texas."

Jessie said, "Hey, Relax; you've got plenty of time. It'll take us a good while to brand 40 percent of the herd for Turner and Bill before we need the JR brandin' irons. As we get the Artesian Well cattle branded, we can send a couple of the boys to the Artesian Well Ranch with 'em to further spread out the load on the water."

"I guess you're right, Jessie."

Rob looked at Turner and said, "Turner, if you'll take care of things here, Jessie and I will go see how the headquarters camp has fared and find a location for the round-up corral. We'll be back before sundown."

Turner nodded, and Rob and Jessie rode out.

Turner watched them ride out and said, to Bill, "I like that boy."

"Me too. How about I ride out to the ranch and check on things? I can pick up the AR branding irons and bring them back. Then we'll have 'em whenever we're ready."

"Good idea, Bill. Hey, bring me back more tobacco too. Bring the whole jar. I'll use what's in it and refill it at Stephenson's store. See how fast you can get back."

On the way to the Dog Canyon Ranch headquarters camp, Rob and Jessie found a huge stack of wood. The flash flood waters had dropped it off and stacked it up in a sharp turn of an arroyo.

Rob said, "Wow, Jessie. This is the biggest stack of wood I ever saw."

"Yeah, and lots of it is big enough for fence posts too. Why don't I go back and get Paco, the wagon and trailer, and some of the boys? Then we can load up a bunch of it and take it to the corral site."

"Okay, sounds good to me, but I'd leave off the trailer. It would be hard to get them both up out of the arroyos. I'll go scouting and pick a location for the corral a little closer to headquarters. Then we can get this rodeo started."

They parted ways, and Rob looked for a location for the corral. He reasoned that the long deep canyon between the triple box canyon and Dog Canyon was the best place for the corral. It was two-thirds of the way between Culp Tank and Dog Canyon with the huge canyon between the coral site and Culp Tank. Rob thought the big canyon had to have water in it somewhere. He rode on to the long deep canyon, Rob found a big arroyo at the mouth of the canyon and moved downstream until the arroyo was close to 150 feet wide. He cut four century plant stalks, tied them in a teepee with his red bandana, and stood it up to make it easy to see from a long way.

Rob remembered Wise Elk had called this Escondido Canyon. He decided to call the corral the Escondido Canyon Corral. He stepped off what he thought was just over two hundred feet downstream in the arroyo and marked that. That gave them a corral of two-thirds of an acre.

Rob rode on up to Dog Canyon to look around and checked on the spring and pool. They looked undisturbed and beautiful. He found a smaller spring about two hundred yards south of Dog Canyon and thought that would be a good place for the house and barn. It gave headquarters its own water supply, separate from the Dog Canyon water. The small rise of the Dog Canyon alluvial fan north of it gave the headquarters a windbreak from the cold north wind in the winter

Except for being disappointed that he would not be able to see the Hernández in Tularosa, Rob was feeling pretty good with himself and thought, maybe he could go to Tularosa later. He looked off to the south and saw the dust of the others coming with the wagon and started off to meet them at the woodpile.

Jessie, the Rodriguez boys, and Pepe came riding up with the extra mules—two with packsaddles and two in harnesses. Paco was driving the wagon, and the goats were following the wagon just like chicks following an old hen.

Paco said, "Señor Rob, we tried to leave the goats with the herd, but they were not having it. I decided not to waste any more time trying to leave them there."

"Oh, well," said Rob. "Follow me. See those century plant stalks with the red top? That is the site of the Dog Canyon Ranch Escondido Canyon Corrals. How do you like the sound of that?"

Jessie said, "Sounds kinda highfalutin for an outfit that don't even have a privy, but I like it. It won't always be this way."

"Jessie, you are exactly right. The first building we need is a privy. Not just any privy but a two-holer—with a roof that doesn't leak."

"Why do we need a two-holer? I'm not going to the privy with you, Rob."

"Señor Rob, you insult Paco by implying that his cooking starts a stampede to the privy."

"No, you guys. It's, nothing like that. It was just that when I was younger, my little sister was afraid to go to the privy by herself. She insisted mama go with her. The only time mama was away in town and couldn't go with her, I stood outside next to the privy and sang *Flies in the Buttermilk* so she would know I was right there. Someday we will have wives and children here, and they will deserve a good privy."

Everyone was silent thinking about Rob's story, and they didn't know what to say.

Paco changed the subject and said, "Are you sure you want to build the corral in the arroyo, Señor Rob? When the Indians do their rain dance in summer, the water might get deep in the arroyo and it goes mucho fast."

"Well, yeah … that's why I came down to where it is 150 feet wide. It can't rain that much."

Paco shrugged and was silent.

Jessie said, "You're the boss. Marco and Pepe, harness the mules to Paco's chain. You can go pull up a big bundle of ocotillo plants from the south face of that hill. They must be taller than Pepe—but the bigger, the better. Be careful when you pull them up so they don't whip back and stick in you. Only pick the healthy ones. The ones with rotten stalks will break off and fall on you. Bundle them up with your lariats and pull the bundle back to the north side of this arroyo with the chain."

Rob said, "Paco, take Julio, go to the corral site, and unload the wagon. When you come back, go to the north side of the arroyo with the red bandana topped teepee. Don't let him use his injured shoulder too much. We will set up camp there while we are doing the branding."

Julio said, "El jefe, I can work. My shoulder is almost healed."

Jessie said, "Yeah, it's almost healed on the outside, but if you are going to be able to do a man's work, it has to heal on the inside, right Paco?"

"Señor Jessie is correct. If you pull the injured muscles apart, they cannot find each other to grow back together—and you will always be weak there. You can drive the wagon, and Paco will do the heavy work. Now come on, Julio."

Jessie said, "Paco, when you get back, stay on the north side of the arroyo. That way, we won't have to go around it each time to get to the corral site."

"Si, Señor Jessie." And Paco cut his eyes up and asked for patience.

When they left to unload the wagon and set up camp, Rob and Jessie went over by the woodpile and started digging out a path downstream in a small arroyo that ran into the big arroyo. The dug down the north side so they could use the mules to drag the wood to the top and load it in the wagon.

While Rob and Jessie were digging, Marco and Pepe returned with the first load of ocotillo plants.

"El jefe, what do you want us to do with the ocotillo?" Marco asked.

Rob went up to look at the bundle and was surprised at the size of it. "Leave it tied up here. Take Jessie's and my lariats and go back to get another one. By then, we will be finished with a path to the bottom."

In a short while, Paco and Julio came back with the wagon and trailer and stopped on the north side of the arroyo at the pathway Rob and Jessie were digging. They took the mules with the packsaddles, managed to get down the new pathway to the bottom of the arroyo, and started toward the woodpile.

Rob and Jessie dug out the roughest spots on the path and rode over to the woodpile. When they got there, Paco and Julio were gathering firewood and cutting greasewood branches.

"Paco, what the hell are you doing? We are not going to cook supper here. We don't need a damn fire."

Just then a rattlesnake buzzed, and Rob jumped. Another snake buzzed. It wasn't loud, but it struck the fear of God in everybody.

"Señor Rob, that's what we are doing. That woodpile is full of the snake."

"Well, are you going to burn the whole damned woodpile? That's the biggest pile of wood we've seen in the whole territory. We need it for fence posts."

"Oh, no, Señor Rob. The snake thinks the woodpile is his house, so he will defend it. The snake has no ears, so he is deaf. Paco cannot talk to him and tell him Señor Rob needs the wood. So Paco starts a fire and adds the greasewood. The greasewood makes big clouds of bad-smelling, black smoke when Paco burns it. The snake thinks his house is burning down and tells his friends Come on, we must find another house. And they all leave."

"Well, shit, Paco. Can't we just kill the damn snakes and be done with it?"

"Señor Rob, you must not say these bad words. You are a very smart man, and you know many words. You can find nice words to say what you want to say. The other hands have not heard you speak this way. What is wrong, Señor Rob?"

"I'm sorry, Paco. All the things that need doin' are gettin' to me, I guess and everything takes too much time. Can't we just shoot the snakes?"

"Yes, we could. But we need the grass for the cows."

"Paco, you are not making any sense. What grass?"

"Ay, Chihuahua. Julio, go get the canteen from the wagon for Señor Rob. Señor Rob, sit down on this rock. Paco will explain. The rabbit and the mouse eat the grass. God saw this and thought they would eat too much grass, so he put the coyote and the fox here to eat the rabbit. They needed help with the mouse, so God put the snake here to eat the mouse. If we kill all the snake, there will become too many mouse. The mouse will eat the grass and the grass seeds, then the cows will be hungry. Here, have a drink of this water and rest a minute. Paco and Julio will tell the snake and his friends to move on and go eat the mouse some other place." He handed Rob the canteen and went back to building the fire on the west side of the woodpile.

Rob said, "Why don't you build a fire on both ends of the pile? That would be faster."

Paco looked up, crossed himself, and asked for more patience, then said, "Señor Rob, here, the wind almost always blows from the southwest. The arroyo runs from the east to the west. So Paco puts the fire on the west end of the woodpile. The wind can't come from the south because the fire is down in the arroyo. It can only come from the west up the arroyo. The smoke goes east up the arroyo through the woodpile. If we put two fires, the snake has to come out on our side of the woodpile. They will not be happy. It is very painful to be bitten by the snake—sometimes you even die. Señor Rob, let Paco do it."

Rob shut up and watched. They built a fire, and Paco had Julio put the greasewood branches on it. The black smoke billowed off the fire and went up the arroyo into the woodpile. Within seconds, a ringtail rattler went slithering east up the arroyo. Several more followed the first. Then two huge rattlesnakes slithered up the arroyo, and Rob and Jessie were shocked at how big they were. A few more went east as Paco let the fire burn. In a few minutes, Paco had Julio throw dirt on the fire to put it out. The greasewood smoke smelled awful and made them choke.

"Paco, why did you let the fire burn so long? This smoke is terrible."

"Señor Rob, sometimes I think you are not so smart. Did you see the smoke go up the arroyo?"

"Well, yes."

"What do you think would have happened if as soon as the snake left the woodpile Paco put out the fire and no smoke was chasing the snake up the arroyo?"

Jessie laughed and said, "We would have been knee deep in ringtail western diamondback rattlesnakes as big around as my leg." He laughed some more before saying. "Paco, I am so glad this not-so-smart Texan had sense enough to talk you into staying with us."

Everybody laughed.

Rob blushed and said, "Come on, you smart cowboys. Let's get this wood loaded."

They loaded the pack mules with suitable fence posts, and Pepe and Marco came back at a trot.

Marco said, "What was all the smoke? We thought something had started a brush fire."

Rob said, "No, it was just Professor Paco talking to the rattlesnakes."

Jessie said, "You are back just in time. Unhook your ocotillo, bring the team down here, and help Rob haul some wood to the top. Leave your bundles tied up with the lariats."

They made several trips with the mules and loaded the wagon.

Paco said, "We need to move all the wood Señor Rob wants to the top because the snake will come back to his house as soon as we are gone. We will have to burn the smoke again before we can get more, and Señor Rob does not have time for that."

"Oh, Paco. Quit it. I'm sorry. I should know better than to question how and why you do things."

"One thing about gringos they get smarter very fast." And he grinned.

Everybody chuckled, and they moved what they thought would be two more loads of wood to the top of the arroyo.

Rob said, "Okay, Marco you and Pepe get your ocotillo bundles hooked up to the team. Julio, follow Paco in the wagon. I will lead the mules with the loaded packsaddles. Paco, tell your da— tell your goats to get out of the way."

Paco feigned a cough and spoke to the goats in Spanish for a moment.

Rob was sure the goats looked up at him before they moved to the other side of the wagon.

Jessie laughed so hard he had to take off his hat. He said, "No el jefe. I will skin the mules. You must lead our band of warriors to your corral site."

Rob snorted and started off toward the site.

When they arrived at the red bandana topped teepee frame, Rob told everybody to take a break for lunch and went looking for a pathway to the bottom of the arroyo. The sides of the arroyo were ten to twelve feet straight up and down each side.

Rob rode up the arroyo a ways then came back and went down it. About fifty yards downstream, he found a smaller arroyo that emptied into the big one that was the right width for the mule team. Twenty yards up, the small arroyo crossed a gravelly outcrop and rose up sharply. He looked up the gravel strip and realized it was the bottom of a draw that fed its water into the big arroyo.

Rob went to the camp and ate a biscuit and drank coffee.

Jessie said, "I guess you found what you were looking for."

Rob smiled. "Yep, it's a much easier place to dig a path down to the bottom. You won't have to work so hard."

They built the corral complete with a gate on the upstream side and another on the downstream side. They used the posts for the fence braces and planted the ocotillo the boys had pulled up as close together as necessary to have the thorny branches fill most of the holes and create a solid fence. They strung their lariats from post to post, weaving back and forth from one side to the other of the ocotillo cactus to hold them up straight. The cactus was as good as barbed wire for holding back the cattle. Rob hoped some of the plants would take root and grow, resulting in a natural fence of thorns. Building the gates used up the wire Paco had in the wagon.

"Jessie, you want to load up and take the camp back down to Culp Tank or send someone to get the others and bring them here?"

Jessie said, "We need to start headquartering at headquarters sometime—might as well be now. By the time the others get here, Paco will have some of his stampede-starting food ready." He ducked just in time for an empty coffee cup to go sailing over his head.

After everybody got over their laugh, Rob said, "Julio, go to Culp Tank and get the others. Leave one man there to keep an eye on things. Let Turner Sutton pick him. Tell the man you leave that a couple of cowboys will bring him some supper and help him nighthawk. If they are not there by nightfall, build a fire so they can find him. They are all new to this country. With any luck by tomorrow we will be able to leave the cattle overnight. They will know to stay close to the water."

They packed up and went to the Dog Canyon camp.

Rob said, "We need to go to La Luz for supplies and more wire. Paco, does Mr. Stephenson have any of that new barbed wire. If we only use it for gates and around the garden, maybe the other ranchers won't care too much. What do you think?"

"I don't know, Señor Rob. The other ranchers don't like the wire with the barbs."

Jessie said, "Let's ask Turner what he thinks."

Rob said, "Good idea. Paco, plan on going in the morning. You can take Pepe with you to help."

Pepe said, "Why can't Julio go? He is unable to do a man's days-work. I can stay here and work."

That brought a chuckle with coughs and snorts.

"I can do a man's days-work," Pepe said, looking around at the others.

Jessie said, "I think that is a good idea, Pepe."

That took some of the sting out of Pepe's hurt.

Rob realized what had just happened and was glad. He didn't want to hurt Pepe's feelings. He said, "Okay, Paco take Julio with you. Now Paco, I'm not criticizing your doctoring, but if there is a doctor in La Luz, if you want to, you might have him look at Julio's wounds. I'm sure he will compliment you on your work, but maybe he is new and has not seen many gunshot wounds before." Rob went on trying to get out of the hole he had dug for himself.

Paco said coolly, "We will see."

The next morning, Paco and Julio left for La Luz. Paco was in the empty wagon, and Julio was riding ahead of him. Paco had spoken to the goats in Spanish for a considerable time, and they were apparently content to wait there for him and the wagon to come back. None of them attempted to follow the wagon.

Rob looked at Jessie who just shrugged his shoulders.

Bill, Turner, Rob, and Jessie talked over another cup of coffee.

Rob asked, "What do you think of using barbed wire to build gates and using it around the garden and house?"

Turner said, "One day it will probably be all right Rob but right now the ranchers are very touchy about any barbed wire."

Jessie said, "Let's not take a chance on upsetting them. For now let's use regular wire for our gates until we can get some lumber to build them with."

"I guess you are right. Pepe, go catch Paco and tell him to just buy five rolls of plain wire. Forget about the barbed wire."

"Si, patron." Pepe jumped on his horse and took off to catch Paco.

Everyone laughed and emptied their cups on the fire. They mounted up and started for Culp Tank.

Rob looked back and saw the goats watching them leave but staying where Paco told them to stay. Rob whistled at Jessie and pointed to the goats. Jessie looked back and laughed.

Chapter 10

Rob Learns a Hard Lesson

When they got to Culp Tank, Rob said, "Boys, what do you say about cutting the herd in half and driving part of it to the Dog Canyon Ranch Escondido Canyon Corrals?"

There was hootin' and howlin'. They were laughing and excited to get started,

When they settled down, Rob walked over to the Mescalero and said, "Wise Elk, you and Little Deer stay here with the rest of the herd and the remuda. They will stay close to the water. So let them range out a little. I think you will not have much trouble."

Wise Elk nodded and looked at Little Deer. Little Deer nodded too.

When the cowboys got to the corral, they drove fifty head of cattle down the dugout pathway and into the corral, closed the gate, and built a fire. Bill produced two AW branding irons and put them in the fire. Jessie's leg was still sore, and he was better in the saddle than on the ground. So Rob and Jessie stayed a horseback, and Turner and Bill worked on the ground. Marco hauled in wood for the fire, drove the branded cattle upstream towards the hills, and helped when it was a particularly ornery cow's turn. Pepe kept the fire hot and handled the branding irons.

When Rob and Jessie roped a cow—one on the head or horns and the other on the hind feet—they stretched the cow out with their cow ponies until it fell. Turner held down the head, and Bill held onto the tail, while Pepe branded the animal's right hip. When a calf came up, it was much easier. One rider roped the calf and dragged it to the fire. One of the ground men threw it to the ground and tied three of the calf's legs together with a small tie rope and the ropers could move on to the next animal. While the ground men held it still, Pepe branded it. If it was a bull calf, Pepe branded it, cut it, and threw the balls in a bucket for the traditional calf fry dinner that night. Then he untied the tie rope to release it. Pepe hung the scrotum on the ocotillo fence so they could keep track of how many bull calves they had cut. He threw a rock on one pile for each cow or heifer calf and one rock on another pile for an older steer. They didn't bother the bulls yet.

The system worked pretty well, but it progressed very slowly. Branding adult cows was hard work.

At noon, Rob sent Marco to the Culp camp for fresh horses and to see if everything was okay there. He said, "Marco, get Little Deer to help bring the remuda to the round-up corral. Tell Wise Elk that at sundown some cowboys will bring him some supper and help him nighthawk."

That slowed things down more because one of the ground men had to help with wood and a rider had to drive the branded animals up the arroyo towards the mountains.

About two o'clock, Marco got back with Little Deer and the remuda.

Rob called for a break and said, "Marco and Little Deer, go saddle everybody a fresh horse. Bill and Turner may not really need one, but give them one anyway. Then Bill if you will go with me, we can take the remuda to Dog Canyon Springs and show them the water. I think, that will make them happy and keep them here." Jessie heated the coffee and got out the leftover biscuits and cold venison from the night before that Paco had left for them.

Jessie said, "Turner, you better sit down and soak that foot that cranky ol' mama cow stepped on when you tried to keep her from her calf." With a smile he added, "Workin' on foot's hell, id n it"

"Jessie, if I shuck my boot, I'll never git it back on. Just pour the damn coffee. Okay?"

"Okay, okay. Maybe Paco can look at it when he gets back."

In a few minutes, everybody came in, sat down, ate, and drank coffee.

Rob said, "Hey, Turner. How's the foot?"

"Not you too, Rob? My foot is fine as frog hair. Drink your coffee."

"Everybody take a few minutes to rest. We'll need it."

That afternoon was hot as blazes, and big thunderheads showed their billowing, curdled white tops over the mountains. The air was heavy, and everyone was sweating profusely. They were unable to go on much longer. The air was dead still. It seemed the later it got, the hotter it got.

Rob called a halt and told everyone to get their canteen and drink plenty of water.

When they had drunk their fill he said, "Little Deer, take the canteens to the spring and fill them with cool fresh water. Be sure to wet the cloth on the outside of the canteens to help keep them cool. Everybody happily gave Little Deer their canteens.

Rob said, "Let's get to it. Maybe we can finish the bunch in the corral."

Rob looked up and saw Paco and Julio's dust in the north. He was relieved. He always felt better when everybody was together where he could see them.

Paco and Julio drove the wagon into camp. The goats got excited when they recognized the wagon and Paco. He talked to them, and they bounced around like puppies.

"Señor Rob, Señor Stephenson only had four rolls of wire. He had no wire with the barbs. He said he could not have it in his store. If he did, the other ranchers would not buy from him."

"Okay, I guess that answers that question. Paco, this crew is dragging their tails. You better go cook up something to perk them up—or they may not make it to their bedrolls. Here, take these bull balls. That will help."

Paco smiled and said, "Si, señor." He turned to the goats. "Vámonos, mi amigos."

The goats gathered up and tagged behind the wagon like baby ducks behind their mama.

The men went back to work and finished branding all but seven of the biggest, meanest cows.

Rob said, "Let them stay in the corral 'til morning. We'll finish them then when we are all fresh. They will be thirsty, but they will be all right for a few hours."

When they got to the Dog Canyon Camp, they tended to their horses and released them into the remuda. The other horses were grazing on the hillsides.

Rob collapsed on a spare upside-down saddle and his bedroll.

Paco had handed out the customary end of the day coffee.

He came over and was looking up at the mountain tops and said, "It is not the correct time of year, Señor Rob, but I think it is going to rain in the night."

Rob said, "Why do you say that, Paco? The clouds are over the mountain—not on our side."

"Señor Rob, look at the goats. They are not by the wagon. They are up on the hill under the cliffs. The mules are not eating the grass in the bottom. They are also high up on the hillside. And the air, she is so heavy and thick."

"Oh, Paco, I think they are just happy to be home. They know this is their new home. That's all."

"I hope you are correct, but I don't think so."

Paco had cooked a great supper of calf fries, fried potatoes with onions, frijoles, venison steak, and biscuits with butter and honey he had gotten at the store. He had a special treat. Paco had a small keg of the cold beer he bought from the gringo cantina wrapped in several blankets to keep it cold. He tapped it and called the cowboys. The thrilled cowboys ate and drank beer until they couldn't move. Then they drank more beer. The seven-and-a-half-gallon keg wasn't full to start with, and it wasn't very strong beer, but everybody enjoyed it and had a good time after several weeks of hard work.

Rob noticed that Little Deer wasn't drinking beer with the others. "Little Deer, do you not like the beer?"

"Señor Rob, the white man's beer makes my eyes not see good."

"You are just smarter than these boys. I'm glad. Will you take Wise Elk some food and guide Julio and Pepe to the Culp Tank camp to help nighthawk?"

"Si, Señor Rob."

Paco had been watching the conversation and was grinning. "Señor Rob, you and Little Deer talk like old friends."

"He has come a long way, Paco. He is going to lead Julio and Pepe and take some supper to Wise Elk. Will you send extra coffee to Wise Elk? He likes it strong."

"You are a good man, Señor Rob."

Rob blushed and walked off toward the arroyo.

The camp quieted down, and Rob and Jessie decided the animals would be all right. They needed to learn that they were home too. But just in case they left the horses they had been riding saddled and hobbled with loosened cinches. Rob didn't put out a nighthawk, and everybody fell into their bedrolls.

A little before dawn, it began to rain. At first, it was just a few huge drops. The drops were so big they made a big "Plop" sound when they hit the ground and one would wet the whole side of your face. Then there were more and more drops until it fell like waves of ice-cold water. Then it was just solid water. It rained harder than Rob and Jessie had ever seen. They were soaked to the bone and cold before they could break out the slickers or put up a tent. The rain washed out the fire, and they were miserable.

Paco put up the fly tent over the cooking area and got a fire going using dry wood from the belly bag under the wagon. In a few minutes, he had the coffee ready. He called out, "Señor Rob," and motioned at the coffee.

Daybreak was barely showing through the black and green clouds. Before Rob could get the coffee, Duke howled a few yards west of camp. When Rob looked up, Duke did his circle dance.

Paco said, "I think he wants you to follow him, Señor Rob."

Rob stood up and started toward the coyote.

Duke took off toward the corral. Rob had a bad feeling and ran to get his horse. He tightened the cinch and followed Duke at a trot. Rob called out to the others to follow. It was raining so hard that Rob could barely see.

Rob realized he had been hearing a low-frequency noise since he woke up, but he didn't know what it was—and it was getting louder. He couldn't hear Duke howling or whining. When he approached the arroyo, where the corral was he saw Duke was doing his circle dance on the edge of the arroyo. The noise was thundering. It terrified Rob, but he looked over the edge of the arroyo. The arroyo was half full of brown muddy water thundering out of the mountains. The violent river roared down the arroyo, and Rob pulled his horse back from the arroyo's edge.

Duke was again showing Rob to follow and took off down the edge of the arroyo. Rob saw that the corral was gone and the cows were gone. Jessie and Bill got there and Rob took off after Duke. He led Rob a quarter mile down the arroyo to a bend of ninety degrees. Rob saw one of the gates wrapped around one of the cranky cows. It was holding her down in the rising water. The water had washed the cow and the gate over to the shallow side, and her head was still above the water. Luckily she was on Rob's side of the rushing water because he could not have gotten to her if she had been on the other side.

Rob retrieved his wire cutters from his saddlebags and started toward the cow. Jessie tried to call him back, but the water was roaring too loud for Rob to hear.

Rob managed to cut the wire in enough places to partially free the cow. She began to struggle and head-butted Rob. He saw stars and then white turned to black, and he fell. When his face hit the cold water, it revived him, and he came up sputtering. He shook his head to clear it, and somehow the wire cutters were still in his hand so he went back to cutting the wire. The water had risen to the cow's nose. At last, he cut her free. The cow got up bawling and ran out of the arroyo to safety. She kept running toward the mountain until she was out of sight.

The water was up past Rob's knees, and he had trouble standing. Jessie threw him a rope loop to hold on to, and he half walked and was half dragged to the edge through the now waist deep and still rising water. Rob shouted, "Do you see any of the other cows?" That made his head explode in stars and pain again.

The other men still on their horses shook their heads as they gazed searching the arroyo and the desert to the west.

Rob could barely stand, and he was freezing. He couldn't believe how cold the water was. Jessie helped him mount his horse, and they rode back to camp. Rob was on the verge of tears. He was ashamed of himself, he was mad at himself, and he was grateful to Duke once again. He didn't see Duke, but he shouted, "Thank you, Duke."

Rob looked at Jessie and said, "Thank you too, Jessie Hatfield."

When Rob got back to camp Paco had him dry clothes and hot coffee ready. Rob was shivering badly. He shucked his wet clothes and Paco handed him a flour sack towel, and he dried himself. He put on his hat, dry clothes, dry socks, boots, and his slicker. Then he said, "Paco, I'm sorry I doubted you. I should have listened to you about building the corral in the arroyo and about the rain coming last night—about everything."

Paco was embarrassed and unable to speak. He made Rob sit down while he checked his head. He looked in Rob's eyes. They had neither dilated nor pinpoint pupils. Paco looked at the goose egg knot on Rob's forehead. Except for that, Rob appeared to be uninjured.

Rob asked, "Paco, why is the water so cold? I can barely move."

Paco rubbed Rob's back and arms to warm him up, Paco explained. "The higher up in the air you go, the colder it is. The big thunder boomers are so high up, the water she freezes—and ice falls out of them. Up on top of the mountains, the ice-cold water falls and runs down the draws into the little canyons, and the little canyons run into the big canyons. The big canyons run into bigger canyons, and the water runs faster to get out of the way. By the time it gets to the bottom, it is a raging wall of ice-cold water. It carries bushes, trees, dirt, and rocks. You saw how fast it fills the arroyos."

Rob drank his hot coffee and said, "Turner, will you and Bill see if you can find the other cows from the corral and check on the unbranded herd. Jessie and I will go check on the other half of the herd down at Culp tank. Paco, will you check the remuda, the goats, and the Dog Canyon spring and canyon. Marco you go check on the branded cows we drove up Escondido Canyon. Be careful of that raging water. Don't anybody risk your life looking for cows. I will bring all the cowboys back here so we can be together and plan our next move. Have some hot food ready when we get back. And Paco feed that damn— feed the duke of Dog Canyon real well."

Everybody put on their slickers, mounted up, and rode out.

Chapter 11

THE NEW CORRAL

ob and Jessie rode south to Culp Tank camp. They took biscuits, frijoles, and venison for breakfast. Rob had asked Paco for calf fries, but they were all gone. They had to ride west a long way to be able to cross the arroyos.

Jessie said, "Can you believe this water? It looks so angry. Muddy and churning, I'm surprised these arroyos are not fifty feet deep."

"Yeah, this morning when that low ground shaking sound turned out to be the water in the arroyo, it frightened the hell out of me."

"If you were so damned scared, why did you go running off in it for a twelve-dollar cow?"

"Well—she was your cow." And he grinned.

"Do you reckon we'll find the other six?"

"I doubt it. That water was terrifying this morning."

Jessie said, "Boy am I glad to find that camp smoke. This pot of beans is getting heavy."

They rode into an empty camp. Rob was nervous until he noticed the coffeepot was on the fire and still hot.

In a minute Julio, Pepe, and Little Deer rode into the camp.

"I am glad you boys are all right. Where is Wise Elk?"

Julio answered, "We are glad to see you also, jefe. Wise Elk rode west to find any missing cattle. We don't know how many are missing—or if any are missing. The big bunch is peacefully eating grass like nothing happened. There are small bunches laying down chewing the—eating—"

"You mean chewing their Cud." Jessie helped as he set the beans and coffee on the fire and added wood.

"Si, señor. Gracias, chewing the cud." Julio said smiling.

Rob said, "Get down and eat. Here is something from Paco. Is there coffee left?"

"Si, señor, but it is very muddy. Wise Elk made it."

Jessie said, "Well, a little water added will fix that right up. This morning we have plenty of water to match the muddy coffee." There was laughter.

Rob knew it was good for the boys to laugh after the time they must have had. He rode to a high spot so he could look west for Wise Elk. After a few seconds, Rob found what he was looking for, Wise Elk was coming east. Rob pointed and hollered, "There he is." Rob had a big grin on his face.

Wise Elk was herding a bunch of cows toward them. It was strange not to see dust.

Jessie whispered to the boys, "Rob is getting worse than an old mama dog when she can't see all her pups."

Pepe said, "I like it. He even cares about orphans and old Indians."

"Yeah, I guess he does at that," Jessie said and observed Rob in a new light.

Rob came back to camp, stepped down, and unloaded his saddlebags of the rest of the breakfast Paco had sent. There was even a mason jar with the last of the goat milk for the boys. Rob handed it to Pepe whose face lit up and said, "Paco said to add this to the muddy coffee, and it will go down better."

Jessie asked, "Where did you get the dry wood for the fire?"

Julio answered, "Last night, Wise Elk said it was going to rain before morning. He made us gather wood. He covered the stack with the tarp Paco left for us."

Rob said in anger, "I guess I was the only one who didn't know it was going to rain."

Jessie said, "No, Rob. Most of us didn't know it was going to rain."

"But Paco knew. And Wise Elk knew. Hell, even the goats and mules knew. How come I didn't know?"

There was silence. Then Little Deer said, "Jefe, you have other things to think on. Let the old men and the animals think on rain."

Rob looked at the boy and said, "I just need to learn to listen when they tell me, but thank you, Little Deer."

Wise Elk came in after rounding the cattle into the herd. He sat on a rock, and Jessie handed him a plate of breakfast. Wise Elk looked up at Jessie, and his face softened. "Gracias," he said, and began to eat.

Jessie had saved Wise Elk a cup of the very muddy coffee before he added the water and handed it to Wise Elk. Wise Elk took the coffee, smiled, and nodded. Jessie couldn't remember seeing Wise Elk smile.

Rob said, "Wise Elk, do you think the cattle will be all right here if we all go to Dog Canyon?"

"The cattles be all right as long as they have grass to eat and water to drink. They be happy to see us leave so they not be bothered with …" He turned to Little Deer and said something in Apache then added "long walks." repeating Little Deer's answer.

"Okay then when you all get through eating, put the camp stuff and some dry wood under the tarp in a safe place. Make sure it is on high ground. We will leave it here in case we need to camp here again. I am going to look at the tank and make sure the cattle have water."

When Rob got to Culp Tank, he was shocked. The draw was full of water. He rode around it and then saw why the tank stayed full of water. At the west end of the tank, there was a natural dam like rise. It didn't wash away when the flash flood water came for two reasons. The little canyon had a split in the arroyo in the bottom. Part of the water went down one side to the tank, but if the arroyo got too full, the rest went into another arroyo to the north of the tank. The other reason was that the natural dam was a rocky outcrop that didn't wash away when the tank got full. It let the overflow go over the rocks and run on down the draw. If it had stopped all the water, it would have been washed away. Rob was gaining more appreciation and understanding for this country.

Rob rode back to the camp, and everybody's horse was saddled and packed. He said, "Let's ride."

When they got back to Dog Canyon, Paco handed them a cup of coffee. Rob took his and sat on a big rock to drink it.

Turner said, "Rob, Bill and I only found one dead cow. We came back and got Paco, butchered it, and hauled it back here. We might as well eat her as leave her for the buzzards since we know what killed her."

"That's good thinking. That leaves five. Paco how is the other stock?"

"The horses and mules are fine. They found dry dirt to roll in under the cliff, and the goats are happy as fleas in the dog casa. Dog Canyon Spring is running fine. The pool has a few new logs at the bottom. We must move them to the fire wood pile so they don't form a dam that will break and cause a bigger flood in the next storm."

"Anybody have anything to add?"

Turner coughed and toed the ground with downcast eyes. In a while he took a deep breath looked up and said, "What you did this morning with that cow was brave ... brave but stupid. A bigger flash flood could have come rolling down that arroyo as easy as not. We need you more than some ol' cow. You have to respect the storms in this country even if you don't fear 'em." He sat down on a rock and drank his coffee.

Rob was speechless. He didn't know whether to defend his actions or acknowledge Turner's remarks. Looking off into the distance, he decided to do neither.

Paco saw it, and after a few minutes of silence, he said, "Julio, how are things at the other camp?"

Julio made his report of Culp Tank camp to the others and asked what happened while he was gone.

Paco told them about the storm and Duke coming to get Rob to follow him.

Jessie added that Rob had followed the coyote and found the cow. He left off the part about Rob going in after it. Paco had raised his eyebrows at him and shifted his eyes to Rob. Jessie got the hint and ended the story in time.

Rob said, "Well—the bad news is we need a corral again. Ours is gone. We worked so hard to build it, and it's gone. I put it in a bad place."

Bill said, "The good news is we brought the branding irons to camp rather than leaving them in the corral. Did anyone count the rocks in the rock-piles and the scrotums?"

Pepe said, "There were thirty-two rocks in the south pile, thirteen in the north pile, and eight scrotums."

Rob said, "So that's thirty-two cows and heifers, thirteen older steers, and eight new ones. That's only fifty-three branded head."

Bill said, "It will be a long, hot summer."

Jessie said, "You know, last year, I saw a contraption in Fort Worth that the stockyard cowboys were usin' to brand cows. It held the cow still while they branded it or marked its ear. It didn't work on the longhorns, but it saved time on the others."

"What did it look like, Jessie?" Turner asked, rubbing his foot.

"I'll have to think about that. I didn't pay much attention to it at the time."

"This is what I think we should do," Rob said. "While my slow-witted partner here thinks on it, we need to build another corral. This time on high ground like Paco tried to tell me. This one will be four sides of fence, so we will need more fence posts, more ocotillo, more everything—twice as much of everything. Paco, give Pepe and Marco all the lariats and rope you have.

"Marco and Pepe, take Julio and Little Deer with you. Harness a team of mules, and gather ocotillo bundles like you did the other day. We will need twice as many. Drag them to east of the big grass flat southwest of here. Watch out for Julio's shoulder. Bill, you and Wise Elk spread out and go find us another wood pile for fence posts. There must be some new piles after this morning. Turner, why don't you rest that foot and ride to La Luz with Paco? You might find some ointment or liniment or something at Stephenson's store. "I will ride out and find a dry location for the new corral, and if my learned colleague here gets through thinking, he can help you guys haul wood.

"Paco, unload the wire into the wagon trailer. We will use the trailer to haul it to the new corral site and haul fence posts until you get back with the wagon. I've been thinking about how to hitch a mule team to your trailer. When you and Turner get to La Luz, see if there is more of that wire. Get us some light rope, heavy string, and canvas to make tents. We will need more lariats too. You better bring Jessie some nails and screws and bolts with nuts. Ask if Mr. Stephenson has any hinges, latches, and stuff like that. We will need hardware for a house and a barn. Fill up the rest of the wagon with heavy lumber for gates. Tell the lumberman we will need lumber for a house soon and for a privy right away. If you need any supplies, get them. This is going to be a hungry crew for a while.

"Turner, why don't you talk to Stephenson and see if he wants to buy any of our beef to resell it. Maybe we can work out a deal. I am running up quite a bill. Can anybody think of anything else?" Rob looked around at the cowboys. "And, by the way, I was scared to death this morning."

The others broke out in laughter.

With a broad smile, Jessie said, "No, jefe. I think that pretty well covers it. There ain't nobody left to tell nothin' else."

Before Paco left for La Luz, Jessie said, "Paco, do you have a pencil and some paper I could draw plans on?"

Paco dug them out and gave them to him.

Jessie thanked him, went up to Dog Canyon Spring, sat down, and leaned against a bolder. It was cooler and peaceful by the water, and it was a good place to think.

The four young gentlemen took the chain, the rope, and a mule team and started off to cactus hill. Bill and Wise Elk saddled up, filled their canteens, and rode out. They talked a minute and then separated with Bill going south and Wise Elk going west. Rob watched everybody head out and saddled his favorite little spotted rump horse and rode southwest.

Rob rode over the ground west of Dog Canyon to west of the El Paso to La Luz trail and from Dog Canyon south to Escondido Canyon. There were a few arroyos between the big canyons, but none were the size of the Escondido Canyon arroyo. The grass flat southwest of Dog Canyon camp was perfect, but he decided he didn't want to disturb that grass The best place for the corral and headquarters was on the high ground east and above the grass flat and west and below the small spring he had found south of Dog Canyon. It was mostly surrounded by red sand dunes containing mesquite bushes.

The open ground was relatively flat and level just below the small spring. Rob marked off a place for the house that had an open, 360-degree field of fire. He tied four agave bloom stalks together with his red bandana and planted the teepee on sandy flat ground. Rob stepped off a 210-foot square and marked each corner with a pile of rocks he carried out of the area of the marked corral. He decided that instead of two gates this corral needed a gate on all four sides. He admitted to himself that mostly only one or two would be used, but since he didn't know what the future held, it was the safest thing to do. Rob found the center of the corral by lining up the four corners and marked it with another pile of rocks. He wanted to have a strong snubbing post planted there when the time came to break horses.

Rob went to the four corners and marked off rounded corners twenty-five feet in both directions from the marked square corners. That eliminated the square corners where the stock would bunch up and try to hide. The corral wasn't round, but it had no corners.

Rob was thinking of a way to get water to the corral when he noticed Wise Elk riding in from the west driving four cows. Rob rode out to meet him.

"One cow muerto. Head go under the water. No good, buzzards." Wise Elk pointed to the cows he was driving, These cow eat grass, happy. Come with Wise Elk."

"Wise Elk, I am happy you found the missing cows. That means only two of the seven I left in the corral died, and we saved one of those for food."

"Coyote man no do wrong. No rain should come. Corn no grow over knee. No dance. No you fault." He went on driving the cows toward the herd.

Rob did not know what to say, so he said nothing. He just watched as the old Mescalero herded the cows east. Rob could see for miles to the south, west, and north. He could see the young hands gathering ocotillo on the foothill to the east. They had one bundle tied and were working on the second. Bill and Jessie were riding toward the Dog Canyon camp and he headed that way feeling less guilty. He pulled out his pistol and fired two shots into the air. That was the prearranged signal to come a runnin'. The boys on the hill looked up, and he waved them north. They hooked up the ocotillo, mounted up, and started down to drop off their gather and head back to camp.

When Rob rode into camp just after noon Jessie, Bill, and Wise Elk were there waiting for him. Jessie was breaking out Paco's leftovers for lunch and had a pot of coffee on the fire.

After a few minutes, the young gentlemen came riding into camp. They had dropped off their gather where Rob had told them to take it, and they had unhitched the mules and watered the saddled horses. They unsaddled them, saddled fresh horses, hitched fresh mules for everybody, and turned the others out to graze. Then they came in, got their coffee, and sat down.

Rob said, "Wise Elk found the five missing cows. One was dead and had already been spoiled by buzzards. He brought the other four in."

Everybody smiled and tipped their hats to Wise Elk.

Rob continued, "The young cowboys have a bundle and a half of ocotillo delivered and ready to plant." They got their well-deserved verbal pats on the back.

"I found a good corral site with soft sandy ground that is flat and level. It is below but not far from the house and barn site. It will not destroy much grass, and it is on high ground. I put up the red-top teepee and marked the four rounded corners, the location of four gates, and the center snubbing post." Not waiting for any acknowledgment, he said, "Bill, did you have any luck finding posts?"

Bill said, "You bet. I didn't find a pile as big as the one you and Jessie found, but I found one. The best find of the day is that Wise Elk says your woodpile is still there. Apparently it's there because the water doesn't pick it up and carry it off. In fact, it may be bigger that when we left it. We will have to let the water go down a little more but he thinks we should be able to get in there tomorrow if the mud is not too soft. After he found that he looked for the cows."

Rob was surprised; he never expected to still have that wood pile.

"Then the biggest question is, Jessie, do you know how to build your Fort Worth cow chute?"

Everyone looked at Jessie in anticipation. He played the drama for all it was worth. He hesitated, and then said, "Does a wild bear shit in the woods?"

Everybody cheered and laughed.

Rob sighed in relief and said, "Okay. Let's eat."

Rob got a pair of biscuits and a slab of the venison from last night and sat by Jessie with two cups of coffee. He offered Jessie one and said, "Good thing Mama Paco wasn't here to wash your mouth out."

"Oh, he thinks you are the only one too smart to talk nasty. The rest of us have to get by as best we can. Where did you get that vocabulary of yours—and how do you know what proper English is anyway?"

"My mama taught me. While I was growing up, she made me sit and write verb conjugations and recite the different parts of speech. Every time I said something incorrectly, she thumped me on the head or made me write it correctly ten times in the sand. If you want to have time to play marbles or go fishing, you learn to speak good English. If I made three mistakes in one morning, she made me muck out the stalls in the barn. And sometimes if she got tired of messing with me, she turned me over to my daddy—and off to the woodshed I went. By the time I was ten years old, I could write clearly, spell all the words in last week's newspaper, and conjugate all the verbs she could think of.

"Even when I was eighteen, if I said something incorrectly, she would whack me with her broomstick. You don't have to be very smart to learn proper English, but you had to be real dumb not to learn it in my house. Pretty soon, it came natural—thanks to my mama. God bless her. You should hear my little sister talk."

Rob realized what he had said and it appeared, Rob might cry. Rob stood up and walked away from the camp as if to take a piss in the arroyo.

Bill walked over, sat next to Jessie and said, "That was a beautiful story. Is it true?"

"Yep, Rob's mama was from back East. She taught school at some college there before she fell in love with Rob's daddy. Mrs. Wilson knew arithmetic all the way through long division and lots of science. She was the book brains of the ranch and could fix the windmill or a well pump and rig up a way to patch almost anything mechanical. Last winter, they all caught typhoid fever and died. I helped Rob bury them. He said he couldn't stay there and sold the family ranch to come here and get a new start. I thought he was crazy, but when I couldn't talk him out of it, I decided to come with him and try to look after him. He is the best friend I ever had."

Rob came back to camp and said, "Well, have you cowboys had enough to eat? Paco will be back soon and will skin us all if we don't get some work done. Pepe, you and Little Deer fill everybody's canteen, it will get dry digging postholes." He started toward the remuda to hitch up a mule team to the little half wagon. The others followed his lead, and they started back to work.

Rob said, "You young cowboys see how fast you can gather three more bundles of ocotillo and drag it to the corral site."

He hitched up the mules to the little wagon and started off leading them with the wagon loaded with wire, one of those newfangled posthole diggers, and three shovels, Paco had bought in La Luz. Paco kept his old shovel in his wagon to dig fire pits and in case of trouble with the wagon.

They unloaded the wire in the new corral, and Rob strung a line off a ball of string from the northeast corner rock pile to the southeast corner rock pile. He drove two stakes on either side of the proposed gate in the middle of the side. He stopped and thought a few seconds and went back and pulled up those stakes and drove them in the ground close to the north end of the line. "We will put this gate closest to the house." He didn't need to explain what he was doing. By now no one contradicted him or questioned his decisions unless they had a very good reason.

They took the wagon trailer and rode to the woodpile Bill had found. It was further west and the water in the arroyo was slowing down to a trickle. The bottom was sandy with gravel mixed in and not too muddy. They managed to throw most of the fence post size wood out of the shallow arroyo and loaded it in the trailer. After two trips, it was gone.

Rob and Jessie rode over to the big woodpile, but the bottom was too muddy. Bill sank up to the top of his boots.

Jessie said, "Hey, what are cowboys for?" He took his lariat, roped a post in the pile, and hauled it up to the top.

They began roping and hauling. They cussed when they got the rope tangled in the wood. One rope they couldn't get loose, and they left it for the next day when they could get to it. They hauled up an impressive pile of fence posts and hauled them to the corral site.

Rob said, "How about Jessie and I start digging postholes—and you keep bringing in wood? When we give out, we'll trade off."

Everyone agreed and went to work.

"Jessie, before we go too far, will you show me your plans? Let's figure out where to build your Fort Worth chute?"

Jessie said, "I'm not finished, but okay if you want to see." He opened his saddlebags and pulled out the paper he had gotten from Paco. They laid it on the ground with a small rock on each corner to hold it still in the breeze.

Rob was impressed and told Jessie so. He could understand the principle right away without too much explanation.

The Fort Worth branding chute was a twenty-four foot piece of wood fence, four rails high, replacing that length of the wire and ocotillo fence on the east side of the corral. Another wood rail fence three feet west of the first one ran parallel to the first. They ended on the south end, fifty feet from the southeast corner of the corral. Both fences had four sets of double fence posts, six inches apart, starting at the south end and then every eight feet and at the north end. Except the inside or west part of the fixed fence ended at the double post, eight feet from the left or north end. The left or north section of the inside fence was a four-rail wooden gate, hinged to an oversized post at the north end. That north section could swing in from the double post that was eight feet from the north end of the inside fence. The gate was the north section of the inside fence.

The swinging or south end of the gate had a lariat fixed to the top, and the bottom of the south end and could be pulled by two riders and closed on the cow in the north section. That would hold the cow still while it was branded and didn't require such rough treatment of the cow. The south and middle section were designed to force the cow to stand, settle down, and relax while the north cow was pinched and branded. They also provided a steady supply of cows to brand.

Jessie and Rob talked about the Fort Worth chute a few minutes more and started digging postholes. Digging postholes is back breaking work, especially in ground with rocks in it. The alluvial fan under Dog Canyon had lots of rocks and was sandy enough so that the sides fell in often. The wetter the sand held the shape of the hole. Today it was very wet. Even so when the posthole-digger hit a fist-sized rock, it broke the side away above it.

They worked until Wise Elk and Bill brought a load of wood. When it was unloaded, Rob noticed the men walking. Wise Elk and Jessie did well on horseback, but they both limped. Rob noticed them limping and said, "Wise Elk, will you ride down to Culp Tank and check on the herd? I'm nervous about them ranging out too far. We don't want to have to round them up again."

Wise Elk nodded but had a mildly grateful expression on his face when he mounted his horse.

"Jessie, we can't dig holes for all these posts today. Why don't you ride over to Dog Canyon to check on those cows and the remuda? Look in on Paco's goats too. I can't believe they mind him like they do. They may be halfway to La Luz by now. Bill and I can dig postholes for a while."

"Robert Wilson, you can't fool me. You just think me 'n Wise Elk can't haul our weight. I'll have you know I'm as good as new."

"If you were as good as new, you wouldn't be limping. Now don't argue with me too much—or I'll ride over and check things out and you can dig holes in the ground. You know what I think? I think these ranchers say they don't like barbed wire fences because they don't want to have to dig postholes."

Everybody laughed, and Jessie mounted up and rode off toward Dog Canyon.

Bill said, "You are a good boss, Rob Wilson. They didn't expect that." and he picked up a shovel.

Rob blushed and took hold of the posthole diggers.

Bill asked, "What in the world is that?"

Rob said, "Paul Stephenson ordered this for me. It is one of those newfangled posthole digger things. It's two shovels fastened together with a hinge kind of thing. A feller named Lindsley from up in Michigan invented last year. Paul says it's 'spose to make digging these holes much easier."

"Does it?"

"I guess it does 'cause if it was any harder, there wouldn't be any new fences in the whole country."

Later in the day Jessie rode back with a coffeepot. He stepped down, set the coffeepot on a rock, drew his pistol, and fired two shots. They could barely see the young cowboys on the hill. The cowboys looked up and started toward them with the mule team pulling two bundles of ocotillo plants.

Jessie built a fire for the coffee while Bill finished the posthole they were digging. Rob took a few steps east and looked back at the line of holes in the ground. "Wow." He wiped the sweat off his face. "We are better than halfway down this side."

It took the young cowboys a quarter hour to get there. By that time, the coffee was ready. Jessie had four canteens of cold fresh water from the spring. Everybody drank their fill.

Wise Elk rode in with a new calf across his saddle. A mama cow was following him. Wise Elk said, "New boy cow. First one here. Good sign."

Rob took the new calf and held it for all to see. He took out his knife and cut two slits in the right ear. "I name you Primo." While everyone applauded, he pointed the calf toward his mama and let it go. The cow bawled, and the calf ran over to her to nurse.

Things were looking better.

They had seen Paco's wagon return to the camp and started for the camp just before sundown. Their spirits were high, but their tails were dragging. They found muscles they hadn't used in a while, and those muscles were complaining.

They rode into camp and were greeted by wonderful aromas. When they got down, Paco handed them a cup of hot fresh coffee.

Turner's foot was bandaged, and he sat with it up on an empty keg. Rob was reluctant to ask about it so he just waited.

Jessie said, "Paco, what in the world is that sweet smell?"

"It is apricot cobbler, you gringos call it. But you cannot eat it before supper, so no ideas from you." Paco said as he wagged his big cooking spoon at Jessie.

Jessie turned around and said, "I swear, Rob, you're right. Paco is getting to be more like a mama ever' day." As he finished saying it Paco's big wooden mixing spoon thumped him on the back. "Ouch!" he said in surprise.

Everybody laughed.

Paco brought fresh new potatoes, carrots, big garden onions, and the fresh apricots. He had sugar, honey, fresh butter, and a gallon of that tangy vinegar from Mr. Stephenson's. They ate like kings. By the time Paco lifted the Dutch oven lids on the cobbler, they had knocked the edge off their hunger, but the aroma brought them in line again for cobbler and more coffee.

When Rob got around to asking about Turner's foot. Paco answered, "When you told me to let the new doctor in La Luz look at Julio's shoulder, I was not sure how I felt about that. I talked to my cousin, and he said I should not feel bad about that. He said you were just trying to give your men the best care possible. He said I was a good desert doctor, but Dr. Peterson was liked very much and had herbs and medicine. I took Julio, and we met the new doctor. He is very nice, and he said I did do well on the wounds. He gave me some salve to put on wounds and said to keep more whiskey on hand. Not to drink but as a cleaner. It kills the little bugs we cannot see. I took Señor Sutton to him. He said the foot is broke. He says wrap it, keep it up, and put this salve on the cut on top. Watch it and if it turns black or red, to rush back with Señor Sutton."

Rob was so proud of Paco. He smiled at Turner and kept eating his cobbler.

After supper, Rob walked over to Paco and asked, "Paco, can I borrow your wagon to take Turner and go to El Paso? I need to register the brand, have our branding irons made and I need to go to the bank and get us some more money. We are running out of gold. If he stays here, Turner won't stay off that foot. So I will ask him to go help me. The other boys can build that fence better than I can."

"You know you can have anything of mine Señor Rob ... anytime."

"Thanks. I wanted to talk to you before I mentioned it to anybody else."

Later Rob gathered Paco, Jessie, Turner, and Bill for a meeting. He said, "Turner needs to stay off that foot. I need to go to El Paso to register our brand and go to the bank. It would help me if he would go with me to show me how to register a brand. Paco says we can use his wagon to go. Maybe we can bring back some things. Jessie, you and Bill are better builders than I am. You can build the corral, and when we get back, we can start branding. Any objections?"

Nobody had any.

Rob said, "Well, all right, Turner and I will leave in the morning."

Chapter 12

THE SURPRISING TRIP TO EL PASO

The next morning, Rob threw Turner's saddle in the back and tied Turner's favorite horse to the wagon. Paco had loaded groceries, a pan, a skillet, a Dutch oven, tin plates, utensils to cook and eat with, and a coffeepot. They had two good bedrolls and a lean-to tent.

Jessie said, "Rob, hold this rolled up blanket on the wagon footboard so I can wire it tight. That will give Turner a place to rest his foot."

They climbed aboard and headed to El Paso.

Rob had to dig with Paco's old shovel in three washed out arroyos while Turner drove the wagon, but they made it to El Paco on the third afternoon.

Rob said, "Let's go register the brand first."

Turner was not in much pain and agreed. When they got to the registry office, the clerk told them, "The JR brand is already taken. Junior Wilkins over by Sweetwater owns that one."

Rob didn't know what to do. He and Jessie had not talked of this possibility. He looked at Turner.

Turner said, "What was that other brand that Jessie suggested?"

Rob remembered, "Oh, How about the RJ brand?"

The clerk shook his head, "No. Robbie Joe Sampson down Del Rio way owns that one."

Rob couldn't come up with another brand.

Turner said, "Let's go have a drink and something to eat. You didn't stop for lunch. That will relax you and help you concentrate. Besides, I'm hungry." He looked up at the clerk and said, "How long will you be open?"

The clerk answered, "I have to wait for the southbound stage to come in. I'll be here 'til at least dark."

Rob said, "We'll be back."

They walked out of the office and across the street to a saloon. Turner was using one of Wise Elk's crutches and getting around pretty well.

They sat at a table and ordered whiskey, then another with steak, fried potatoes, frijoles, and tortillas. The food wasn't as good as Paco's, but they hadn't eaten since breakfast, and they ate with enthusiasm. After they had eaten and were having more coffee, Rob jumped up and said, "I've got it."

Startled, Turner said, "What?"

Rob said, "The brand … DOG. Do you think DOG would be all right with Jessie?"

Turner smiled and said, "See? I told you this would help. Go over to the clerk. I'll pay the bill and be along."

Rob entered the clerk's office. The clerk looked up and Rob said, "DOG, How 'bout DOG?"

The clerk smiled and said, "If I'm not mistaken, that is open. Let me check the brand book to make sure." He opened a big ledger book and turned the pages until he found the one he wanted and fingered down the page. "Yep, that's open. Here, draw it out on this form exactly like you want it. List the owners' names and addresses and sign it."

Rob wasn't sure what to do. He wished Jessie was there to take care of that part. He was holding the pencil above the paper when Turner limped into the office. Rob said, "He wants me to draw the brand the way I want it. Jessie usually does this sort of thing. And, I don't know our address."

Turner was quiet a second then he laughed and said, "Just write DOG in big letters. You don't have to draw it—just write it. Then put your names and put La Luz, New Mexico Territory."

"Oh, yeah." said Rob, and he did that. When he was through, he looked up at the clerk and handed the paper to him.

The clerk took the paper, and wrote on it and then he made a copy, and stamped it with a stamp that had the words: "Registered Brand, Texas." around a small map of the state of Texas. He looked at Rob and said, "That will be two dollars. And it has been an honor to register your brand, Mr. Wilson."

Rob almost fainted. He handed over the money, took his copy of the registration, and Turner guided him out of the office.

When they got outside, Turner said, "Rob, what's a matter with you? I was afraid you were going to pass out in there. I thought maybe you didn't have the two dollars. I've got money if you need it."

Rob collected himself and said, "Oh, no nothing like that. I was afraid he was going to ask me how old I am and tell me I couldn't register a brand until I was twenty-one."

Turner laughed and said, "Why didn't you ask me about that? I could have told you. Hell, on some ranches, all the sons have their own brands so they can keep track of a few head of their own."

"I didn't think about it until he looked up at me in there."

Turner laughed and slapped Rob on the back. "You'll do, Rob Wilson. You'll do."

Rob said, "Let's go find banker Bloomberg. We need more money."

They walked in the bank as it was closing.

The banker smiled and said, "Hello, Mr. Wilson. I see you're back."

"Yes, this is Turner Sutton, another rancher friend of mine."

They all shook hands.

"How do you do, Mr. Sutton? Could you fellers hold on a minute? Please sit down."

Rob and Turner sat in front of the only desk in the bank.

The banker finished with the last customer, came over to his desk, and sat behind it. "I am so happy to see you back, Mr. Wilson. First, I want to tell you I am sorry for your loss. The Texas banker wrote me about your family and why you came west. I have been hearing about all the good things you have been doing up in New Mexico Territory. I only know Mr. Sutton by reputation. He's the rancher who stepped his horse in an artesian well isn't he."

This surprised the two ranchers. They had no idea anybody outside the Tularosa Basin knew anything about them.

Turner acknowledged the story was true. Bloomberg offered them cigars. Turner took one, but Rob declined.

Rob said, "I'm running a little short on cash. Did you receive my money from the Texas bank?"

"Oh, yes. Your money came in last month. Here is the five hundred dollars in gold you requested if you are ready for it." He placed a leather poke on the desk. "One thing though," Rob tensed up ready for the big screw up with his money. Mr. Bloomberg continued, "Your uncle John Wilson found a mason jar of cash in the corn crib when he was cleaning out your place to turn it over to the new owner. I'm happy to report you have $6,254 on deposit in this bank and not $4,100. Of course, that's before this withdrawal."

Rob was dumbfounded. He didn't know what to say. He was happy, but he felt stupid for not knowing his daddy had more money stashed somewhere. Finally he said, "Thank you, sir. I'm shocked. I expect we can find something to do with that extra money."

They all laughed.

The banker said, "Mr. Wilson, if you need to withdraw more money or make a deposit from time to time, Mr. Stephenson from La Luz banks with us. His brother has a store here in El Paso, and he banks with us. The freighter that hauls supplies and beer to the miners at White Oaks delivers parcels and mail back and forth for us. You can send a message with him if you need cash, and I'll send it on the next trip. If you have a deposit to make, I have found the freighter to be honest to a fault."

Rob was silent for a while, and then he said, "Well, that's good to know. That will make things easier in a pinch, but coming to El Paso is worth the trip. I'm hoping to bring my whole outfit back for some fun this summer. They are all looking forward to it. I like the idea of the freighter hauling the cash better than one man riding back and forth. It seems safer. Where is Stephenson's store? We are in need of some things."

Bloomberg beamed with pleasure and gave them directions to Stephenson's store.

Rob said, "Turner, why don't you stay here? I'll go get the wagon—and we can see if the store is still open." Turner agreed and Rob picked up the leather poke of gold, put it in his vest, and turned to leave. "I'll be right back."

The banker said, "Here Mr. Wilson, you need to sign this draft for the gold."

Rob signed the draft and left.

After Rob had gone, the banker said, "Mr. Sutton, that's quite a remarkable young man. Few young men his age possess the sense to handle money the way he does. I never met anyone with the self-confidence to take on an operation like the one he is starting."

Turner smiled and said, "Yes, sir. He'll do to ride the trail with."

Rob came back driving the wagon and stopped in front of the bank. Bloomberg and Turner were standing on the boardwalk out front. Rob got out of the wagon, they shook hands, and Rob helped Turner up on the wagon. They tipped their hats to the banker, and Rob said, "Thank you again, sir."

Rob and Turner followed the directions to the store and it was still open. They went in and were shocked to see Mr. Stephenson. The man came over to them and said, "May I help you?"

Rob was speechless, Turner said, "What are you doing down here? We were looking for your brother."

The man laughed. "Oh, you thought I am my twin brother. Paul is tending his store in La Luz I 'spect. I'm Levi Stephenson."

They laughed, shook hands, and introduced themselves.

When the ranchers introduced themselves, Levi Stephenson froze and stared at them ... Finally he said, "Are you the Mr. Rob Wilson and Mr. Turner Sutton from New Mexico Territory?"

Turner said, "Why Yes. Have you heard of us, too?"

"In a manner of speaking, I feel like I know you."

"Turner, I bet he has been talking to his brother."

Rob gave Levi the list of their grocery needs Paco had given him. Then Rob added, "I am looking for some items for our ranch headquarters. Do you have any furniture and kitchen stuff?"

"Well, yes. I have some very nice things out in the shed. We received a new shipment from Saint Louis last week. Would you like to look at them?"

"Yes, sir—if you have time."

Stephenson called out, "Martha, I am going out to show these gentlemen the shed. Will you watch the store please?"

An attractive woman stuck her head out through the doorway to the back room and said, "Sure, dear."

When they walked in the shed Rob was awe struck. It was full of beautiful furniture, rugs, lamps, lanterns, pots and pans, sets of dishes, candelabras, and tea sets. Rob remembered his mama and how she loved her things. He vowed to fill his home with fine things and hoped someday his wife would like them too. He wondered if Emily Hernández liked this style and quality of furniture and accessories.

Then he saw it. It was the biggest wood stove he had ever seen. It was five feet wide and three feet deep, and it had two oven doors and front access doors to the fireboxes on both ends. There was a high back with a warmer at the top like his mama's. It had shiny nickel-plated corners and feet and ceramic handles on the oven doors, the firebox doors, and the warmer box on top. A tank with a spigot was up there too. Rob said, "What's that?" and pointed at the tank.

Stephenson looked at what Rob was pointing at and said, "Oh, that's a newfangled water heater. You can fill it with water, and by the time dinner is cooked, the water is hot and ready to do the dishes or for your bath. The instructions say you can pipe water to it and keep it full all the time. I'm not sure about that though. This is the hotel model. You notice it has a firebox on both ends. When you are busy and need the whole top and both ovens hot, you can build a fire in both ends. If you are only in need of part hot and the rest warm, one fire will do."

"I'll take it. Can you have it ready to load along with the rest of our order by morning? I also need five rolls of wire, a set of gate hinges, and some other things."

"Well, yes, Mr. Wilson, but don't you want to know how much it costs?"

"No, sir. That might scare me out of buying it for Paco."

"The other one is still in the crate. It would need to be assembled, but—"

"No, I want this one just like it sits. I don't have time for Jessie and Paco to spend putting the other one together. They would fight like two wet hens before we could have supper. You better give me a mess of hotel-size pots and pans too. Paco will need them. Also, I need a barbeque spit strong enough to hold a whole side of beef with locking skewers to prevent it from slipping on the spit and supports to turn it on. I need the support rods to have variable height notches so I can raise and lower the spit. Can you assemble the hardware for a whole house for me? I also need three blocks and tackle, an anvil, a forge with a bellows, and blacksmith tools. Only the things I can't get from Paul. I mean no disrespect, but if your brother can sell it to me, I owe it to him to buy it from him in La Luz."

"I understand, Mr. Wilson, and I admire your loyalty. Paul and I are partners in both of the businesses. Why don't I ship all the hardware to him in La Luz, and you can pick it up as you need it? I have the barbeque spit, but the supports you describe will have to be fabricated special. I'll ship it to Paul when it's ready for you."

"That would be fine, sir. If you know of other things a new ranch needs, forward him those too. I had no idea you had all this. The bill will be substantial. Now, I want to pay you with a draft on the bank we both use. Please check with Mr. Bloomberg and verify my funds. I will go there and pick up a pack of drafts first thing in the morning."

"Mr. Wilson, I like your style. Consider it done."

"Oh, one more thing, could I have ten or twelve dozen hen eggs?"

"I'll have to ask Mrs. Stephenson about that, but you are welcome to all we have."

"We will see you in the morning. Please apologize to Mrs. Stephenson for keeping you late."

"That's all right. She's used to it. Give me until, say, nine o'clock in the morning and all will be ready and thank you for your business."

"Come on, Turner. Let's go have some of those green chili chicken enchiladas at that cantina of Mr. Dell's. Mayhap we should have a tequila or two with 'em."

"I thought you'd never ask. My foot is bothering me a little. I may need more than two."

"I'll tell you what; let's go see if the barber is still open. We can get a hot lather shave, and he can soak your foot at the same time. I better not get a store-bought haircut. Paco might get his feelings hurt, but you are welcome to. Did you bring the salve the doctor gave you?" Rob didn't need to shave often, but he could tell the trip had taken its toll on Turner.

"Yeah, I think it is in my saddlebags. You think very highly of Paco—and I don't blame you. I just didn't know how highly."

"You sit still. I'll get the salve," Rob said.

Rob rooted out the salve from Turner's saddlebags, and they found a barber who was still open. "Howdy," Rob said to the barber who was finishing up with a tall skinny man. "Are we too late for a shave and a haircut and another shave?"

The barber said, "Not at all, that will be fine. My wife has gone to Ysleta to a church ladies' meeting and won't be back in time for supper."

"Well, then, why don't you join us? We are going to Dell's cantina for some of those green chili enchiladas." Turner didn't add that they were planning on having a few tequilas.

"That's mighty nice of you. I will. My wife doesn't like to go there. She thinks it's a might rough."

"Good. One more thing: Turner here injured his foot. Could you provide him a pan of hot water to soak it in while we're here? Oh! By the way, I'm Robert Wilson, and this is Turner Sutton."

Startled, the barber said, "You are the New Mexico cattlemen who went to the Pecos and into the Llano Estacado. Then you fought the Comanche, rounded up all those cattle, drove them west, and fought your way through the Mescalero Apache? Yes, sir, I'd be proud to help you in any way I can."

Rob looked at Turner, and they both broke out in knee-slapping laughter. "Rob, I didn't know when you sent for me n Bill you was goin' to make us famous." And they laughed again.

"So you are that Rob Wilson? Wow. Oh, there is a wash basin and soap and towels in the back if you are of a mind."

Rob and Turner laughed again. They went to the back of the barbershop and washed their hands, necks, and faces in a washbowl with hot water from a stove. They dried off with clean white towels and returned to the front of the barbershop.

The barber said somewhat in awe, "Please sit down, gentlemen."

Rob had Turner sit in one of the chairs, and they took the bandages off of Turner's foot, Rob was pleased. The foot was bruised, but otherwise, it looked pretty good.

The barber poured hot water from the stove into a small washtub and added half a scoop of white crystals.

Turner eased his foot into it and said, "Ouch. That's hot."

The barber splashed some cool water in it from the water butt and said, "Is that better?"

"Yeah, thanks."

Rob said, "I didn't get your name."

"Oh, I'm John Henry, John Henry Adams."

"Okay, John Henry. How about a shave while Turner soaks?"

"Yes, sir. And a haircut while you are in town?"

Rob said, "No, sir. I'm sorry, but it might hurt my cook's feelings. He's the one who usually cuts my hair."

When they finished in the barbershop, the cowboys looked and felt better. They started toward the door while John Henry turned out the lanterns, as the lanterns were turned out, several children's silhouettes were revealed in the front window. John Henry saw the children and said, "I'm sorry, gentlemen, but we don't get many famous Indian fighters here anymore."

"We're not Indian fighters. Two Mescalero are part of my outfit. Come on, John Henry. Let's go eat. Let me help you up, Turner."

When they arrived, they got down from the wagon and walked into Dell's cantina. When they entered the cantina, the bartender shouted, "There they are."

The people stood up and started applauding and shouting. The bartender Rob remembered as the Dell brother came over to the door, wiped his hands on his apron, and held out his clean right hand. "Welcome back to my establishment, gentlemen."

The crowd cheered again.

Rob and Tuner were becoming uncomfortable with all the recognition they were getting. They nodded to the crowd and shook hands with the proprietor.

Dell motioned them up to the bar and said, "I have six rounds of drinks waiting for you—paid for by some of your admirers. And besides that, your money is no good here tonight. What'll you have?"

Turner answered, "Tequila."

The crowd cheered again.

Dell poured the drinks and said, "Ladies and Gentlemen, these are the famous New Mexico ranchers who took on old Mexicans and Indians, orphans, kids, and an Indian scout to form a gathering expedition. They rode all the way out into the Llano Estacado and fought the Comanche to a draw. This man's pet ghost coyote warned him of a Comanche attack and led them to a lost herd where they rounded up five thousand head of lost longhorns. His partner trained a longhorn steer to lead the herd, and they drove them back across the Pecos to my brother's trading post. They paid ten dollars for three beers and—though starving—refused to eat because my brother didn't want to feed their savages in the dining room. They fought their way across the mesa through hundreds of Mescalero, leaving untold numbers dead and wounded. This man's ghost coyote roared and deafened everybody, encouraging them to stop the fight. In a magnanimous gesture, they gave the Mescalero five hundred head of beef and sixty-seven goats for their starving families even though the group had sustained many terrible injuries. They drove the starving herd for days without food or water—sustained only by roots and rattlesnakes and sucking the moisture out of cacti—all the way back to New Mexico Territory." Dell stopped to take a drink of his beer, paused, and said, "Welcome back to my establishment."

Everybody hooted and hollered applauded and stamped their feet.

Rob and Turner were so embarrassed that they wanted to crawl under the bar. Rob was his customary shade of red, and Turner was turning pink. They didn't know what to say, so they said nothing. The ranchers clicked their glasses, licked the salt from their hands, downed the tequila, and bit their limes. That brought another roar from the crowd. Rob recognized Sam Bloomberg and a small woman he assumed to be the banker's wife. He saw Levi Stevenson and his lovely wife and the brand registration office clerk. He tipped his hat to each of the ladies and nodded at the men. Rob tugged on Turner's sleeve and pointed out the locals they had met.

Turner smiled and tipped his hat, too.

Dell refilled the glasses and put out more lime wedges. Turner saluted the crowd, and they drank another. They broke out in another round of laughter, and the crowd went wild. It seemed there was nothing they could do that didn't please the crowd.

When things settled down, Sam Bloomberg walked over and said, "Won't you join us at our table?"

Rob and Turner approached the big round table in the middle of the room, bowed to the ladies, and shook hands with the men. The Brand Registry clerk, Sam Bloomberg, and Levi acknowledged John Henry and shook his hand. One more chair swiftly appeared, and they sat down at the big round table. There was one man at the table Rob and Turner hadn't met. Levi introduced him as Art, the newspaperman. The crowd had quieted and now they were listening intently.

Mrs. Stephenson said, "Mr. Wilson, do you really have a pet ghost coyote?"

"Oh, no, ma'am," Rob said. "Ma'am, please call me Rob. He is not really my pet, and he is not a ghost. I have been sort of accepted by a he-dog coyote that has helped me out a few times."

Turner jumped in and said, "What do you mean? Sort of accepted by. Didn't that coyote save your bacon when he growled at that Comanche in time for you to duck? What about the time he howled at the Mescalero to make you a supernatural cowboy in the eyes of the Indians? And who came and got you so you could risk your own life to go into the flash flood to save that cow? I'd say he had much more than 'sort of accepted' you." Turner downed another tequila.

"Turner, that was different. Duke helped me out, but he is not my pet."

Mrs. Stephenson said, "Duke? Is that his name? If he has a name and has done all those things, he sounds like a pet to me."

"But he's not mine, ma'am, I don't own him. He just comes around when he wants to."

Turner said, "Yeah? Well, what about that story Wise Elk told us about the coyote being the ghost of one of your ancestors looking after you. Duke shows up out of nowhere whenever you need looking after. You can't tell he's not a ghost coyote by me."

"I'm sorry, ma'am. You must excuse my friend here. He gets carried away sometimes." All the attention was making Rob turn red again.

Mrs. Stephenson said, "I would like to know how you took such a diverse group of cowboys and turned it into such a formidable fighting force that you were able to fight your way through almost a thousand miles of hostile Indian country with a herd of thousands of cattle with only ten men, counting yourself."

"Well, ma'am, you make it sound like a lot bigger deal than it really was."

Mrs. Stephenson said, "It is a big deal. Your partner Jessie almost died from an arrow wound from the Mescalero battle. And what about your Mexican cook Paco, that went through the whole battleground doctoring friend and foe alike while he and Mr. Sutton's friend cooked a feast for hundreds? That is a pretty big deal. Did you know the Mescalero Indian agent also said that after the battle your young Indian wrangler Little Deer, I believe his name is, told some of his cousins that your whole outfit decided they would ride through the gates of hell and try to put out the fire if you asked them to!"

Rob turned red again.

The newspaperman was taking notes.

Rob said, "Hey, you are not writing this nonsense down, are you?

"Mr. Wilson, this is not nonsense. These facts clear up some of the hazy spots in the story. And they make it more interesting for my readers."

"What do you mean?"

"Mr. Wilson, I'm hurt. Have you not read the ongoing accounts of your escapades that I have been printing in the *Rio Grande Times*?"

"No, I have not. We don't get the newspaper at Dog Canyon. How would I have been reading about it?"

Art looked at Stephenson and said, "Levi, I need to send more papers to La Luz for Paul. Mr. Wilson doesn't realize how famous he is. Mr. Sutton, have you seen the papers?"

Turner said, "No, we have been busy building two ranches and have not been to town much."

"Oh, my. I will put together a complete set of "The Chronicles of the Ghost Coyote" for you. It spans the last four issues of the paper. How long will you gentlemen be in El Paso?"

Rob said, "We are leaving as soon as we can get loaded in the morning. Where did you hear all these stories?"

John Henry jumped up and hurried over to the door. He took a woman's hand that had just come in, and she whispered something in his ear. She was very primly dressed. He smiled and led her to the table. Another chair appeared. The men stood, and Sam Bloomberg introduced her as Mrs. John Henry Adams. She sat down next to John Henry.

Art said, "Mr. Dell, could we have some coffee for Mrs. Adams and another round here please? Mr. Wilson—"

Rob interrupted, "Call me Rob. My daddy was Mr. Wilson." He said more aggressively than he intended.

Art continued, "Okay, Rob. The freighter that delivers for Levi overheard your cook talking to his cousin about the coyote warning you about the Comanche. He heard the part about the Mescalero from a southbound trader who got it from the Indian agent at Mescalero."

Rob said, "There weren't many more than fifty Mescalero in that little fracas. It wasn't really a battle."

Mrs. John Henry Adams said, "When Mr. Dell's brother attempted to apologize for his stupidity, Mr. Sutton, in speaking of your friend Mr. Wilson, you have made the phrase 'He'll do to ride the trail with.' a household saying in the Southwest."

The clerk said, "A deputy sheriff from Las Cruces told me about Mr. Sutton and a trained witch horse that finds artesian wells that spurt up hot, sweet water better than a divining rod."

Turner said, "That horse was not a witch. He stepped in a hole and broke his leg. I had to shoot him and drag him off—and then the hole filled up."

"Was it hot, sweet water?" the newspaperman asked.

"Well, yeah. I didn't know it was sweet until the other horses started to drink it. I was afraid it might be poison. So I tasted it myself."

Everyone laughed.

The newspaperman went on, "This week when the freighter was in town, he told me, he was in the saloon and witnessed, the horse rancher's beautiful daughter, Emily Hernández, horse whip a cowboy in the main street of Tularosa when he accosted her and attempted to molest her. Supposedly it was a shiftless man that needed a whippin'. Is she your sweetheart?"

Rob's chair careened across the floor as he jumped up with fire in his steel blue eyes and his hand on his gun. "Art, if you print one word about Emily Hernández, I'll hunt you down and shoot you like a rabid dog. I swear I will."

Turner was on his feet standing between Rob and the newspaperman trying to calm down Rob. The whole place was so quiet you could hear a drop of sweat hit the floor.

The color had completely drained from the newspaperman's face. "Rob, I'm sorry. I won't print anything about Miss Hernández. I promise."

While John Henry picked up Rob's overturned chair, Turner got Rob calmed down enough to sit back down.

In an effort to change the subject Levi Stephenson said, "And today, you didn't buy that huge stove for yourself—you bought it for Paco, the cook. In fact you didn't even buy yourself a new hat, which you really do need, by the way. You didn't buy one thing for yourselves—neither one of you."

Mrs. Bloomberg added, "Look at you. Two successful New Mexico ranchers in worn-out trousers, scuffed up boots, and sweat-stained shirts. But look at those handguns. Samuel Colt was dead twelve years before his widow Elizabeth, began manufacturing single-action Colt .45 army pistols. She didn't start until seventy-three, and you men already carry them. Your kind have to have the newest, finest, most powerful handguns in the world. They are clean and shiny, and every loop in your belts has a shiny cartridge in it. Gentlemen, that is the stuff American heroes are made of."

The crowd went wild; they applauded, whistled, shouted, and beat on the bar.

Rob and Turner were stunned. They couldn't move. They sat and looked down at the floor.

People started coming by the table shaking hands with them or patting them on the back. The people seemed to want to just touch the men they had been reading about.

Art said, "Mr. Sutton, You just mentioned a story we haven't heard about yet, Duke leading Mr. Wilson to save a cow from the flash flood?"

Rob jumped up and said, "Turner, if you tell that story, I swear I'll tell the one about you getting your foot busted by that mama cow."

Everybody hooted with laughter, and then they cheered and applauded again.

Mrs. Bloomberg said, "Gentlemen, I rest my case. These are the kind of stories that have made America great in the eyes of the world."

Turner said, "Rob, I'm afraid we are certified heroes from the West."

Rob said, "Yeah, Turner … what are we going to do?"

Turner said, "Well, I think we should get drunker 'n hoot owls."

The cantina erupted in shouts and laughter, and people crowded up to the bar. Dell was pouring drinks as fast as he could. He called the cook and dishwasher out of the kitchen. She was drawing mugs of beer as fast as it would come out of the tap, and the dishwasher was cutting limes.

Rob said, "Can we have some of Mr. Dell's world-famous green enchiladas now?"

Everybody laughed again.

The food and more tequila were served with an unusually good white wine for the ladies.

Mrs. Adams pointed to the wine and said, "May I have one of those?" When her husband looked at her questioningly, she said, "Well, John Henry, it's a celebration."

The food was outstanding, the tequila and wine flowed, and everybody had a wonderful time. When they were ready to leave, Levi suggested Rob and Turner send the wagon home with him. He would feed and care for the mules and the horse and put them in his barn for the night. That way, the wagon would be there in the morning.

Rob and Turner agreed. Rob walked out to get their saddlebags. When everybody was gone, the cowboys staggered across the street to the hotel and fell into their beds.

The next morning, they were up and dressed when Rob said, "Let's have breakfast in the hotel dining room. You don't need to be walking too far."

After breakfast, Turner said, "Here Gimme that. I'll pay this bill. Say, how about while you go to the bank and get the wagon at Levi's, I'll go visit John Henry and see if he will soak my foot again. That felt good, and I think it helped."

"You got it. Come on. I'll walk you over. You stay with John Henry until I bring the wagon over and pick you up."

"Okay, mama. I swear, you are getting just like Paco. I wonder if it's from driving the wagon."

Turner walked in the barbershop, and Rob took the saddlebags and walked down the street to Levi Stephenson's store.

Levi had two men helping him load the stove. They loaded it in the wagon and tied it down so well Rob was sure nothing could move it. It was crated and padded with quilts.

Levi said, "I put in a few things you will probably need. Oh, and your eggs are inside the right oven of the stove. Return anything you don't want to Paul for credit. Have you thought of anything else you need?

Rob looked embarrassed but after a pause, he said, "Levi, I need some help. There is this girl—"

Levi said, "Let's get Mrs. Stephenson. She is very good at this sort of thing."

They walked inside, and Levi told his wife that Rob needed a gift for a young lady and was not sure of what would be appropriate. Rob was red again, standing with his hat in his hand, toeing the floor.

Mrs. Stephenson smiled and said, "Mr. Wilson—I mean Rob— how old is this girl?"

Rob said, "I think she is eighteen or so, ma'am. I'm not sure."

"Is she your sister or your cousin?"

"No, ma'am."

"Rob, is her name Emily Hernández?"

Rob looked up at her in surprise. "Yes, ma'am. How did you know?"

"I was there last night. Remember? I take it you like her some. Romantically I mean."

"Well, yes, ma'am. She gives me the tingles."

"Oh." It was all she could do not to burst out laughing. After she composed herself, she said, "Have you spoken to her daddy yet?"

"Oh, no, ma'am. I haven't even spoken to her yet."

Mrs. Stephenson gave Rob a strange look and said, "Levi, why don't you ask the boys to watch the store? Let's go to the hotel for coffee. This may take a while."

They walked across the street and into the hotel dining room where they sat at a corner table.

When their coffee had been delivered, Mrs. Stephenson said, "Rob, what do you mean you haven't spoken to her yet?"

"Well, the first time I met her, she said, 'Hello. My name is Emily Hernández. May I help you?' I opened my mouth to talk but nothing came out. Luckily Paco was there, and he sort of covered for me. Later I did say 'Thank you for the coffee, ma'am'." Rob said proudly. "I bought ten horses and four mules from her daddy. I am going back to visit her as soon as the herd is branded and the privy is built."

"I hesitate to ask, but why must the privy be built?"

"Well, I figure she might want to look over the ranch first, and a girl should have a privy."

Mrs. Stephenson did not pursue that line of questioning and said, "Rob, a gift from a man she doesn't know is a big step for a girl. What makes you think she will accept the gift?"

"When she poured my coffee, she looked me right in the eye." Rob said as he pointed to his eye with his right index finger. He paused, and said, "I believe she will accept it."

"Rob, you live a long ways away. We will pick out a couple of things. You can speak to her daddy, and if he says okay, then after a while you can give the first gift to her. If she accepts it, that will be a good sign—if she is a nice girl. Some not-so-nice girls accept gifts from men they don't really like, but they the like the gifts. Do you understand?"

"No, ma'am."

Levi spilled his coffee and feigned a cough. He wiped the coffee off his hand.

"Yes, well, ah … it doesn't matter. After a while, if her daddy says it's okay, give her the second gift. If she accepts that, that's very good. Then you have to talk to her, Rob. You have to know if she … if you give her the tingles too. If you get along after a while, you can talk to her more seriously. And then after a while—"

"Ma'am, I get the idea, but I don't have all those after a whiles."

"Rob Wilson, if she is as good a girl as I think she is, you will just have to find all the, after a whiles she wants if you want her for your own." Mrs. Stephenson took a deep breath. "Now, we'll pick out one last thing, so you will have it if you need it. If you end up not needing it, you can send it back to Levi."

"Yes, ma'am."

They walked back to the store. Mrs. Stephenson took Rob by the arm and led him over to the jewelry counter. She said, "Rob, is she Catholic or Protestant?"

Rob said, "Oh, ma'am. I don't know. Her daddy is Mexican, but her mama was not. I don't think. Most Mexicans are Catholic, and most gringos are Protestants, I think. I just don't know, ma'am."

"Okay listen. Here is a nice little silver cross necklace, here is a very dainty rosary, and here is a small cameo brooch. If she is Protestant, give her the little cross. If she is Catholic, give her the rosary. If she is Jewish, give her the brooch. If you can't find out what religion she is, give her the brooch. After a while, you can give her one of the other things. But if she is not Catholic, don't give her the rosary. Send that back to Levi. I am going to give you—as a gift from Levi and me—a silver sewing thimble to take care of the old tradition.

"Now, here is a new kind of ring. It's called an engagement ring, but instead of a plain gold band, it has a diamond in it. It costs more, but now that they have found diamonds in Africa, diamonds are not so dear. It is much more impressive for the young lady. If after you are sure she has had all the after a whiles she needs—and you are sure you give her the tingles—offer her that and ask her to marry you. If she turns you down, she is not smart enough for you anyway. If she says yes, give her the silver thimble. We will select a gold wedding band at that time."

She wrapped the gifts in little boxes, tied them with string, and handed them to Rob. "Give her all the after a whiles she needs—and then one more. Got it?"

Rob smiled and said, "Yes, ma'am."

"And Rob, girls like well-dressed men when they are courtin'. Buy yourself a new hat and some new clothes. Not dude clothes—just new, clean, ranch clothes."

Rob smiled at Mrs. Stephenson and offered her his hand. "Thank you, ma'am. I am truly grateful."

She ignored his hand and hugged him and gave him a kiss on the cheek. "Good luck, Rob."

Rob blushed and said, "Thank you, ma'am."

He paid the bill with one of his new drafts and climbed up on the wagon. The Stephensons waved their so longs and watched Rob drive down the street. Martha Stephenson said, "Wow, that man has buried his whole family, moved across the country, taken on a huge responsibility, traveled to the Llano Estacado, fought the Comanche, fought the Mescalero, fought drought, fought floods, and amassed a huge herd of cattle—yet he is an innocent young boy who is in love and doesn't have the first idea of what to do about it."

"He knows she gives him the tingles," Levi said with a smile. "Looks like he is doing all right to me."

After a minute, she said thoughtfully, "Levi … do I give you the tingles?"

Levi looked her in the eyes, grinned, and said warmly, "Every time I see you."

She smiled, and they walked arm in arm back into the store.

Rob drove the wagon to the barbershop and went inside.

John Henry was bandaging Turner's foot. "We saw you comin'. Just one minute."

When Rob walked back outside, Art came trotting over to the wagon. "Mr. Wilson, I'm so glad I caught you. Here is a complete set of "The Chronicles of the Ghost Coyote" for you. Only these have been published. I'll remember what you said."

Rob looked at the newsprint bundle, pushed back his hat, and said, "I'm not sure I should thank you, sir, but I do appreciate you bringing us this. We will read it."

Art shook Rob's hand and walked away with a big grin.

Rob looked in the back of the wagon. It was nearly full. He took his saddlebags and opened one side and put the package from Mrs. Stephenson and the bundle of newsprint in it and buckled it back up and placed both his and Turner's saddle bags in the wagon. Turner came out carrying a bundle. He showed it to Rob and said, "Mrs. Adams fixed us some fried chicken and biscuits for lunch."

"Wow, Mrs. Stephenson filled one of those new pots with stew. We will have supper for tonight too."

"That's good. No offense, but you don't cook like Paco."

"Well, thank you very much."

On the drive back to New Mexico, Turner said, "Rob, I been thinkin'. You know that spring you found south of Dog Canyon?"

"Yes."

"Have you measured where it is to see if it is on your homestead claim?"

"No, I haven't. What if it's not?"

"Someone else could stake a claim to it. This is open range, but it is also range you can homestead. If you have a claim on the water, you control the land around that water. You don't have to claim all of it because it's not much good to anybody else without the water. But, you can only stake one claim."

"But I'm not old enough to stake a claim."

"Paco is."

Rob said, "Yeah, and that would leave me able to stake one where we need it next year."

"I thought you should check if you haven't."

"Thank you, Turner Sutton."

They made it back to Dog Canyon in good time. Because of the stove, Rob took them far out west in the basin to avoid the arroyos, and then turned east when they were due west of Dog Canyon.

Jessie and the others saw them coming and rode out to meet them. When the cowboys got close, everybody stopped.

Rob said, "How are you boys? Did any work get done while we were gone?"

Jessie said, "You can come and see for yourself. It may not suit you, but work got done."

"If you boys did it, I bet it suits me."

Jessie said, "Come on. If Paco sees us out here lollygagging, we will all be in trouble."

Rob laughed and said, "See? It's not so easy running things, is it?"

When they arrived at Dog Canyon, Paco said, "Señor Rob, I'm so glad you have returned. These no-account cowboys need constant supervision."

Jessie said, "Damn. Rob's been gone less than a week, and Paco starts talking in three-syllable words."

"What do you mean three-syllable words, Jessie?"

"Well, *no-account* is a three-syllable word id'n it."

The cowboys all laughed.

Rob asked, "How is the herd?"

Marco said, "The cows are doing very well, jefe. We have more new calves."

"And the remuda?"

Little Deer said, "Very good. I think soon we have little horses."

"Okay, here is the deal. Paco, have you picked the spot you will use as the kitchen until the house is built?"

"Si, Señor Rob. I thought that was settled."

"I wanted to make sure you hadn't found a better place. Okay, you cowboys unload that wagon here in Paco's kitchen. And be careful—there's hen eggs in there. Come on, Turner. Let's see if there's coffee."

Turner hobbled over to a big rock, and Rob handed him a cup of coffee.

The cowboys unloaded the small stuff first—oohing and aahing at all the new things.

Rob winked at Jessie. "You boys bring Paco all that produce over here, and maybe we will get some for supper."

Jessie looked in the back of the wagon, whistled his approval, and called for help. They unloaded the stove and carried it over by the fire pit. Paco had his back to them and was admiring all the fresh produce. When they sat the stove down it clinked on a rock, and Paco turned around.

After looking at the stove for a few seconds, Paco whispered, "Aye, Chihuahua." He walked over to the new stove and touched it tenderly. His eyes teared up, and everyone had to turn away.

Rob said, "This is for you, my friend."

Paco said, "It is the most beautiful stove I ever saw. Thank you, Señor Rob."

"Oh. Unless you are going to have baked eggs, you better unload the right oven. I had Levi put in an extra section of stovepipe so you won't have smoke in your eyes all the time."

Jessie said, "Who's Levi?"

"Oh, partner, have I got some stories to tell you."

Chapter 13

Branding the Herd

Rob started telling Jessie about the trip to El Paso. "The trip down was without much trouble. We had a few washed-out arroyos, but we made it through them okay. Because it was the most important thing, we went to register the brand first."

Turner interrupted, "Jessie, I thought we were going to have to come back and get you to help Mr. Wilson here with the registering of the brand. He kept saying, 'Well, Jessie usually does this' and 'do you think this will be all right with Jessie?' But he finally got an inspiration and got it done just before he almost passed out."

Paco turned and said, "Passed out?"

Turner said, "Don't get upset about your boy Paco. He did fine. At the last minute, he thought the clerk was going to tell him he wasn't old enough to register a brand. He was so scared. I thought he was goin' a pass out." Turner laughed.

"Oh, Turner. It wasn't that bad. Jessie, the JR and the RJ brands were already registered. I finally thought it should be Dog—for Dog Canyon Ranch. Is that all right with you?"

Jessie was stunned. "Sure, Rob. Whatever you think." Jessie appeared to be touched that Rob wanted it to be okay with him. He said, "Okay, you Dog cowboys."

They all shouted, "Dog cowboys. Yeah, Dog cowboys."

Rob said, "After we finished there, we went to the bank. Mr. Bloomberg had our money ready, and best of all, he told us about Uncle John finding a Mason jar in the corn crib with a bunch of money in it. Mr. Bloomberg informed me we had more money than we thought—even after the withdrawal for more gold and what I spent at Levi's store."

Jessie asked, "Who is this Levi you keep talking about?"

"I'm getting to that." Rob noticed the silence and looked around at everybody. The whole camp was frozen still as the North Star, listening to him talk. Turner had a grin on his face, but everybody else was mesmerized.

Paco was listening intently while he silently cooked supper.

Rob decided it was their story too, so he was going to tell the whole story ... to everybody.

"First, Pepe and Marco, does Paco have everything he needs to feed this mangy-looking bunch?"

Pepe looked to Paco, who nodded. Pepe said, "Si, Señor Rob."

Rob said, "Little Deer, are all the horses unsaddled and the mules unhitched and tended to?"

Little Deer said, "Si, jefe, and they have drunk water and all but this many," he held up all his fingers, "are turned out to eat. Those are saddled with loose cinches and hobbled so they can eat too."

"Well, I'll be. Turner, I guess you and I should go off more often. This outfit is whipped into pretty good shape."

Jessie said, "Ah, shit, Rob. You knew this outfit was in good shape before you left. Now go on with the story."

Everybody laughed and looked around proudly.

"I will, I will, but before I go on, Julio could I have some more of Paco's coffee? I really missed that."

There was laughter as they moved closer to Rob and Turner while Julio poured coffee all around and sat back down on his rock.

Rob said, "When we left the bank, Mr. Bloomberg gave us directions to Paul Stephenson's brother's store. We walked in the store and there stood Paul, big as life. Well, 'course we were shocked to see him in El Paso and said so. Then he told us he was not Paul—he was Paul's twin brother. He is as nice as Paul, and his name is Levi Stephenson. His beautiful wife's name is Martha. I gave him Paco's grocery list and told him about some of the other stuff we needed."

Turner interrupted again, "I thought Rob was going to buy out the store. Then he told Levi that if Paul could sell it to him, he would have to buy it from Paul in La Luz. Well, Levi was proud to hear that and told us so, and he told us they were partners in both stores. Then Rob says, 'Do you have any kitchen stuff? Paco needs a few things.'"

Everybody laughed and looked at Paco as he cooked on his new stove.

Turner said, "Levi took us out back to his shed, and I thought Rob was going to have an apoplexy. He started telling Levi all the things he wanted for the house and barn ... and then he saw the stove. He just stood there admiring it, and then he said 'I'll take it.' Levi asked if he wanted to know how much it cost, and Rob said, 'No. It might scare me out of buying it for Paco.'"

There was complete silence, and everybody looked at Paco. Paco just kept cooking. He didn't turn around, but he had to take his towel and wipe his face.

They all smiled silently and turned back to Rob and Turner.

Duke told the sun good night, and Rob looked up and said, "Boys, that's the most famous coyote in the entire West."

Rob said, "Oh, shoot. Turner, I forgot about the newspapers." He stood up to go to his saddlebags, unbuckled one side, and took out a bundle of newspapers. He carefully returned all the other things to his saddlebag and buckled both straps.

"Here, Turner. Look at this. This is what that newspaperman brought me the morning before we left. I clean forgot about them." He handed the bundle of newsprint to Turner.

Turner opened the bundle and unfolded the newspapers. He began to read them and said, "My gawd. Rob, when you get through with your story of El Paso, you should read all these to everybody."

Rob said, "I was afraid of that. We finished with Levi, agreed to pick up the order the next morning, and walked out on the street. It was a beautiful late afternoon, and we decided to clean up some before supper. We found a barbershop and walked in. When we introduced ourselves for the third time, the people acted funny. It was like they knew us or about us anyway. Turner's foot was a little sore, and we asked the barber if he would soak it while we took a shave and Turner had a haircut."

Paco turned around and looked at Rob's hair. Rob saw him, took off his hat, and turned around to show Paco that he had not gotten a haircut. Paco smiled and went back to cooking.

Rob looked at Turner, and they laughed.

Turner said, "You can't believe how good it felt to soak my foot in that hot water with some kind of salt in it. Some new thing … Edison salt I think it was."

Rob interrupted, "It's Epsom salt, magnesium chloride. It's named after a town in England where it was discovered about a hundred years ago."

"You mean it's not new? Why haven't I found it before? Rob, how do you know this kind of stuff?"

"I read about it in a history book my mama made me read. Then she would test me to see if I remembered everything. I had to learn it."

Turner said, "Anyway, we washed up and got shaved. I got a haircut. We were feeling pretty spiffy. We invited John Henry—that was the barber's name, John Henry Adams—to go to supper with us at Dell's cantina."

Everybody oohed and aahed and smiled at each other at the mention of Dell's cantina.

Pepe asked, "Señor Rob, did they have the music and the dancing lady?"

Rob said, "No, I guess they only have that on Saturday night. But you wouldn't have believed the crowd there. When we walked in, it was almost full. Mr. Dell hollered, 'There they are.' And everyone cheered."

Turner said, "I never saw the like. They guided us up to the bar and told us our money weren't no good that night. We each took a shot of tequila and toasted the crowd, and they went wild again. Then Rob saw the banker and his wife, Mr. and Mrs. Stephenson, the brand-registry clerk, and another man. They invited us to their table. We sat down with them, and they started telling us all the things they had heard about us—you all too. They knew so much about you guys. Rob and I were speechless until the newspaperman mentioned Emily Hernández and the boss here jumped up with his hand on his shootin' iron and threatened to shoot up half the state of Texas if one word about her was printed in the newspaper. I think the exact words were: 'If you print one word about Emily Hernández, I'll hunt you down and shoot you like a rabid dog. I swear I will.' I thought Art was going to piss his pants and die of fright right in the cantina."

There was total silence in the camp. Only the crickets and a quail calling broke the silence.

Jessie slapped his knee and said, "See, Paco. I told you so."

Rob was as red as he was in El Paso, but he continued, "Well, the long and the short of it is that the Texas banker told Bloomberg why we came to New Mexico. The freighter that hauls the beer to White Oaks told them about hearing Paco talk to his cousin Juan. Jedidiah Dell told them about us going through there and all about that story—complete with the story of Jessie's trained steer leading the herd away from food and water to perish in the waterless mesa. Some trader got the story of the Mescalero fight from the Indian agent in Mescalero. Paul told the El Paso Stephensons about Paco's doctoring and of how much you cowboys can eat and how spoiled you are."

Turner said, "Yeah—and that your boss has a pet ghost coyote that keeps him out of trouble. And of how the boss here tries to keep you boys healthy, in line, and make you wise."

They all cheered and applauded. Rob turned red again and said, "Paul Stephenson told them about Little Deer whispering to the horses in Apache and turning them into … what was it he called them, Turner?"

"Uncommonly reliable mounts. Yeah, that was it. And of the man of the coyote spirit' callin' his pet coyote down and scarin' the Mescalero half to death."

"No, Turner. The freighter said that. Well, I think. Anyway, you are all famous heroes throughout the West, and everybody around here has a big mouth."

There was silence again. Rob looked around. Everybody was looking into the twilight and thinking.

Rob said, "Pepe, light all three lanterns. After supper, we'll read the newspapers. Paco, how is supper coming anyway? That stove not broken in yet?"

"No, Señor Rob. Supper is coming fine. It is Paco who is slow. I have been listening to the story. While you boys wash up, I will put it on the table. Pepe, will you help me pour the coffee when you finish with the lanterns?"

"Si, señor."

The cowboys formed a line at the washbasin outside the tent. When everybody had washed, they took their seats at the wooden table with benches on both sides. There was a new chair carved from mesquite wood on each end of the table. Paco told Rob to sit on the north end of the table and for Turner to sit on the south end. They were impressed with the workmanship of the chairs.

Rob asked who made them.

Paco said, "Wise Elk—as surprises for you two."

"Thank you, Wise Elk. I had forgotten how good you are with your hands."

Wise Elk nodded and sat down on the end of the west bench.

Pepe started to take a biscuit, and Paco swished his towel at him. "Pepe!" Then he said, "Señor Jessie, will you say the blessing?"

Jessie bowed his head, paused, and said, "Dear Lord, smile on us in mercy and give us thankful hearts for these and all the blessings we beg for Christ's sake. Amen."

The cowboys said, "Amen," raised their heads, and started passing the food just like everything was normal.

Rob just sat there with his mouth open. He was stunned. He said, "Paco, what has happened around here? Why I'd be proud to have the preacher over for Sunday dinner if you boys are going to act like that."

Paco said, "Oh, Señor Rob. Nothing has happened. It's just that we decided we were going to treat this tent like it was our home."

Rob still didn't know what to say.

Jessie handed Rob the steak platter and said, "Pass the 'taters."

Turner looked at Rob, shrugged, and passed the biscuits to Paco. "Paco, before you send me off on another trip with Rob, you need to polish up his cooking skills. I thought he was trying to poison me. I tell ya, I'm sure glad to get back to your table. We haven't had a decent meal since we left here, and I'm starving."

Paco beamed again.

After supper, they had fresh cherry cobbler and more coffee.

Rob said, "Now, listen to me. I don't want you bo—I don't want you men to get the big head over all this stuff in the newspaper. If it is like what those El Paso people told us, the stories are greatly exaggerated."

Everyone pulled up their bench or a rock a little closer to the table and moved around a little so they could all see Rob's face as he began to read the newspaper stories. As he went on, their jaws dropped a little, then their mouths were just hanging open. Their eyes in their suntanned, wind-burned faces got bigger and bigger until they all looked like huge raccoons in the dim light of the lanterns.

Occasionally someone would say something like, "They knew my name?"

Or "That was not really the way it was."

If the newspaper didn't give the source of the information, Turner would explain how the story had reached El Paso.

After Rob had read all four of the articles in the Rio Grande Times, he lowered the newspapers and looked around the table and said, "I apologize for causing you all to be famous and to have your names in the newspapers all over the West. The newspaper man told me he had been contacted by the *San Francisco Examiner Daily*, the *Santa Fe New Mexican*, and the *Denver Rocky Mountain News* about syndicating the series to their papers. They all seem to think you cowboys are the cream of the crop and represent the best of the men who tamed the West. I don't think I can do anything about it. I'm sorry. But I want you all to know I think you are the finest bunch of men I have ever known, and I am proud to call every one of you my friend."

Pepe said, "Señor Rob, the stories are not all true, but they are not all lies. Like you said, they are just exaggerated. The numbers are not correct, but most of the things they talk about we did do. Maybe not in as big a way as they say, but we did them. I am not ashamed to be the most famous Mexican orphan in New Mexico, and I am proud to call you my patron."

The others all agreed. There was a chorus of "yeah," and "you're right" and "you bet". Then Jessie raised his cup and said, "To the patron of Dog Canyon."

Everybody cheered and raised their tin cups.

Rob's eyes welled up and he said, "Thank you." He had to turn and walk toward the arroyo.

Paco said, "Señor Rob, the privy is over there."

When Rob had collected himself, he came back to the table. "How is the corral coming along?"

Jessie said, "Well, when we got that first big one you laid out for us built, we all agreed that we needed a smaller one to keep the horses and mules in if we wanted to keep them hemmed up for some reason. So we built a smaller corral between here and the big one."

Bill said, "You will be amazed at Jessie's Fort Worth cow chute. It works like a fine watch. You start the cows through it, and by the time they get to the third section, they are calm. We pinch them in the hinged section, brand them, and they are out the end of it before they know what happened."

Marco said, "It is so easy compared to the old way. While some of us are branding the old stuff, one roper and Pepe can brand and cut calves."

Jessie said, "We are glad you two are back though. The longhorns and the bulls won't fit through it, so we need you to help double-rope or maybe triple-rope them so we can brand all the cattle. We even tried the chute on the horses. We had to add a top rail, but it works for them too."

Turner said, "I can't wait to see it in the morning."

Duke called up the moon, and Rob took a plate of food out into the darkness. Everyone watched him, but no one said anything.

The next morning, Rob woke early and enjoyed a few minutes of private coffee time with Paco before the others had their boots on. Paco told Rob how hard the boys had been working, trying to finish before Rob and Turner got back. They finished the big corral and started the second then they decided to try Jessie's cow chute. It worked so well that they branded 114 cows in one afternoon. They were ecstatic, and so proud. They talked all through supper about how proud Señor Rob would be.

Paco said, "Now you be proud. Don't let on that Paco talk too much."

"I will, Paco. Thanks."

Jessie walked into the kitchen, area scratching his head and wiping the sleep from his eyes. "Well, are you ready to watch the cow chute work?"

"You bet. I can't wait."

Paco took an iron rod and beat on his big iron triangle, "Breakfast you DOG boys. Breakfast; Come eat with Paco before the sun makes it hot. Today is going to be mucho caliente. Come drink coffee with Paco in the cool."

Rob said, "Paco, how is Julio's wound?"

"Señor Rob, Julio has been very good. He is healing. It won't be long until he is whole again."

"Thanks to you and your doctoring, Paco. Did his back close up?"

"Almost. He tries to hide it from me when he comes into camp, but I see that there is almost no blood on his shirt now."

"Has Jessie had any trouble with his leg?"

"No, and he has almost stopped limping."

Wise Elk came riding into camp.

Paco said, "Wise Elk, where have you been? I didn't know you were gone."

"Paco, Wise Elk hears big cat high up mountain. I think she hungry. I go see."

"Did you find her?"

"No find."

"Well, come eat." Paco opened one of the ovens and took out a pan of biscuits.

"Señor Rob, look how even the stove browns the biscuits—beautiful. Almost good as a Dutch oven but much more easy."

"I'm glad you like it, Paco."

After breakfast, they rode over to the new big corral to show Rob and Turner the Fort Worth cow chute in action. Jessie was explaining how it worked. Then he sent Marco and Julio to go get fifty head of cattle that needed branding.

While the boys were gone to get the cattle, Jessie had Pepe built a fire in the fire pit and got out the branding irons. When Marco and Julio returned with the cattle, the cowboys were mounted and ready to haze the cattle into the chute. Little Deer and Wise Elk had their lariats tied onto the hinged chute gate. Wise Elk's was tied to the top of the gate above the cow's backs. Little Deer had his lariat tied to the bottom of the gate and let the rope go slack, and fall in the dirt.

The cows were held in the individual compartments with separator poles run through slots that had been built for that purpose.

With one cow in each of the three compartments, Pepe shouted, "Ready."

Wise Elk and Little Deer backed up their horses and took up the slack. The hinged gate closed on the cow in the last compartment.

When she was held tight and still, Pepe branded the cow on her left hip.

The Mescalero walked their horses forward to release the pressure on the cow. Bill pulled the separator poles out of the last section of the chute complex, and the cow was free to run out and join the rest of the herd in the corral.

Bill reinserted the separator poles on the end section into their slots, and Jessie pulled out the ones in the second section. The cow in the second section was free to move into the hinged gate section.

Jessie replaced the separator poles, and Marco removed the poles in the first section. The cow in the first section was moved to the second section. Marco reinserted the separator poles between the first and second section, and a new cow was driven into the first section. Marco reinserted the separator poles on the south end of the first section to keep the system loaded.

Julio stayed mounted and kept herding the cattle into the first section as needed. When a mother cow and her calf came up, he roped the calf and dragged it over to the fire pit area for one of the ground men to throw and tie so Pepe could brand and cut it if it was a bull calf. It was then ready to rejoin its mother when she was finished and came out the end of the chute. Pepe threw a rock in the appropriate pile or hung the scrotum on the fence after he put the balls in the bucket.

The thing worked like a well-oiled machine. Rob and Turner watched in amazement.

Rob said, "Turner, I have to go to La Luz to the blacksmith Paul told us about and have the DOG branding irons made. These boys are going to run out of Artesian Well cattle to brand before I get back if I don't hurry. Do you want to ride to town with me? I'll buy you one of those cold beers from Mr. Masterson, and you could get your foot soaked at the barbershop."

Turner pondered a minute and said, "Yeah. That sounds like a good idea. I believe I will."

Rob and Turner walked over and shook Jessie's hand and told him how much they liked the cow chute. They bragged on all the cowboys for their part in the branding operation.

Rob said, "I'm taking Turner to the barbershop, and we are going to the blacksmith to have the Dog branding irons made. I must hurry back with the new branding irons before all the Artesian Well Ranch cattle are branded."

The cowboys cheered, and Rob was proud.

When Rob and Turner rode into La Luz, they stopped at the blacksmith's shop to inquire about the branding irons. Rob showed the blacksmith his registration and asked, "How long will it take?"

The blacksmith said, "Mr. Wilson, I know about you. I don't need the registration papers. I can have one branding iron this afternoon, but the other one won't be ready until about noon tomorrow."

Rob said, "If that's the best you can do, that's fine. I'll be back for the first one this afternoon. It might be a day or two before I will be back for the other one."

They headed for Masterson's cantina for lunch. Masterson greeted them warmly and set up the cold beer.

Rob asked, "How are things going?"

"Rob, things here is fine, but you must a' been havin' the time o' yer lives, what with all 'at Indian fightin' an' cattle drivin' an' all. When ya first come in here this spring, I had no idee I was talkin' ta a legend and one of them heroes of the West."

"Just goes to show you the power of the press. Mr. Masterson, I'm not a hero and will never be a legend. I'm just an honest cowpoke, trying to make a living in the cattle business."

"And I 'spose this gent with ya never rode 'is magic hass off in an artesian well, too."

Turner said, "Ah, shit, Masterson, you know that horse wasn't magic. I use to ride him over here all the time. He was just a horse … a good one, but just a horse."

"I know. I know. But you guys don't un'erstand. Those newspaper 'counts may have stretched the truth a might, but they give us people 'at read 'em somethin' ta dream 'bout and somethin' ta admire.

Somethin' ta talk to each other 'bout. It gives us somethin' ta be proud of that we knowed you boys and your hands. People need heroes and fascinatin' tales to pass back an' forth ta make up fer the dull hardworkin' days o' most of our lives. You should be proud 'at ya give us that."

Turner said, "Damn. I never looked at it that way. I laughed at it and told Rob it was all right and that we should get drunk and enjoy bein' famous. He is the one havin' the most trouble with it. He don't like being famous."

Rob said, "I didn't say I didn't like being famous. I'm just not sure of it when the facts are being exaggerated so much."

Masterson said, "Rob, ya know how a story 'at gits tol' an' retol' grows, whether it's in a town, er a cow camp, er a ter'tory like our'n. People like to know somethin' important 'at other people don't know. It makes it funner ta tell the story. I bet that newspaperman wrote the truth as he knowed it. By the time the stories got from you and where ya done all that stuff all the way ta El Paso, they had done been tol' and retol' an' they jus' growed they own self. All he can do is write it like he heard it."

Rob thought about what Masterson had said. He said, "I have to admit, what you say makes a lot of sense, but I wish it was somebody else they were talking about. That's all. It makes me feel like a fake or an imposter. I'm not a hero."

Turner said, "Rob, sometimes you don't have to be a hero. You just do what has to be done as best you can. It's the people that make you a hero when they hear of what you did and the way you done it. You can't make yourself a hero, and if they make you one, you can't help it—and you can't do nothin' about it."

"You make it sound like I'm stuck with it."

"Well, I wouldn't say it that a way. I'd say you earned it—so enjoy it. Quit worryin' about it. You can't change it."

"I sure hope you're wrong, Turner. How am I going to face Emily and Ignacio Hernández?"

"What do you mean 'How are you going to face 'em? They are goin' to be proud of you. You don't have to do nothing—just be you."

"Turner, will you pick up the DOG branding iron and tell the blacksmith I'll be there tomorrow to pick up the other one. Tell Paco not to worry. I'll be at Dog Canyon by tomorrow night. I don't want anybody but maybe Jessie and Paco to know I'm going to Tularosa."

"Rob, don't you think all the boys are smart enough to add two and two? All that book learnin', and you don't have sense 'nough to pour piss out of a boot. I won't tell nobody nothin', and they will all have a pretty good idea where you are. Don't worry about it. It's okay. Now let's eat before you go. I'm starved."

They ordered lunch and more beer. When they finished, they shook hands. Rob walked out to his horse, mounted up, turned north, and rode off.

"Masterson, that was good talking you did. That man is having trouble being a hero."

They both laughed, and Masterson got them both another beer.

Chapter 14

GOING BACK TO TULAROSA

*I*gnacio watched the rider coming and recognized Rob. He was in no hurry to finish what he was doing in the barn and looked for something else that needed doing. Ignacio figured the young people needed a few minutes to talk. They had plenty to discuss.

He smiled, remembering how hard it was to say the simplest things when you were young. Emily's mother would finally stop and say, "Ignacio, just say what you want to say." That would shut him up, and he couldn't say anything. Besides, she seemed to know what he wanted to say anyway. She would stand there and wait until he worked it out and could say what needed saying.

Sometimes he would start talking, and she would finish it for him. He would ask, "Why did you make me try to say it if you knew what I wanted to say?"

She would say, "Because you had to say it—not me."

Ignacio hoped Emily had inherited that from her mother. It would make it much easier on that boy.

Rob rode straight to the Hernández place without even going through town. He rode into the yard, got down, and tied up his horse.

Rob walked up to the door, and knocked. He stood there holding his hat.

Emily came to the door and when she looked up at him she said, "Oh. What are you doing here? I would have liked to comb my hair and straighten up some before you saw me. I mean, I wish you had sent word you were coming."

"I'm sorry. I didn't know I was coming. You look wonderful … uh … you look fine. You don't need any fixing up."

"Rob Wilson, I know when I need fixing up."

"Yes, ma'am. Is your daddy home?"

"Why do you want Papa? I thought you came to see me."

"Well, I did, but I need to talk to you both … if you don't mind."

"He's in the barn. I'll get him."

"No ma'am. You can do what you wanted to do. I'll go get him."

"Are you saying now I need fixing up?"

"No Emily. I think you're beautiful right now. You don't need anything. I just thought it might make you feel better and then you wouldn't be mad at me. That's all."

"Rob Wilson, I'll never understand you. Okay, you go get Papa." She turned to go back in the house, stopped, and said, "Rob, I'm glad you came." and she hurried into the house.

Rob walked down to the barn and found Ignacio. "Hello, Mr. Hernández."

"Hello, Rob Wilson. How are you? It's good to see you."

"I'm fine. Thank you, sir. If you have time, I would like to talk to you and Emily together."

Ignacio looked at Rob curiously and said, "All right. Let's go up to the house."

While they walked to the house, Rob thought, *What am I going to do now?*

When they got to the house, Ignacio said, "Come in, Rob." As they walked in, Ignacio called out, "Emily, it's Rob and me. Can you join us? Is there coffee?"

"I'm coming, Papa, and yes I put on fresh coffee. It will be ready in a few minutes. You two go in the kitchen and sit down. I'll be there presently."

Ignacio smiled at Rob and motioned toward the kitchen.

They sat down at the table, and Rob said, "Thank you for taking time out of your day to talk to me. I …"

Emily came walking in the kitchen and Rob jumped up and held a chair for her.

She said, "We have been reading all about your exploits in Texas—and your cattle drive back to Dona Anna County."

"That's what I want to talk to you about."

"Why do you need to talk about that? We read all about it in the El Paso newspaper."

"Because what's in the newspapers is not true."

Emily said, "You mean you didn't go to Texas and round up cattle?"

"Well, yeah. We did go to Texas and rounded up cattle, but we didn't round up five thousand head of longhorns. We only rounded up less than 1,800—and only part of them were longhorns."

Ignacio burst out laughing. "Rob, do you know how many ranches in southern New Mexico Territory have 1,800 head of cattle?"

"No, but 40 percent of them are Turner Sutton's, and we gave some to the Mescalero."

Emily said,"

Yes, you gave five hundred cattle to the Mescalero. That is the nicest thing I ever heard."

"No, that's another thing. We only gave two hundred to the Mescalero."

"So you gave two hundred head of your cattle and sixty-four goats to the starving Mescalero for nothing—out of the goodness of your heart?"

"No, there were only ten goats and ten horses."

Emily teased, "And you did it out of the *meanness* of your heart."

Ignacio said, "Rob, are you aware of anybody who ever gave the Mescalero ten beeves and one horse?"

"Well, no sir, but I don't know this country very well."

Ignacio said, "No one but the Indian agency ever gave any tribe one old skinny milk cow much less two hundred head of beef. Madre de Dios, son, that alone will make you a living legend in the entire West. It puts the whole United States of America to shame."

"Well, I didn't do it to be famous. It just seemed to be the right thing to do at the time, and besides, I wanted to stop the fighting."

Emily said, "All the more reason for us to be proud of you. You didn't do it for yourself. You did it because it was the right thing to do."

"You're proud of me? You don't think I made all this stuff up?"

Emily said, "Let me get this straight. You were afraid we would be ashamed of you because you gave some young and old Mexicans and Indians a chance to make a decent living. You took them to the Llano Estacado, fought the Comanche—"

Rob interrupted, "That's another thing. We didn't have a big battle with the Comanche. One brave let fly one arrow at me, and I shot back."

"And Duke didn't bark at him to warn you?"

"Well, no. He only growled at him."

Ignacio and Emily broke out in laughter.

Rob was embarrassed. He didn't understand why they were laughing.

Emily said, "Let me go on. You rounded up 1,800 head of cattle in the Llano Estacado and drove them five hundred miles through hundreds of hostile Mescalero with no water—and you don't want to be a hero?"

"There weren't much more than fifty Mescalero in that bunch, and it was closer to four hundred miles."

"Okay, you drove them four hundred miles through Mescalero with odds against you of at least five to one. Rob, that's what's so wonderful about this story. You lived it, you were there, and you don't understand how the rest of the world looks at it. Nobody has a wild coyote that growls at Indians to protect his friend. Hundreds of people have gone into the Llano Estacado and perished. You go and come back with a herd of cattle, a herd of horses, mules, and a bunch of goats. And you did it with three other gringo cowboys, two old men, and four teenagers. Do you understand why you are heroes?"

"No, Emily. I'm no hero."

"Robert Wilson, you are a hero. Whether you want to be or not, you are my hero." She put her hand to her mouth and blushed.

Ignacio smiled and said, "So you only have about a thousand head of cattle, a ranch, and a registered brand?"

"How did you hear about the brand?"

"The freighter who brings beer from El Paso told the people in the saloon about it. I just heard about that yesterday."

"I want to be a rancher and try to make a living here—not a character in the newspapers."

Emily said, "I'm sorry, Rob. I'm afraid it's too late for that. The stories are already in the newspapers."

"But that's what I've been trying to tell people it's all exaggerated."

Ignacio said, "Rob, the story may have grown in the telling a little, but it is basically all true. Let people have their heroes. It's not only you. Do you know how proud the Rodriguez family is about their boys? You gave them that. And Pepe, he was just a Mexican orphan living from hand to mouth, now he is a hero too. You gave him that. I talked to Juan Morales in La Luz the other day, and he is so proud of Paco that he doesn't know what to do. You gave him that. An old Mescalero and a young Mescalero boy are a famous chief and a renowned horse trainer who will always be able to find a job. You gave them that. Not one person I have talked to has any ill feeling toward you at all."

"Coffee's ready, gentlemen."

Rob said with a sigh, "Good. I need it." then perked up and added, "And I remember how good your coffee is."

"Would you like a piece of fresh cherry pie to go with it?"

Rob looked up at her in adoration and nodded.

The look didn't go unnoticed by Ignacio. "No, my darling. I will take my coffee to the barn. I need to finish mending that saddle. Rob, stop by the barn before you leave."

"Yes, sir."

Ignacio walked to the barn and said, "Well, my baby girl did get what her mama had." He smiled happily.

Emily served the coffee and pie. "My friend Juanita is Marco and Julio's sister. She is so proud of her brothers. Two jobless Mexican boys from Tularosa are now proven cowmen and brave Indian fighters who have faced the Llano Estacado and returned. Their whole family is so grateful to you. You gave them that too."

"Emily, I didn't give them that. They earned every bit of it."

"So, you admit the Rodriguez boys are heroes?"

"Well, sure. They are good boys. I couldn't have done it without them."

"Rob, if they are heroes, why aren't you a hero?"

"Did you mean what you said about me being your hero?"

Emily hesitated a few seconds and said, "Yes. I meant it, but you were not intended to hear it."

"And you don't mind that the stories are not true?"

"Rob, the stories may be exaggerated, but you admit that they are not lies. I don't mind. I am very proud of you."

"You are? Well, maybe this hero business is not so bad after all." They both laughed.

Rob said, "Emily, do you know what 'after a whiles' are?"

"I have no idea. What are they?"

"I'm not sure, but I'm working on it."

She looked at him strangely and frowned.

"Emily, I will be back as soon as I can." Rob stood up and reached for his hat. He looked at Emily and said, "Are you Catholic?"

"Yes. Why do you ask?"

"I just wondered. It has to do with the after a whiles."

"Rob Wilson, sometimes I don't understand you." As he walked out the front door, she said, "Don't forget to go talk to Papa in the barn."

"Yes, ma'am." He smiled, tipped his hat, and went to the barn.

"Oh, Rob. Here, hold this up for me, will you?" Ignacio handed Rob a saddle fender to hold up while he re-stitched the saddle under it.

Rob said, "Mr. Hernández, Emily gives me the tingles. I would like your permission to come calling on her."

Ignacio burst out in laughter. "Oh, Rob. I'm not laughing at you. I'm laughing at your choice of words."

Rob looked at him in fear.

Ignacio said, "Of course I give you my permission to come calling on Emily—but not to tell anyone else that she gives you the tingles." He laughed more and slapped his knee.

Rob stood in confusion and looked at Ignacio.

Ignacio said as he cleared his throat, "Rob, the fact that she gives you the tingles is not a bad thing, but some people might not understand that you mean it in a respectful way. Just tell them that you are calling on Emily. Okay?"

"Wow. Anything you say, Mr. Hernández. Thank you."

"Call me Ignacio. If Emily is as much like her mother as I think she is, you are a lucky man—but you will be in for some hard times."

"I have noticed that if Emily says, 'Robert Wilson,' I better pay attention to what she says after that, but when she bows up, if I just backup a little and wait, she mostly works it out for me."

"You have a big head start on me. When I was courting her mother, it took me a lot longer to figure that out."

"I bought her a rosary when I was in El Paso. May I give it to her?"

Ignacio said, "Well, sure, Rob, but I don't know if she will accept it. Maybe you should wait, and then after a while—"

"Oh, no. There are those after a whiles again. I will chance it now."

Ignacio laughed again. He patted Rob on the back and said, "Well, okay. Good luck."

"Thank you … Ignacio," Rob said with a grin.

Rob rode to La Luz the same way he came to the Hernández place, without going through town. When he got there, he looked for and found Juan Morales and invited him to the cantina for supper and asked if he could spend the night in Juan's camp.

Juan said, "Sure. You may camp with me if you don't mind the goats."

"That's one thing I want to talk to you about. We have fifteen goats that found us in the Llano Estacado. Would you take them off our hands? Paco wouldn't mind keeping a couple of nanny goats for goat's milk, but they might be happier with you."

Juan said, "Paco didn't tell you?"

"Tell me what? We haven't had time to talk much."

"Paco tried to give me the goats. When you were in El Paso, he brought the goats to me. He talked to them, but they didn't listen. The second morning after he brought them here, the goats were at the camp when he got up to cook breakfast. We decided they would have to stay at the Dog Canyon Rancho."

"Well, I'll be." Rob said.

The next morning, Rob rode to Stephenson's store. "Hello, Paul. Has Levi sent you anything more for me?"

"Hello, Rob. Yes, he has. The freighter delivered it yesterday. I have a fancy barbeque spit and a bunch of hardware for a barn. I guess there is enough hardware for a whole house. Are you ready to build?"

Rob said, "Well, not quite, but I'm getting close."

Paul said hesitantly, "Rob, I'm not trying to tell you how to run your ranch, but you sent an order for enough wood to build a barn and a house. May I suggest that you build an adobe barn and house? It will be some cheaper, and it will be much cooler in the summer and much warmer in the winter—and it is bulletproof."

Rob said, "What do you mean, bullet proof?"

"Well, you know … bullet proof. You can't shoot through it and you can't burn it down. If you put a Mexican tile roof on it, it is almost indestructible. I can give you the name of a good adobe builder. Rob, I took the liberty of ordering only enough wood for an adobe house and barn. If you insisted on them being built of wood, we could get more lumber."

"Thank you, Paul. I am glad someone is looking after me. I'm new in this country. I didn't know much about adobe buildings before I came here."

"Rob, there are a lot of people who would like to help look after you. They are a little in awe of you right now. They will warm up. Just give them a chance."

"Give the name of the adobe builder to Paco. I'll send the wagon to pick up the stuff from Levi and whatever else you have for us." Rob hesitated and said, "Paul, Where do I get the adobe bricks?"

Paul laughed and said, "Rob, the builder will make them at your ranch. Don't worry about it. He will take care of it all."

Rob had lunch with Masterson and then he went to the blacksmith, and picked up his other branding iron. It was beautiful. He tied the branding iron on the back of his saddle and started for home. He liked the sound of that, home.

Chapter 15

Rustlers in Dog Canyon

ob rode into Dog Canyon camp got down and walked in the tent to show Paco the branding iron he was so proud of.

Paco handed Rob a cup of coffee and said, "Yes, they are beautiful. Señor Sutton showed me the one he had."

"Paco, we haven't had time to talk much. Juan told me about the goats. I think it is funny. Do you mind having them around the ranch?"

"No, señor Rob. I don't mind. I will make us some goat cheese when we have more fresh nannies. I wonder what happened to all the kids. Some of the nannies were still fresh. The kids had not been gone long."

"Hum, I didn't think of that. I bet the Comanche or the coyotes got them. I stopped by Paul Stephenson's today. He has some things for us to pick up whenever you have time. Or you can send one of the boys with the wagon."

"I will go myself. It will give me a chance to visit with Juan."

"Paco, what do you know about adobe houses?"

"Ah, Señor Stephenson must have talked to you. I have not had the chance. Señor Rob, in New Mexico, it does not rain often. When it does rain, it does not rain for a long time. Usually it rains hard and fast—but not all day or all night—only for one or two hours. Adobe bricks don't have time to get soaked and will not melt and wash away. The adobe is cool in the summer and warm in the winter. If you plaster the outside of the walls, they will last many, many years. If you plaster the inside and whitewash it, the bugs will not come. I think the lime in the whitewash burns their feet."

"Paul said the adobe builder would make the bricks here. Where do we get Mexican tile for the roof, Paco?"

"The builder will know the best place to get that."

"Do you think Paul is right? Do we need to build the house and barn out of adobe?"

"Si, Señor Rob, I do."

"Okay, that's it then. When you go to La Luz, get the name of the builder, contact him, and tell him I want him to start as soon as possible."

"Señor Rob, it would be best if we wait until after the Indians dance for rain and the rains are over. While it is raining every day is not a good time to make bricks. They will not dry."

"How long will that be Paco?"

"Señor Rob, what is the hurry? We still have to brand the cattle, dig a well, and make a water hole. And after a while, it will stop raining."

Rob drank his coffee and drooped his shoulders. "There's that after a while thing again. I guess after a while will be fine."

About that time Wise Elk rode into camp in a hurry.

Rob said, "Hello Wise Elk, where have you been? Your horse looks about plum tuckered."

Wise Elk said, "Some cattles gone. I look. I find track this many horses." He held up five fingers. "The track go up Grapevine Canyon with many cattles. You call big canyon. I send Little Deer for Mescalero. They come maybe one day more. They track for you."

Rob stepped out from under the tent and fired two shots in the air. "Good work, Wise Elk. Paco, cook supper fast. We will leave as soon as the men have eaten. Make extra biscuits and cook more steak so we can take some with us."

Jessie came in and said, "I was at the cow chute with the others. I gave orders to shut down the branding and bring everything to the camp."

Rob asked, "How did you know to do that?"

"I noticed Wise Elk riding in, in a hurry. When I heard your shots, I figured it was trouble. Things have been too smooth around here. What's up?"

"Wise Elk noticed some cattle missing. He investigated and found the tracks of five horses driving a bunch of cattle up the big canyon, he calls it Grapevine Canyon. He sent Little Deer for more Mescalero to help track. Paco is cooking supper early and making extra bread and steak for us to take with us. Will you please break out plenty of ammunition for the boys?"

"How come you called it Grapevine Canyon?"

Wise Elk said, "White mans call it Grapevine Canyon."

Jessie said, "Wise Elk, why didn't you tell us that before? We've been looking stupid callin' it the big canyon"

"You no ask."

Rob and Paco laughed. Jessie looked embarrassed, and then he laughed too.

Rob said, "Wise Elk, will you get a fresh horse for yourself, and round up some of the fresh horses for the others. Get two horses saddled with packsaddles. Check your guns and ammunition. Was Little Deer armed?"

"Yes. Little Deer have long gun, no short gun. Not many bullets."

Rob said, "Jessie, load an extra .44 for Little Deer and take plenty of ammunition for all our guns. Paco, load supplies for five days. If we haven't found them by then, we will have to organize a long hunt."

Jessie said, "Rob, what are we going to do with 'em when we catch 'em?"

"I haven't decided yet. You better think on that, too. What are heroes 'spose to do when they catch rustlers?"

"Paco, bring plenty of rope."

The other cowboys came in with questioning looks on their faces.

"Jessie, tell 'em what happened and what to do. I'm going to the spring to wash and think."

Wise Elk nodded in approval, and everybody followed instructions.

Rob walked up to Dog Canyon Spring, took off his shirt and hat, and washed the dust off his head, face, and upper body in the pool then drank his fill from the spring. He looked up and saw Duke. "Hello, Duke. You know what happened. What should I do?"

Duke sat down on his haunches, scratched his ear, and sat with his tongue hanging out, looking at Rob.

Rob said, "I am thinking. We don't have any law this side of Las Cruces on the Rio Grande. We can't let the rustlers get away with it—or we won't have any cattle left by Christmas. Yet they will shoot back, and I don't want any of the Dog Canyon crew to get hurt."

Duke cocked his head, like he was really listening. Then he jumped up, and looked down the trail.

Paco was walking up with all the canteens. "Everything is ready. Did he help you decide?"

Rob looked around, but Duke was gone. He smiled and said, "Well, he told me to think about it and be careful. At least I think that is what he said."

"That is good advice."

"Okay, Paco. Fill those canteens—and let's ride."

It was mid-afternoon by the time they left and that night, they camped on a grass flat in Grapevine Canyon. The tracks they found showed that the rustlers were easing along in no hurry.

Wise Elk said, "Bad mans no hurry. Try make no dust. Hope we no see."

Rob said, "Are there only five?"

"Now this many." He held up six fingers. "One looking from up there." He pointed up toward Tabletop. "He come down, follow others after they go. Maybe together now."

Rob said, "Damn. They had a lookout. They are smart and organized. We will do well to be careful. Wise Elk, go see if you can figure out where they are going. They will be watching their back trail. Maybe we could get in front of them."

Wise Elk said, "Good," and started to ride off, up grapevine canyon.

Paco called out, "Wise Elk, take this." And handed him a bundle of cooked meat and biscuits.

Wise Elk nodded to Paco, and his expression might have had a hint of a smile.

Rob said, "Everybody, check your guns and ammunition. Check your knives. Check everything. Unsaddle your horses and hobble them so they can graze. We will need them tomorrow. This may be a bad fight. The rustlers know the penalty for stealing cattle. Remember they will shoot back fighting for their lives."

After they had eaten and had coffee, they sat around the fire and watched the sun meet the horizon and flatten on the bottom as it spewed the sky with color.

Rob said, "Jessie, what do you think?"

"I wish Wise Elk would get back."

"Yeah, me too. We have to get the cattle back—or rustlers will plague us and run us out of business. How are we going to do that without getting anybody hurt?"

"We will have to play it by ear and be as careful as possible. These are good men, they will be careful, and they are tough."

"I like it that you call them all men. Remember when we use to call the young ones boys?"

Then Rob addressed the whole crew, "We will go back to the nighthawk schedule we used in the roundup. Jessie and I will take the first watch. Turner and Julio, we will wake you in four hours. You can call Bill and Marco to wake up the sun. Come on Jessie, you take the high ground. and I'll work the bottom."

The night was uneventful. Rob was able to think about Emily, and his heart hurt as he remembered her magnificent eyes. He wondered what she meant when she called him her hero. The first shift passed quietly. He and Jessie woke the graveyard shift and crawled into their bedrolls.

When Rob awoke, he heard people talking around the fire. He got up, put on his hat and boots, went and relieved himself, and walked up to the fire.

Paco and Wise Elk were talking. Paco handed Rob a cup of hot coffee.

Rob said, "When did you come in, Wise Elk? Why didn't you call me, Paco?"

"I come now. You sleep. I drink coffee, Paco."

"What did you find, Wise Elk?"

"Bad mans go up Grapevine then turn south. I think go mesa to Texas. They must go mountains. Much slow with cattles. We go south now wait on mesa. They come. We shoot. Get cattles back."

"Sounds good to me. Have you heard from Little Deer?"

"No. Little Deer come soon."

"Wise Elk, it is dark as pitch since the moon has gone down. Little Deer can't see."

"Little Deer no see. Let horse see. He come."

Sometimes his Mescalero friends still amazed him. They were capable of many unbelievable things. The noise and commotion woke the others as the eastern sky paled.

Paco passed out beans and biscuits, and Bill and Marco came into camp.

Rob said, "I believe we should try to get in front of the rustlers and ambush them."

That was it. Rob had spoken, so that is what they would do.

About that time they heard horses coming down the canyon, they took cover and drew their short guns. It was Little Deer. His pinto pony was recognizable in the faint light. He had four Mescalero with him.

Everybody relaxed. The Indians hobbled and released their horses to graze and came into camp. Wise Elk nodded to Little Deer and handed him a cup of coffee. Paco passed out coffee to the others. Little Deer spoke to Wise Elk in Apache. After that, he turned to Rob. and with Paco translating for everyone, said, "We smelled them from up the canyon. We eased down the canyon, but they had turned south. We could see their fire. They are headed for the mesa. My cousin and five others went on south to keep the herd in sight."

Jessie asked, "What do you mean? How could you smell 'em?"

"Wind come from southwest. Come up canyon. Cattles smell loud. We smell."

"Good work, Little Deer. After you eat and rest, we will go south and set up an ambush for them."

"Señor Rob, I let horse see. I sleep. I ready to go."

Rob shook his head and looked at Wise Elk who was looking proudly at Little Deer. "You and your friends still need to eat." He turned and said, "Paco?"

Paco said, "Little Deer, come and bring the others."

Duke called the sun up over the mountain, and they rode south. They crossed two ridges and rode down onto the mesa. Rob picked up the pace when they got to more level ground. They found a small water hole and stopped to noon and make a plan.

Rob said, "Wise Elk, where is the next water for the herd?"

Wise Elk told Rob of a well-known permanent waterhole about five miles to the south. Wise Elk thought the rustlers were headed there. "Send Mescalero. Go see cattles. Meet at waterhole with ..." he looked at Paco.

Paco said, "Report, with the report."

Rob said, "Okay. Do it. Come on, you heroes. Eat up—and let's go."

They rode easy so as not to make much of a dust plume and stayed down in the bottom of draws until they reached the waterhole.

Rob said, "Water your horses. Little Deer, see if you can find a draw where we can hide the horses and build a fire without them being able to see it tonight."

Jessie laughed and said, "Rob, you're turning into an Apache right before our eyes."

"I may be a slow learner, but I do learn. Wise Elk, can the other Mescalero move out as scouts? The rustlers had a lookout back there. They might still have a point man out in front."

Wise Elk spoke to the three remaining Mescalero, and with Little Deer taking the south; they disappeared to the four points of the compass.

Turner said, "Rob Wilson, it's a pure-t-pleasure to watch you work. You didn't get this kind of learnin' from one of your mama's books."

"Oh, yes sir, I did. She made me read the army's *Book of Tactics* my daddy brought back from the war."

They all laughed. The laughter released the tension and was good for everybody.

In a short time, Little Deer came back,. He told them about a place a little way south and around a curve in the draw that had grass for the horses and was low enough to be invisible to the rustlers as they approached.

Rob said, "Julio and Marco, give your horses to Pepe and stay here on watch. Keep your hardware. If you see something, one of you come running. Everybody else, let's take our horses and go make camp at Little Deer's spot."

While they ate the steak, beans, and biscuits Paco had cooked, the cowboys talked. Rob said, "I've been thinking. There is a rise on both sides of the draw that leads to the waterhole. If we could lay behind the crest of the rise on the west side, they could not see us. We could get the drop on them. And the sun would be behind us, shining in their eyes."

Turner said, "That sounds good to me, but remember that lookout, we need to find him."

Rob looked at Little Deer.

Little Deer said, "I find." He finished his supper in a hurry and rode out.

Turner said, "Okay, Julio. It's our turn." They rode out into the coming darkness.

While the others were drinking coffee and resting on their bedrolls, one of the Mescalero came in from the north. He talked to Wise Elk, left, and rode back out.

Wise Elk said, "Young brave see bad mans fire. He say they be here tomorrow. After midday, before night."

"All right, you heroes. Make sure your guns are loaded and clean. Let's get some rest."

Jessie said, "I wish you would stop calling us heroes."

"But you are heroes. Not only all those newspaper readers' heroes—you are my heroes."

Jessie shook his head and looked at Rob.

Rob walked over to his bedroll and shucked his hat and boots.

The next morning, Rob let everybody sleep late. The sun was full up melting away the wispy morning clouds, when it finally woke them.

Turner came over to the fire scratching his head and said, "How come you didn't wake me?" He nodded thanks to Paco for the coffee.

Rob said, "For what? If the Mescalero is right, and I am betting he is, we will have to wait around all morning. Waiting is the hard part. I decided to let 'em sleep."

"I reckon you're right, but sleepin' this late don't seem right somehow."

Paco said, "Pepe, make sure the Mescalero all eat. They are a little shy. You may have to offer food and coffee to them pretty forcefully. They hesitate to take it. I will ask Wise Elk to speak to them."

"Si, señor."

Paco said, "Wise Elk, do the other braves have food and water?"

Wise Elk said, "No. Mescalero no need. He eat after fight."

Rob nodded his agreement to Wise Elk. "If that's how you want it, it's okay with me."

Rob explained to everybody what he wanted to do. He said, Eat, rest, and clean your guns. Be careful not to fire a shot accidentally. That would give us away. We will lay close to the top of the ridge, west of the draw that leads to the water. Spread out with ten to twenty feet between you. Have your saddle guns pointing at the rustlers. When they come toward the waterhole, I will stand and order them to surrender. Likely as not, they will refuse. They might even shoot at us. If they shoot, you shoot—and shoot to kill. Shoot as fast as you can shoot, reload, and shoot accurately. Remember, if you don't hit your target, how fast you shoot doesn't amount to nothing. Stay down, and don't give them a good target. The most important thing is that no DOG cowboys or Mescalero get hurt."

Rob drank his coffee, thought a minute, and said, "Wise Elk thinks their lookout may scout the waterhole before they come in. We must watch for him. When we find him, we must kill him silently. After that, the one of us dressed the closest to him will take his hat and vest or coat and sit on his horse—in full view of the rest of them—and wave them in. After that, we will play it by ear. Look to me for orders. If I go down, look to Turner or Jessie or Bill and Paco. Good luck."

Paco translated for the Mescalero, and they nodded.

The possibility of Rob falling surprised the cowboys, and they didn't like it.

Everybody was in place before noon. The air was still, and it was hot on top of the shade less ridge.

About two hours after midday, a quail called from the east. Rob looked up to see Little Deer pointing to the east-southeast. Rob looked where Little Deer was pointing and saw the lookout riding toward the waterhole. He had gone around and come in from below the waterhole. It was just luck that everybody was out of sight. He stopped and looked at the waterhole for a long time. Then the lookout began to ride toward the water and suddenly was hit by two arrows— one in the chest and one in the neck. The lookout fell off his horse like a pole-axed hog.

Little Deer and one of the Mescalero scouts appeared out of nowhere, picked up the lookout, threw him over his horse, ran down to the bottom of the draw, and led the horse with the lookout slung over the saddle. Rob and Jessie worked their way back down and around the rise to the camp.

Little Deer took the lookout's guns and gave them to the other scout. He took the man's hat and vest off and brought them to Rob. "Jefe, you are most look like lookout. You wear hat and clothes?"

Rob put on the hat and vest, mounted the lookout's horse, and rode back to the top of the rise. He smiled at Jessie who had walked along with him, shielded from the rustlers' view by the lookout's horse Rob was riding.

Jessie dropped off on the line with the others and dropped to his belly. By then they could see the dust from the herd.

Rob said, "Relax ... settle down ... everything is going according to plan. Remember, look at your target, bring your gun up, align the sights on the line between your eye and the target, and squeeze the trigger. Don't jerk it—squeeze it."

The rustlers were driving the cattle from behind. When the cattle smelled the water, they could not hold the herd back. The cattle ran toward the water.

Rob had the lookout's hat in his hand, waving in the rustlers. He could barely see them through the dust. He thought the rustlers could not see him any better because of the dust. He put on the hat.

The cattle ran to the waterhole and into the water to drink. As their dust settled, the five rustlers rode toward Rob. When they were about twenty yards away, Rob pulled his .45, and said, "Hold it right there. Drop your guns."

The closest man to Rob drew his gun and fired at Rob. Rob returned fire, knocking the man off his horse. After that, there was mass confusion. The DOG cowboys opened up on the rustlers. Two more went down in a storm of bullets and arrows. One turned his horse around and rode back north in time to be hit with several arrows from the Mescalero that had been trailing the rustlers. There were a few more shots fired, and the last rustler threw down his gun and put up his hands.

Rob ordered, "Hold your fire."

Everybody stopped shooting. Rob was impressed with the discipline of his cowboys, and he was proud of them. He looked around, counted heads, and found all his men were standing apparently unharmed. Rob let out a big sigh and reached up to push up his hat. He was not wearing one. He didn't remember taking off his hat during the gunfight.

Turner came walking up holding the rustler lookout's hat, and his finger was sticking out through a bullet hole. "Are you looking for this?" He handed it to Rob. "An inch lower—and your brains would be splattered all over the mesa."

Rob swallowed hard. "Well, I'll be."

The dust cleared, and they crowded around the one rustler who was still standing. He was young, about the age of the Rodriguez boys.

Rob said, "What's your name?"

The boy said, "My name is Jimmy. What are you going to do to me?"

"I haven't decided yet. I should hang you."

The boy went white. "Oh, mister. Please don't hang me. I was just tagging along with my big brother Curley." He looked around at the Mescalero mounted and looking down at him. And the ones standing with the gringos with their guns pointed at him. "Mister, please don't let them shoot me. We didn't expect a whole Indian tribe to be with you. Curley said you were some old men and boys who had more cattle than you knew what to do with. He said you probably wouldn't miss a few and couldn't catch us if you did miss 'em. Did that damn coyote hunt us down? Where is Curley anyway? He was here ahead of me. Where is he now?"

Rob said, "If Curley was your lookout man, he's dead. He died of an arrow through the heart and one through his neck."

The boy said, "No, the lookout wasn't Curley. Curley was leading us to the lookout."

Rob said, "Well, then, I'm sorry for you. I killed your brother. I told him to surrender and put down his guns. He refused and drew on me. He shot a hole through the hat I was wearing. I had to shoot him before he killed me."

Jimmy was silent. Tears ran down his face, but he didn't break down and sob. He wiped his nose with his dirty sleeve and looked at Rob.

Rob said, "Paco, go stir up lunch and make some fresh coffee. We need to have a ranch meeting. Turner and Bill, you are invited as part of the ranch. Marco and Julio, tie this cur up and take him to camp. I'm tired of looking at him. Wise Elk, invite your men to lunch and to the meeting."

On the way back to camp Jessie asked, "Would you really have hung him?"

Rob grinned and said, "Nah, but he doesn't know that."

When they got to the camp, Paco handed Rob a cup of coffee, not fresh coffee, but coffee. Rob tasted it and looked at it funny.

Paco said, "Señor Rob, I will have fresh coffee in a little while."

"Well, that's better than after a while. Paco, what do you think I should do with this boy?"

"You can take him to the sheriff in Las Cruces. Or you could hang him and tie a sign around his neck, telling others why we hung him. Or you could try to save him. He is young and was following his big brother."

Rob threw out the old coffee and handed Paco the cup. "Paco, you are a very wise man. Did you bring a shovel?"

"Si, señor Rob. You know I did."

"Pepe, get the shovel from Paco. Then you, Marco and Julio, take this Jimmy the rustler and help him bury his dead. Don't do it for him just help him."

"Si, señor Rob." They said in unison.

While the burial detail was gone, Rob looked around at all the cowboys and Indians. "Is everybody okay?"

They all checked themselves again and indicated that they were all fine.

Rob said, "We don't have a tree within twenty miles big enough to hang him. And I don't want to waste the time to take him to Las Cruces."

Paco poured fresh coffee all around and offered the Mescalero beans and biscuits from breakfast. It surprised him when almost everybody ate again.

The sun was low in the west when the burial detail returned. Jimmy was wet with sweat and had his head bowed low.

Paco gave them all water and gave coffee to everybody except Jimmy.

Rob said, "Jimmy, you are a very lucky man. I don't have a tree to hang you from, and I don't have the time to take you to the sheriff in Las Cruces. I'll tell you what I have decided to do with you. I will turn you lose under these conditions. You go to El Paso. Go to that newspaperman—Art is his name—and tell him what you saw here today, exactly like you saw it. Tell him why you and your friends were trying to steal our cattle. Tell him your life depends on him writing another one of his stories about what happens to cattle thieves on the Dog Canyon Ranch.

"After you have done that, you have two choices. You can go to the hideouts and places other lowlifes frequent and tell them what happened here or you can bring me a copy of the paper with that story in it. If you can convince me and these other men you have straightened up and are ready to lead a good, respectable life, I will give you a real job working with the best group of men in New Mexico Territory. If, on the other hand, you don't do exactly like I told you, I'll hunt you down and shoot you dead like the rustler you are. I swear I will."

Duke took that time to say good evening to the sun.

Jimmy said, "Yes, sir. Yes, sir. I'll do exactly like you told me, sir. Thank you, Mr. Wilson."

"Okay then. It's too late to leave now. Have something to eat and get some sleep. You can leave in the morning—if you don't do something to change my mind."

Jessie had to fake a cough and turn around to keep from laughing.

Rob, Jessie, Bill, and Turner walked up on the top of the rise.

Turner said, "Did your mama make you read a book on justice too?"

Rob grinned and said, "Yep, the Bible. Remember, 'Train up a child in the way he should go: and when he is old he will not depart from it.' Proverbs 22:6?"

Turner said, "Well, I'll be damned."

Everybody laughed.

Bill said, "Why did you let that rustler go, Rob?"

"Jimmy is not a rustler. He's a boy following his big brother—who was a bad man. And I am trying to learn. You heard Jimmy. They have been reading the papers and learned we have a bunch of cattle we drove back from Texas. They have read that we are gringos, old men, and young boys. The stories have made us heroes, but they have also made us targets for rustlers and thieves. I am hoping the story Jimmy tells Art will paint a picture of a bunch of strong, tough men with the whole Mescalero Apache Nation as allies. That can and will track thieves down and kill them in the desert. I am trying to use this hero-manufacturing machine to manufacture an image of strong, mean but just men who should be left alone by crooks—and to scare the bejesus out of rustlers."

"Rob, you are amazing." Turner shook his head. "Come on. Let's go find out if Paco is feeding people yet. I'm starving."

They walked back to the camp.

Rob asked out loud, "Paco, what's for supper?"

"The three B's of the trail, Señor Rob: beef, beans, and biscuits."

"Paco, what a silver-tongued fox you are."

"Jessie, will you please set out some nighthawks? Ask Wise Elk to put out some Mescalero on each shift. They are amazing at night."

"You got it, Rob."

Rob walked over to the fire pit. "Paco, fix Jimmy up a sack of groceries with biscuits and cooked beef. In the morning, give him the sack and this five dollars to eat on and buy supplies to get back to Dog Canyon. Tell him what the money is for. Tell him I'll take it out of his first month's wages. Also, here is a note for Art. Tell Jimmy to give the note to him. It will identify Jimmy and help make sure Art doesn't think he is an imposter."

"You think he will come back?"

"Yes, Paco. He'll be back … he has no other place to go."

Rob walked over to Wise Elk. "Do your people need any of this beef, Wise Elk?"

"No. Mescalero have cattles from gifts you give."

"Wise Elk, tell your braves thank you very much and that they are always welcome at Dog Canyon Ranch. They are welcome to stay with us as long as they want, but we will understand if they need to get back to their families. Wise Elk, tell them that if they ever need anything, all they have to do is ask. If it is within my power, it's theirs."

The next morning, Rob said, "Jimmy, remember what I told you."

Jimmy said, "Mr. Wilson, I won't forget nothing."

"Jimmy, what is your last name?"

"Jackson, sir. I'm James Lee Jackson."

"Okay, Jimmy Lee. We will look to see you at Dog Canyon Ranch soon."

Chapter 16

BACK TO WORK

*A*fter they said goodbye to Jimmy Lee the next morning, they started back to Dog Canyon.

Rob asked, "Turner, do you and Bill want to move the branded cattle to your ranch? We have about five hundred head branded and ready."

Turner said, "I think that would be a good idea. They're drinking a lot of your water."

"Why don't you and Bill take Little Deer and Marco and ride on ahead. You can make much better time than we can with the herd. Little Deer can help you separate the horses. They seem to mind him amazingly well. What do you think?"

"That would be great ... if you can do without us."

"You could be back to help finish up the branding by suppertime tomorrow. Why don't you go ahead? We'll be fine. We have the Mescalero to help."

"Little Deer, Marco, you two go with Turner and Bill and move the Artesian Well cattle to their ranch. We will look for you at supper tomorrow. Be careful."

"Si, Señor Rob."

"Paco, we can't make it home tonight. Why don't you go on ahead and make camp in Grapevine Canyon and fix us one of your

181

world-famous trail suppers? We'll follow with these lazy cows. Did you bring anything to make one of those cobblers? I'm wishful for cobbler."

"You have been hanging around that sugar-craving partner of yours too long. Okay, I will be waiting for you. Adios."

Paco left with his pack animals. Rob, Jessie, Wise Elk, Julio, Pepe, and the Mescalero drove the herd to Grapevine Canyon without incident. When they were about two hours out, Rob sent Pepe on ahead to help Paco with the camp and supper.

When they reached Grapevine Canyon, the Mescalero decided they would turn north and head for the reservation. Everybody said their so longs and goodbyes, and the Dog Canyon hands were sad to see the Indians go.

When they rode into camp and stepped down, Paco and Pepe handed them their end of the day coffee.

After enjoying his, Rob said, "I'll take the first watch. These critters are tired and won't be much trouble for a while. Jessie, you, Wise Elk, Julio, and Pepe split the other two nighthawk shifts. I have time to eat before dark, don't I, Paco?"

"Si, Señor Rob. It is almost ready. I found a bucket of little wild plums up the canyon to make you a cobbler. I think you will like it."

Jessie said, "I wish you had some of that heavy goat's milk to pour on it."

"It is always something. You are never happy with Paco's cooking."

"Paco, I am always happy with your cooking, but I remember my mama putting whipped cream on the cobbler. Your goat's milk is the next best thing."

"Maybe those two rams will have done their work—and we will have fresh nannies soon. If they have, you can have goat's milk. Goat's milk cheese is also good on pie and cobbler."

Rob ate a wonderful trail supper with wild plum cobbler. He thought about how lucky they were to have Paco.

Duke talked down the sun, and Rob took a plate of food out toward the sound.

The next day, they reached the Culp Tank herd, and Rob ordered them all driven to the corral. He thought they could brand and process up to two hundred head a day with the new cow chute. He believed they could make it all right on the water they had.

Later that day, they dragged themselves into Dog Canon Ranch camp, tired and dusty. Paco outdid himself again, and they enjoyed themselves.

Jessie said, "Rob, we need more water. The AW cows have been drinking our water for so long."

Paco said, "You know, in La Luz, they have a mule-drawn dirt-moving machine. It is like an iron barrel with one side cut away, and an iron blade is attached to the bottom. It has a long handle on the back and a flat shovel-like blade on the front. The mules pull it along with a doubletree, and you scrape up the dirt by controlling the depth of the cut with the handle. When you are ready to dump the dirt, you lift the handle. The blade catches on the ground, which makes it flip over and dumps out the dirt. The old man says it is much faster than a man with a shovel and a wheelbarrow. If we borrowed it maybe you could dig an earth tank to catch part of the runoff water when it rains this summer."

"Paco, you are unbelievable. Where did you see this machine?"

"The old man west of La Luz has it. I saw it while riding by in the wagon. He invited me to stop for a cool drink of water. I think he calls it a drag bucket."

"Will it fit in the wagon?"

"Si, señor."

"Okay, you and I will take the wagon and try to rent it or buy it while the other cowboys are branding cows tomorrow. Do we have enough harness to pull it?"

"Si, Señor Rob we do."

"You hear that, Jessie? Paco just saved you cowboys a bunch of backbreaking work. You better be nice to him."

"Hell, Rob, I'm always nice to my little ol' Mexican." He ducked in time for Paco to miss him with a big wooden spoon.

The Artesian Well Ranch crew came into camp. They were tired and dirty. Paco had prepared piles of food. That outfit could eat like crazy.

After the cowboys started toward the cow chute the next morning, Rob and Paco hitched up the wagon and headed for La Luz.

Before noon, Rob and Paco drove up to the farm with the dirt-moving machine. An old man walked out to meet them.

Paco said, "How are you today, amigo? I want you to meet my boss, Mr. Rob Wilson."

Rob and the old man shook hands.

Rob said, "Paco tells me you have a dirt-moving machine. How does it work?"

The man explained the dirt mover, and Rob inquired about the possibility of buying or renting the machine.

The old man said, "I will sell the machine for two hundred dollars, but if you want to use it, you are welcome to take it. I have moved all the dirt I will move this year."

Rob said, "I would be happy to rent your machine."

"No, Mr. Wilson. I would be proud if the Dog Canyon Ranch just borrowed my machine."

After a cool drink of water, they loaded the machine in the wagon and shook hands.

Rob said, "Paco, let's go on into La Luz and have lunch. We can go to see Paul Stephenson and see if more things have come in from El Paso."

They stopped by to visit with Juan and invited him to lunch with them. They went to the Mexican cantina for lunch and afterward stopped by Stephenson's store to talk to Paul.

Paul said, "Hello. How is the Dog Canyon bunch?"

"We are doing all right now, but we had some trouble Paul."

"How's that?"

Rob told Paul about the rustlers and the Mescalero helping catch the rustlers. He told Paul how they were forced to kill all but one rustler and how he had handled Jimmy Lee.

Paul was stunned and stood there in a daze.

Rob gave him time to digest what he had told him and waited for him to respond.

"Rob, you are quite a character. Few people around here would have handled it that way. I think it was brilliant. I can see where all the newspaper stories would make rustlers think you are an easy mark. What a great idea to use the same thing to make yourselves look like very strong ranchers with the Mescalero tribe behind you. That makes it look like you should be left alone. I had no idea you had developed such a relationship with the Mescalero. This story will reflect well on them too."

"I hope so. We would have had a hard time without them. Have you had any word from Levi?"

"He sent more hardware for the house. It is ready anytime you are ready to pick it up."

"I have a wagon load today. Paco can come back in a day or two to buy groceries and pick up the hardware. Just give me some fresh fruit for Jessie so Paco can make him a cobbler."

"Señor Rob, I will wait while you go over to the church and make your confession."

"Okay. Paul, give me some fresh fruit so Paco can make a cobbler or two. I like it almost as much as Jessie does."

They all laughed, loaded their fruit, and shook hands.

Rob and Paco climbed into the wagon and headed home.

Chapter 17

ROB'S NEW WATER TANK

hen they arrived back at Dog Canyon camp, Rob hitched up a pair of mules and tied them to the back of the wagon.

"Paco, let's drive back to the draw that emptied into the arroyo I found. Remember when Jessie and I dug the trail down into the arroyo when they were building the first corral?"

When they arrived at their destination, Rob untied the extra team of mules, led them up the trail, and tied them to a mesquite. "Paco, help me back the wagon up against the bank so the back edge of the wagon bed is almost level with the ground." Rob hitched the extra mule team to the machine, and they pulled it off the wagon onto the trail.

After the dirt-moving machine was unloaded, Rob said, "Will you take the wagon back to camp? Please have Jessie bring a horse and come back to pick me up in time for supper."

"Si, Señor Rob. You be careful with that drag bucket and my mules."

"I will, Paco. You sound like my daddy."

That was the first time Rob had talked about his daddy in front of Paco. Paco was sure it was a good thing.

Rob drove the team fifty yards up the draw and found an area of sandy loose dirt that was easy to move with the machine. If Rob held the long handle down and pointing backwards, the machine would skid over the top of the ground without scraping up any dirt. If he held the handle up a little, the iron blade dug into the ground, filling the bucket with dirt. When he wanted to dump the dirt, he lifted the handle up high and the iron blade dug into the ground and flipped over the bucket, emptying the dirt.

It only took a half hour of practice before Rob could move almost a full barrel of dirt each time he loaded the machine. By late afternoon, he had a sizable depression dug out of the draw. The dirt from it would serve as a dam.

Jessie rode up and was amazed at the amount of dirt Rob had moved in less than half a day by himself. "Wow. You really have been working."

Rob said, "Well, what did you think I was doing?"

"I didn't think you were working this hard." After a demonstration, they unhitched the mules and started for home.

When they rode into camp, Little Deer took the mules and horses, and Paco handed them their end of the day coffee.

Turner said, "Rob, these men have done very well today with the cows. They worked their butts off."

Jessie said, "Rob, Marco is becoming a roper who will give you a run for your money."

Marco blushed, and everybody laughed.

"I can't wait to see it. We can have a rodeo and show off a little when we get these cattle branded."

They ate another of Paco's wonderful suppers and sat around talking while the sun sank behind the Organ Mountains, spewing bright gold and pink on the puffy little clouds that were scattered across the velvet blue sky.

Rob started out with a plate of food and saw Duke with a female coyote on the edge of the arroyo. "Well, Duke, I see you have a friend. Good for you. I hope you are very happy together. Start with this plate. I will go back and bring more for you and the lady."

Duke told the sun good night, and the duchess joined in his song.

Rob laughed and started back to the camp. When Rob got back to camp, he said, "Duke has a girlfriend."

Everybody stood up to look, but it was too dark to see them.

Rob picked up another plate of food and walked back out into the darkness.

The next morning, the cowboys rode back to the corrals to work on the branding.

Rob led a team of mules behind his horse to the tank he was building. No one else could be spared from the branding, but Rob enjoyed working alone with the mules. It reminded him of his boyhood back in Texas plowing the garden with his daddy's mule team.

Paco brought him lunch, a fresh canteen of cool water, and a cask of water for the mules. Paco said, "I am glad the dirt machine works so well."

"Yeah, Paco. This machine is a great labor saver. It would have taken us weeks to move this much dirt by hand. I have dug out a depression about four feet deep and about thirty feet by thirty feet."

"Si, Señor Rob. I am mucho impressed."

By the end of the week, Rob's tank was about one hundred feet by eighty feet and the dam was well packed and lined with rocks. The branding was almost finished, and Rob was eager for rain to test his tank.

In camp that night, Jessie said, "How about we move the rest of the Artesian Well Ranch cattle out to the basin ranch for Turner and Bill?"

Because of the water situation, they all agreed that was a good idea.

The next morning, while the cowboys drove the AW-branded cattle to Turners Ranch, Rob finished his tank. In the early afternoon Rob watched Duke and his girlfriend running through the mesquite, enjoying their freedom and their togetherness.

Rob walked the mules back and forth across the dam to compact the soil. Their small hooves were not as good as sheep's tiny feet would be for compaction, but they were the best he had. He fine-tuned his water tank and made sure the dam had a rock-lined spillway so the water would not wash out the dam if it overflowed. When he was finished with the water tank, he took the animals to the camp.

Rob had finished the tank up early, and he and Paco were able to sit and talk before the others returned from the AW ranch. Paco said, "Señor Rob, the Mescalero will start dancing for rain soon. You will be able to find out how well your tank holds water."

The Mescalero started their rain dance after the summer solstice, and sure enough it rained a little. A few days later, it rained one of those huge raindrop storms.

Rob was excited and couldn't wait to check his new water tank. The next afternoon after the water levels in the arroyos receded, Rob and Jessie rode over to the new water tank. It was beautiful. It was three-quarters full of water, and the dam looked fine.

Rob was so happy and so proud. He and Jessie laughed and hooted as they rode back to camp. They talked about how many cattle to move to the new tank area to spread out the load on the water.

While the other cowboys branded the Dog Canyon Ranch cows, Rob and Jessie gathered up about two hundred branded cattle, including the first calf, "Primo and his mama. They drove them to the new tank and on the way decided that would be the name of it, New Tank.

When they arrived at New Tank with the cattle Rob was so excited about the new water supply.

Rob and Jessie rode back to camp talking about how this country wasn't so hard to ranch. You just had to be willing to work a little harder in the beginning.

After a pause, Rob said, "Jessie, Emily gives me the tingles—and I don't know what to do about it."

Jessie laughed and said, "Well, I'm glad you finally figured out what everybody else has known for months. What do you want to do about it?"

"Well, damn it, I know what I want to do, but I just don't know how to do it."

"And that is?"

"Ah, hell, Jessie. If I was sure, I wouldn't be asking you now, would I? Just study on it with that steel-trap mind of yours. You might come up with something I haven't thought of."

They helped brand cattle for two days. The next afternoon, Wise Elk came in with the split-eared calf, Primo, over his saddle. Primo's mother was right behind them.

Wise Elk said, "Primo come home. Something wrong. You go see."

Rob and Jessie saddled fresh horses and took off to New Tank. When they got there, they were shocked. The tank was empty. Only the bottom of the tank was wet and muddy, and they couldn't see any of the herd they had brought down to range there.

Jessie said, "What are we going to do? We needed that water. Where did it go—and where are our cows?"

Rob sat his horse quietly for a while. Finally he said, "My daddy told me when you can't figure something out, you need to go to the person who knows the most about what you are trying to figure. Usually the hard part is figuring out who knows the most about your problem. In our case, that's easy. Nobody knows more about this country than the Mescalero who have been living here for thousands of years. And which Mescalero knows the most about this country? Come on. Let's go talk to Wise Elk."

Rob and Jessie rode back to camp and found Wise Elk.

Rob said, "Wise Elk, I built New Tank just like I thought Culp Tank was built. Now the water is all gone. Where did our water go?"

Wise Elk walked over to get Paco to interpret for them.

Wise Elk said, "A long time ago the children of the Great Spirit had much water, fruit, squash, and corn. They did not have to work hard. They had spare time and played and forgot about the Great Spirit. The Great Spirit became angry with his children. In his anger, he hit this basin with his fist. It drove the basin down and left the mountain up there." Wise Elk pointed to the top of the mountains.

"The Great Spirit decided to teach his children a lesson. He crumbled up the earth's surface, breaking most of the rock under the soil. The water ran through the broken earth, and the land dried up and cracked. It was hard for the people to make a living on the dry earth, and they prayed to the Great Spirit and remembered him. They promised not to forget him ever again. He said that was a good thing, but to make sure, he left much of the earth's surface broken so it would not become too easy for his children lest they forget him again. After that, he built Culp Tank and other water places for the animals to drink. The animals had done nothing to offend the Great Spirit. You must find a place where the Great Spirit was happy and did not crumble up the earth surface rock and build your tank on unbroken earth rock."

"How will I know where that is, Wise Elk?"

"Look at the top of the mountain. See the layers of rock? Some are tilted up. Some are tilted down. Some are folded and bent. You must find a place on top of the mountain where the Great Spirit left the rock layers level, flat, and whole. Go to the place in the basin that matches the rock layers on top, if it were still up there with the top before the Great Spirit smashed it down. You will feel it. Close your eyes and listen to the feelings of the coyote spirit. Bring the raven-haired girl here. Walk with her. When she is happy and you are happy, feel it. If it matches the straight and level rocks on top and feels like a good place, mark the spot and dig. That is where you need to put your water hole."

Rob, Jessie, and Paco sat in silence and thought about what Wise Elk had said. He said so much in so few words. They needed to digest it.

Rob said, "Wise Elk, if you knew all these things, why didn't you tell me before I built New Tank?" Rob laughed. "I know, I know, because I no ask, right?"

Wise Elk nodded and drank his coffee.

Chapter 18

Jim Healy Hunts for Rob

They saw Duke more often—sometimes with the duchess and sometimes alone—but he was still too timid to come very close. Wise Elk and Little Deer wanted to go to Mescalero to check on their family in light of the recent famine. After branding the herd, they were given leave to go. Rob discussed their compensation and offered them jobs at Dog Canyon.

Wise Elk needed to make his contribution as one of the senior chiefs of the tribe and would go back to Mescalero, but Little Deer would take the job and stay. Rob sent Little Deer with Wise Elk who was still limping and using his crutch, Rob told them he would go get them when it was time to go to El Paso.

A few days later as they watched the basin light up as the sun came up over the Sacramento Mountains. The morning sunlight hit the top of the Organ and San Andreas Mountains and then tumbled down the face of those mountains across the basin before it raced toward them on the basin floor.

Rob said, "Paco, let's go to Tularosa and talk to Ignacio Hernández."

Paco smiled and said, "That is a good idea, Señor Rob. I can stop by and visit my cousin in La Luz and pick up fresh fruit, vegetables, and supplies at Señor Stephenson's store." He closed up the chuck wagon and gave the stove a wipe or two. He saddled his horse and packed a few things on a mule.

They rode hard, but Paco didn't complain. They finished their doings in La Luz and reached Tularosa that afternoon.

Rob, Paco, and Ignacio looked over the stock and walked inside for coffee and pie. They sat at the big dining room table.

Rob said, "As a reward for their hard work, I plan to take all the hands to the Fiesta de Las Flores in El Paso in September. Paco and Jessie suggested that we invite you two to go along with us."

Paco nearly exploded with a feigned cough and bent over with a napkin over his face.

Emily said, "Oh, Papa, can we go?"

Ignacio smiled. "I think it is a good idea. I haven't been to a big fiesta in a long time."

Emily was excited and rose to pick up the cups and pie plates.

Rob said, "Here, let me help you." In doing so Rob was able to look at Emily and spoke a few words to her, when they got the dishes to the kitchen, he pulled out the box with the rosary and held it out to Emily. "I got this for you when I was in El Paso registering the brand."

He held his breath. It seemed like forever while she opened the little box and looked in it. She looked up at him then back at the contents of the box. She said softly, "I don't know what to say."

Rob was petrified with fear but he took control and said, "I have let lots of after a whiles go by. Please say you will accept it."

"Oh, no … not that."

Rob almost passed out; he was afraid she was refusing the gift.

Then Emily said, "I love it. It's beautiful. I will gladly accept it, but I don't know how to say thank you enough."

Rob's face lit up. "Do you really like it?"

"Oh, yes. But, Robert Wilson, you should not be wasting your money on me. You have a ranch to build."

"Miss Emily Hernández, sometimes you just have to get your priorities in order. The ranch will be fine."

Rob was the only person who did not know that everybody knew why he was there, including Emily—in that unique female way. When Rob ran out of excuses and could not think of anything else to say to Emily, he said, "Paco, we better go."

Rob and Paco rode to La Luz.

It surprised Emily that she was so sad to see Rob go.

After seeing Rob and Paco ride through town, Jim Healy saddled his horse and watched for them to come back through town. When they did he followed them. He hated Robert Wilson for all the notoriety he was getting. Healy was like a huge pocket of pus ready to explode all over Rob Wilson. After he finished with Rob Wilson, he would go see that little tramp of a meskin girl, and she would receive his attentions—whether she wanted to or not.

Rob was so excited that Emily was going to the fiesta that he did not watch his back trail in his usual way. Rob rattled on about how good that pie was, how clean and neat Ignacio's house was, and how good the coffee was. He said, "Paco, is that the same coffee we use at the ranch? It seems to be better when Emily makes coffee."

Paco smiled in silence.

When they got to La Luz, Rob and Paco located Juan and the three of them had supper at the Mexican cantina.

Healy snuck up to the outside of the building and listened outside the window where he could hear them talking. He heard Rob tell Paco and Juan that he planned to take the boys to El Paso for the Fiesta de Las Flores. Rob planned to leave the Dog Canyon Ranch, go up the Langford trail, up the Sacramento River, and due north overland to Mescalero to pick up Wise Elk and Little Deer. Then they would ride down Tularosa Creek to Tularosa and meet the others. They would stop for Juan in La Luz and send Pepe to the Artesian Well Ranch to tell Turner Sutton and Bill to meet them at

Dog Canyon Ranch. When they were all together, they would all ride to the fiesta in El Paso.

Jim Healy left La Luz at once and rode toward Dog Canyon.

That night Rob and Paco camped outside La Luz with Juan and started for Dog Canyon the next day.

The next day, Healy traveled past the triple box Canyon and on around to the Langford Trail at the base of Tabletop. He rode up the trail to the bench under Tabletop and around the bench on the north side. Healy decided that where the trail dropped down from the end of Pasture Ridge to the bench below Tabletop was a good place for the ambush He rode over the top and a ways up Pasture Ridge to Pasture Ridge waterhole so he could water his horse and so the horse would not give him away when Wilson approached. Then he moved off the trail south to the waterhole. That put his camp and horse out of sight. He staked out his horse and made camp.

The top of Pasture Ridge is flat with a slight downward tilt to the south southeast; it channels all the rain runoff into the natural waterhole at the bottom of the draw. Most people missed it because they did not expect to find a waterhole that high on the ridge. Pasture Ridge waterhole holds water because the rock strata up that high, at almost 6,600 feet, is flat and not folded and broken like most of the rock on the Sacramento Mountains.

Healy waited three days. He waited at his post until long after dark and was back at it before sunrise. Healy was tired of watering his horse and trying to cook in the dark, but he expected Wilson to come by there between a couple of hours after daylight and about noon. That would give Wilson time to leave his Dog Canyon camp and get to the ambush location. He felt he could not take a chance on missing Wilson or on being discovered.

Rob saddled his little spotted rump horse and a packhorse. He said, "Paco, I will try to kill a deer for Wise Elk and his family. Don't get excited if you hear a shot or two up the canyons." Then he said, "Pepe, ride to the Artesian Well Ranch and tell Turner and Bill that we will pick them up to go to El Paso in a few days. I'll send someone to tell them when to meet us here at the Ranch. After you have done that, hurry back here to help Paco." He headed south toward the Langford Trail on his way to Mescalero.

Rob was enjoying the early morning ride. He looked over his ranch and watched for deer. The sound of running deer over the rise into Bug Scuffle Canyon interrupted his thoughts. He decided that to try to follow them for a shot was too far out of the way and rode on up the trail.

Rob was daydreaming about Emily as he was going up the trail. She was so beautiful sitting at the table in the late afternoon sunlight the other afternoon. He was thinking about how directly she looked at him as he was telling the stories. Rob decided he would ask Paco what it meant when a girl looked you in the eye like that. He wondered if enough after a whiles had passed.

When Rob got up to the bench under Tabletop, he was looking to the left and down in the canyon for deer. He was about to start up on to Pasture Ridge when Duke snarled and warned him in time for Rob to draw his Colt and pull back on the reins to stop his horse.

Jim Healy was on Rob's right about 15 feet above him, and about 25 yards away when he called out, "Turn and face me, Wilson. I'm going to kill you."

Rob shouted, "Not if I can help it." As quick as a rattlesnake, he turned to his right and fired. He hit Healy low in the chest and put him on the ground.

But, Healy had gotten off a shot that hit Rob in the chest. The shot knocked Rob off his horse, and he hit the ground with a thud. Rob did not know it at the time, but his shot had exploded Healy's heart and lodged deep in his spine. Healy was dead before he hit the ground.

Rob was in terrible shock. When he hit the ground, it knocked the wind out of him. He was conscious for a few seconds but unable to move or breathe. Then everything faded to black.

Paco, Pepe, Jessie, Julio, and Marco heard the shots, but they were so close together and distorted by the echo of the canyons that they appeared to be one shot from a saddle gun.

Jessie said, "Well, it sounds like Rob found his deer for Wise Elk."

Duke howled over and over, but Paco thought Duke had moved up the canyon and was letting his kind know, he was claiming the area for himself and his mate.

The men closed down Dog Canyon headquarters, satisfied that all the stock was secure, and rode to meet Rob.

They found Juan in La Luz. Paco said, "We are going to Tularosa to meet Rob and pick up the others. We will be back in a couple of days to pick you up to go to El Paso."

They rode to Stephenson's store, and bought supplies for the trip, including a peck each of fresh apricots and cherries. After they packed the wagon, they stopped at Masterson's cantina and Jessie bought everyone a mug of cold beer. After they enjoyed the beer, leftover biscuits, and venison, they proceeded toward Tularosa to set up camp at the Hernández place and wait for Rob.

Back on Pasture Ridge, Rob was unable to move. He drifted in and out of consciousness. The young appaloosa had become a good saddle horse and had been trained to stay hitched to the ground when both reins were dropped on the ground. He stayed with Rob almost ground hitched but when Rob was shot off his horse only the left rein fell to the ground. So the spotted rump horse felt free to move around a little. During a lucid moment, Rob applied his kerchief to his chest wound and passed out again. As luck would have it, or maybe something else, he slumped back on the ground with a flat rock under his back wound. The flat rock, which was about the size of his hand, acted as a pressure bandage and helped control the bleeding.

At the base of the cliffs, rising to form Tabletop a small spring seeped more than enough water for the young horse and Duke. They were on the north side of the big tabletop mountain, where the most luscious vegetation is. The young appaloosa was content to stay close, cropping the green grass. Unlike the packhorse, that after a while, holding his head out to the side, being careful not to step on his lead rope, headed back to the ranch headquarters camp.

Paco, Jessie and the crew unaware of anything wrong had left for La Luz and Rob's pack horse arrived at an empty Dog Canyon camp. The horse missed his expected oat ration but was content to join the remuda in the familiar surroundings even though the packsaddle was still on his back.

That afternoon, as the appaloosa horse was grazing by, Rob was able to grab the stirrup and pull himself up to stand. He told the young horse "Whoa, whoa boy," as calmly as he could and managed to uncinch the saddle and let it and the blanket slide off and fall to the ground. Rob slumped down and greedily drank some water from his canteen and washed his chest wound. He took out his spare long johns from his saddlebags and used them to try to re-bandage his wounds Rob looked at the blood around the flat rock, realized what the flat rock had done, laid down on it on purpose this time and passed out. Sometime after dark, he came to again, drank from the canteen, and managed to unroll his bedroll and partly cover himself before he passed out again. By the time he regained consciousness, the sun was full up.

Rob woke and opened his eyes enough to notice the buzzards had gathered at the top of the cliff where Healy had been and remembered what happened. Rob drank the last of the water in the canteen and it came to him, he was in trouble, big trouble, he needed water.

Choking down panic, Rob inventoried his wounds. He decided that if he had been going to die, he would already be dead. About that time he saw or thought he saw, Duke drink from the spring, and turn and look at him. Rob realized that if he could crawl that short distance, he too could drink from the spring and might be able to refill his canteen. He was too tired right then, but resolved, he would attempt it after a rest.

After another nap, Rob crawled to the spring, dragging his canteen. When he got to the spring he drank deeply, rested, drank again, and filled the canteen. He made it back to his saddle and bedroll before he passed out. But this time he was more asleep than unconscious. He rested most of the day, nibbled on the traveling food from his saddlebags, and drank spring water from the canteen that evening.

Rob looked at the old juniper wood. He was not aware of it, but the climate had changed ever so slightly over the past hundred years and gotten just dry enough for most of the juniper trees on that bench to die. There were dozens of mature trees, many still standing, with their bare limbs reaching up at the sky. His feverish mind thought they were reaching up with their arms and complaining to their Creator.

Rob gathered what wood he could reach without getting up and built a small fire. He was too weak to make coffee or try to cook. The warmth of the fire made him a little more comfortable and improved his spirits, but he was still seriously wounded and *Alone on Pasture Ridge*.

Drifting off to sleep, Rob dreamed of whom he had come to think of, as "his" Emily, and enjoyed watching her in his mind as she stepped off the porch and said, "Hello. My name is Emily Hernández. May I help you?"

Following their plan, after Rob left, Jessie, Paco, Pepe, and the Rodriguez boys had gone to La Luz's, talked to Juan, and gone on to Tularosa. The Dog Canyon crew made camp on the Hernández place and settled down to wait for Rob.

Ignacio and Emily were so glad to see Pepe that they almost forgot they were upset about his disappearance. Emily hugged him, looked at him, and realized he had changed. He was not the little orphan boy she remembered. It was not so much that he was taller, but he was more muscular, and had a manlier look because of his confidence and attitude.

Emily said, "Pepe, you scared me so bad when you left and I couldn't find you. The next day I remembered you did tell me you wanted to go with the cowboys. When I got over my fright, I forgave you for disappearing like that."

The Rodriguez boys proudly returned Ignacio Hernández's two horses and told him and Emily about their adventures. After the stories Marco said, "Señor Jessie, may we be excused to take our extra horses to our family and visit with them?"

Jessie said, "Enjoy your stay with your family. You've earned it. We will come for you when Rob gets here."

Ignacio Hernández invited the rest of the Dog Canyon crew to his home for dinner. They readily agreed. Pepe remembered what a good cook Miss Emily was. Jessie and Paco found out that good coffee is not the only thing Emily could prepare.

They enjoyed a wonderful dinner and related the stories of their trip to the Pecos and on to the Llano Estacado, the trail drive back, the cattle rustlers, Jimmy Lee's capture, and how cleverly Rob handled it. Emily and Ignacio Hernández sat and listened intently, thinking about the newspaper articles. Paco noticed that Emily asked several questions about Rob.

On the second day, Paco and Jessie expected Rob, Wise Elk, and Little Deer to show up by that afternoon. That night they became concerned and met with Ignacio and Emily to discuss what to do. They decided it would be best to wait until morning. Additionally, they decided that if Rob did not show up by noon, they would have to decide whether to go back to the Dog Canyon headquarters and track Rob from there or to go up Tularosa Creek to try to locate him by backtracking his planned route.

Jessie said, "Wise Elk and Little Deer are much better trackers than any of us. Let's send the Rodriguez boys to Mescalero to find Wise Elk and Little Deer and backtrack down the Sacramento. The rest of us can go to Dog Canyon Ranch and track Rob up the trail he took."

Paco said, "Jessie, Pepe, and Ignacio Hernández will ride their horses. Emily will ride in the wagon with me. An extra horse for Juan, Emily's horse and Paco's horse can be tied to the back of the wagon. We can pick up Juan in La Luz on the way to Dog Canyon

Ranch. If Rob is not there, we can go on south to Grapevine Canyon and start up the Langford Trail at the bottom of Tabletop. Juan is familiar with the area, and I am sure we can follow the trail."

After more discussion they decided they would do both.

Jessie said, "Pepe, help Paco pack the wagon. I'll go get Marco and Julio."

When Jessie reached the Rodriguez home, he knocked on the door and waited.

The door opened, and a beautiful girl said, "Yes sir. May I help you?"

Jessie was stunned but said, "Good afternoon, ma'am. I'm Jessie Hatfield. May I speak to Marco and Julio? Something has come up, and we have need of them."

"Why yes sir. Won't you come in? I'll call them for you."

"Thank you, ma'am." Jessie was distracted from his purpose by the girl's attractiveness. She was beautiful, and her posture was awesome. She was tall and lean, and when she walked away, it was a glide with just the hint of a prance. Jessie had a hard time keeping his mind on his business.

The boys came in the room, and he explained what had happened and what they had planned. They would meet at the Hernández place as soon as they could gather their things and saddle their horses.

Marco noticed his sister standing behind him and said, "Señor Jessie, have you met my sister?"

"No, I haven't."

"Señor Jessie, may I present my sister Juanita Rodriguez."

"How do you do, ma'am? It's a pleasure to meet you." Jessie gave a slight bow.

"It's nice to meet you, Señor Whitfield. We have heard much about you. Thank you for being so good to my brothers."

Jessie nodded and knuckled his brow as he said, "Ma'am." And backed out the door.

That afternoon, Julio and Marco started up Tularosa Creek to Mescalero and had no trouble locating Wise Elk and Little Deer. By sundown they were explaining what had happened.

Wise Elk and Little Deer hurriedly packed and they headed south. Wise Elk checked with other Mescalero along the way and learned that nobody had seen or heard from the man of the coyote spirit. They became more concerned. The men pushed hard and made good time.

By the next night, they were at the head of the little lake in Sacramento Canyon where the trail leaves the Sacramento River Valley and turns off to the west.

The group with the wagon stopped in La Luz, long enough for Juan to ask a friend to take care of the goats, gather his possibles, and they rode south. They drank and watered the stock at the creek at Alamo Canyon and were back out in the desert and headed south by afternoon.

While they rode south, Emily asked many questions of Paco, and being inclined to help the young people's relationship along, he answered them. They arrived at what served as the headquarters of the Dog Canyon Ranch late in the afternoon.

The work done at Dog Canyon impressed Ignacio Hernández. There was a big fly tent about twenty feet by twenty feet. The stove was on the east end of the tent, and a metal smokestack went through the tent to vent the smoke out of the kitchen. A long wooden table with benches on both sides was big enough to seat twelve cowboys. The tent had rolled up side walls that could be unrolled if the weather turned bad. The wagon trailer under the tent held bedding and other supplies stored in it to keep it in the dry. Even though there were no big buildings yet, there was a sturdy two-holer outhouse.

There were two bull strong, horse high corrals: one was considerably larger than the other. Attached to the east fence of the larger corral was a chute that was wide enough for the adult cattle except the longhorns and long enough for three head. It had slots for separator poles to separate each of the three compartments and the end compartment had one side that hinged so it could be closed hard against its occupant to hold it still. Ignacio had heard of these contraptions but had never seen one. He made a mental note to ask

Rob about it when they were together again. The stock appeared to be thriving, and he especially approved of the condition of the horses.

Pepe and Paco built a fire in the pit and in the big stove.

Paco and Emily cooked dinner, while Jessie skinned a deer he had killed and hung on their teepee poles. Paco showed Emily and Ignacio his famous stove. Juan scouted the spring and the arroyos.

Paco heard Duke howling in the distance, far up the canyons but he thought Duke had moved because they had been gone.

Ignacio Hernández replaced a loose shoe on one of their horses.

They had fried deer liver, venison back strap, fried potatoes with onions, frijoles with Emily's extra touch, and fresh cherry pie. Of course they had hot biscuits and the big chuck wagon coffee pot full of hot bitter goodness.

They had a bad feeling about Rob and were anxious to get on his trail in the morning. Paco, Emily, and Pepe packed the wagon that night, leaving only the chuck table down so they could have coffee and leftovers in the morning.

The next morning, Wise Elk and his group headed west over the top of the ridge and down the ridge above Pine Spring Canyon. They rode above Rock Waterhole Canyon and over Jake's Ridge. By late morning, they were riding west on the east end of Pasture Ridge.

In the gray of the predawn, Jessie and Paco's bunch coffeed up and ate breakfast while Paco and Emily packed the wagon. Ignacio finished his coffee and watched Emily. He marveled that, like her mother, Emily could even on a trail drive, appear the next morning washed, combed, clean and pressed, looking like she had walked out of her room at home.

The men saddled the horses, hitched up the team, and gathered extra packhorses and mounts.

Ignacio Hernández found the packhorse with the packsaddle. That scared everybody ... Something was definitely wrong.

They started off south with Ignacio and Jessie leading, Paco and Emily in the wagon and Pepe and Juan herding their small remuda. By mid-morning, they rounded the foothill under tabletop and stopped when they crossed the Langford trail. They unhitched the wagon and set up a base camp west of the mouth of Bug Scuffle Canyon. Having learned their lesson about the flash floods, they located their camp on top of the first rise away from the arroyo coming out of Grapevine Canyon and below the beautiful little round mountain in the mouth of Bug Scuffle Canyon. They staked out the mules to graze.

The men were going to start up the trail, leaving Pepe to lookout for Emily when she threw a fit and said, "You are not going to leave me here. I'm going to look for Rob." She tightened the cinch on the saddle of the spare horse.

Ignacio did not argue with her. In fact he was relieved at not leaving her behind alone with Pepe. He was not sure Pepe could protect her. He had not seen Pepe in a gunfight shooting Indians out of the saddle, shooting rustlers, herding cattle and horses or branding the stock and did not realize how much the young man had matured.

They headed up the trail and by noon, they were on the bench below Tabletop. As they rounded the western point, Jessie saw Rob's horse a little over a mile ahead of them on the east end of the bench and took off at a gallop. The rest of the group followed.

Duke howled, whined, and danced around, leading them to Rob, who was unconscious and burning up with fever.

Emily and Paco bathed him with cool cloths. Paco told Pepe to build a fire and boil water in Rob's coffeepot. Emily was almost in tears, but she put on a good face and talked to Rob the whole time putting on a show of everything being just fine.

Jessie scouted around where he saw the buzzards and found Jim Healy—or what was left of him. The evidence made it clear what had happened, and Jessie wondered how long Healy had been waiting, to have wallowed out such a hole. He gathered Healy's gun belt and Henry rifle and checked his clothes for money and papers. He followed the tracks back to Healy's camp and led his horse back to the group. Nobody even suggested taking the time to bury what was left of Healy.

They needed to get Rob to a doctor as soon as possible and were trying to decide if the wagon would make it up the trail. Juan told them it might but it would take longer to go back down, get the wagon, and get it up that steep, treacherous trail than it would to build a travois with the long arms of juniper wood and the tarps from the packhorses. Then, with their gentlest horse pulling the travois and two cowboys holding it steady with ropes, they could get back down to the wagon. Everyone agreed and started working.

While the cowboys were building the travois, the medical team worked on Rob to reduce the fever. Pepe built a fire and made willow bark tea. They bathed Rob with cool water, and Paco gave him the tea. They tried to get him to drink more water. Rob was only semi-conscious and much of it ran down his chest and belly, but he did drink part of it.

In less than an hour, they were starting around Tabletop with Emily walking on the uphill side beside Rob and Paco walking on the other. Jessie and Ignacio each had their lariats looped around the lower end of the main drag poles. They were steadying the travois as it moved down the trail. Juan led the horse that pulled it. Pepe was in charge of the other horses and brought up the rear.

Rob was delirious and said, "You are so beautiful, Emily. I missed you so much. I am so happy you came to go to the party. Promise me you will save more than one dance for me."

Emily was un-nerved by his boldness but she acted as though nothing was unusual and said, "Why, thank you, Mr. Wilson." She blushed and added in a whisper. "I missed you too." She held Rob's hand and periodically bathed his face with cool spring water from Rob's canteen she had hung on the travois.

Paco said, "Pepe, take the extra stock down the trail as fast as you can. Build a fire and get water boiling for willow bark tea. Open the wagon's chuck table, wash it with boiling water, and clear it so we can work on Rob. Find all the empty flour sacks we can use for bandages, and put some of them in another pot of boiling water. Now hurry."

"Si, señor." Pepe left with the horses in a cloud of dust.

When they had gotten off the bench and down the steepest part of the trail, they stopped to rest.

The men gathered for a discussion while Emily talked to Rob and bathed his face with cool water.

Jessie raised the possibility of going straight to El Paso, about two and a half days.

Juan said, "There is a new doctor in La Luz—only one long day away—but I do not know much about him."

Ignacio Hernández said, "There is an excellent doctor in Tularosa. He has a lot of experience with gunshot wounds during the War Between the States. However, that is an extra half day farther away than La Luz."

While they were talking, they heard horses coming around Tabletop. The men shucked their saddle guns and took defensive positions. They placed Emily and Rob behind the horses, and Paco helped Juan anchor the horse attached to the travois.

Before the riders came into view over the edge of the bench, Duke howled and did his circle dance.

Paco relaxed, and as the riders appeared over the ledge, the others recognize Wise Elk, Little Deer, and the Rodríguez brothers, who joined the group and dismounted. Everybody was talking at once and Wise Elk raised his hands and motioned for quiet. He spoke to Paco, looked at Rob, and smiled ever so slightly at Emily.

While the Rodriguez boys related their story, Paco explained to the Mescalero what had happened. They listened to the story of Wise Elk and the other riders and learned they had had a very uneventful trip until a little while ago when they found the ambush site.

Everyone mounted up and started down the mountain for the wagon camp. Julio and Marco rode on to see if they could help Pepe. Little Deer followed Paco along walking beside Rob with his horse un-tethered but following Little Deer like a well-mannered puppy. Wise Elk silently brought up the rear on his horse.

It was late afternoon when they got down to the wagon camp, the boys had gathered wood, built a fire, boiled the water, made coffee, and cooked the beans. At Pepe's direction, they had washed the wagon table with boiling water. Pepe had arranged the bandages and their only bottle of whiskey on the chuck wagon table and found Paco's sewing kit and set it out. Then he had filled and hung all three of their lanterns up over the table and made the willow bark tea.

Pepe said, "I'm sorry, Paco. I did not know what else to do."

Paco smoothed Pepe's hair and said, "My son, you did a very good job."

They carried Rob to the table and gently placed him on it. He groaned when they moved him, but was out of his head with fever.

Paco washed his hands and asked Emily to wash hers. "Pepe, light the lamps. It will be dark soon."

Paco crossed himself. Emily followed Paco's example and added a little prayer.

While Emily was spooning willow bark tea into him, Rob asked, "How many more after a whiles are you going to need?"

Emily had no idea what he was talking about but said, "I don't know, Rob—not many more."

That seemed to satisfy him, and he was quiet while Paco and Ignacio took off Rob's shirt and performed a more thorough examination. There was a small entry wound on his chest and a larger exit wound on the left side of his back that had an unusual shaped bruise around it.

Paco had seen the blood around the flat rock where they found Rob and suspected he knew the source of the bruise. Paco said, "You men all help hold Rob as steady as possible. Emily, are you sure you want to help? There will be blood. Are you positive you can assist me?"

She was offended and said, "Paco, I am an accomplished nurse. I will have no trouble seeing a little blood."

Paco shrugged and washed Rob's wounds with hot water. Using the torn strips of flour sacks that had been boiled, he washed the wounds with whiskey as the Doctor had instructed. Then he took his tweezers and plucked the shreds of fabric out of the chest wound with little complaint from Rob.

Emily dabbed at the wounds with a whiskey-soaked cloth behind Paco as he cleaned the wounds.

Paco broke off the arrowhead from one of Little Deer's arrows, took a boiled strip of cloth, pulled it into a notch on the arrow shaft tip and tied it. He soaked the shaft and the cloth in whiskey. Paco passed it through the path of the bullet to sterilize the wound in Rob's chest. Rob tensed up, whimpered, and passed out.

Paco said, "Bueno … good … good."

Emily blotted the perspiration from Rob's face.

Paco took his sewing kit, put a few neat stitches around the chest wound and did his best to close the wound on Rob's back.

Emily was there with the small scissors to snip the stitches as Paco tied the knots, and she blotted the wounds with the whiskey-soaked cloth. Paco was impressed with Emily.

Wise Elk had gathered spider webs for Paco to place on the wounds to help stop the bleeding. Paco started to slosh whiskey on the webs, but Wise Elk said, "No. Es no necesario. They pure."

Paco placed the spider webs on both wounds, and Wise Elk made a poultice from lichens, moss, leaves, and roots from desert plants and handed it to Paco.

Paco put part of the poultice on each wound, and he and Emily wrapped Rob with the bandages.

Rob was delirious and burning up with fever. He was humming a tune and babbling to Emily about how he was sure his little sister would really like her.

Jessie was startled and thought with dread, *I will have to tell this girl all about Rob's sister and family.*

Emily continued to bathe his head and face with cool water. She regularly spooned willow bark tea into him.

He thanked her for the lovely soup and hummed away.

Paco washed his hands and said, "The bullet passed through Rob's chest without hitting his heart or lungs or large blood tubes. As bad as that was, he survived. Somehow he stopped the bleeding that usually kills most people who get shot in the chest."

Pepe poured coffee for everybody, and Paco said, "As good as all that is, the wound has putrefied. The fever is trying to kill the putrefaction. The doctor in La Luz called the cause of the putrefaction germs. He said the fever was good for killing the germs, but the fever can kill the patient while making war on the germs. We must control the fever—but still let it do its work on the germs."

After cleaning up the chuck table and covering Rob, Paco said, "The doctors may have medicine to help, but Wise Elk's poultices probably are as good as anything. The spider webs help the blood clot, and the herbs and whatever is in the poultice helps work on the germs. The amazing thing is Wise Elk and his kind don't know about germs. They just know what they know—and it works."

The group discussed where they were going to take Rob. They agreed that because time was the most important factor; Rob would be taken to La Luz.

Ignacio said, "I will send for the doctor in Tularosa and ask him to meet us in La Luz. Marco, at first light, take my horse and ride as fast as you can without killing him to Tularosa. Tell Dr. Esteban Chavez to meet us in La Luz at Dr. Peterson's office. Julio, ride to La Luz and tell Dr. Peterson that Dr. Chavez is coming. Tell him what has happened and that we are on our way."

Juan said, "Julio, when you get to La Luz, go to the church and find the padre. He will help you. Tell Father Ryan that I asked him to help you find Dr. Peterson. Explain what has happened—that Dr. Chavez is on his way and that we will be there as soon as possible."

Duke stayed on the edge of the light of the lanterns and watched Rob.

In his delirium, Rob broke into song. Duke sang along with him in coyote harmony, which shocked everybody. They had never seen Duke stay so close to camp, and they had never heard him sing up close.

Emily took one of Rob's hands and let it hang down. Duke timidly eased up to it and sniffed Rob's fingers. That seemed to satisfy him, and he walked out into the night. Duke did not go far, and every time Rob broke into song, he would sing his own tune in duet.

That seemed to please Wise Elk and he kneeled on the ground beside Rob, and started an Apache chant, and shook a beaded rattle in rhythm with the chant.

Paco cooked supper, and everybody but Wise Elk ate with little relish. He was still chanting and shaking the rattle. The supper and the hot coffee were good for their spirits, and they felt a little better.

Sometime around midnight, Rob's fever broke.

Emily observed his drop in temperature and called Paco.

Wise Elk was still chanting and rattling the beaded gourd. When Emily called Paco, Wise Elk stopped, looked at Rob, and nodded.

Emily continued to bathe Rob's face with the cool cloths as he began to come around.

When Rob opened his eyes, Emily said, "Hello."

Rob smiled and said a little thickly, "I've heard you say that before."

Emily said, "Yes, Mr. Robert Wilson, and I hope you hear it many more times."

Wise Elk said, "Man of coyote spirit will come back to be with raven-haired girl now."

The Duke of Dog Canyon did a little dance and told the moon good morning. Just like he understood everything would be fine now. He stretched a big dog stretch—all the way down low—, then went trotting off to find the pretty duchess.

Cover Copy

While the landscape and the landmarks of southern New Mexico are real, the story and characters are figments of my imagination.

Rob Wilson is a young man whose family dies of typhoid fever in East Texas in the 1870s. To forget the pain of his loss, Rob sells the home place, and travels to southern New Mexico with his friend Jessie. Rob is befriended by a coyote and meets an old Mexican cook, a gringo rancher, and his foreman, a Mescalero Apache chief, a young brave, two teenage Mexican cowboys, and a stowaway Mexican orphan. They integrate all these characters into a wild adventure to the Llano Estacado to find a lost herd of cattle. While assembling this unusual group, Rob meets a beautiful Mexican girl and tries to win her for his own.

Unbeknown to Rob and the others, the accounts of their adventures filter back to a newspaperman in El Paso. He writes a series of articles about Rob and his outfit, publishes them in the newspaper, and makes them all famous.

Rob has trouble accepting being a hero and is ashamed of the exaggerations of his exploits. When he finally adjusts to being a hero, he finds a way to use the process that painted him as heroic to paint a new word picture of his outfit as a fearsome fighting force. It discourages outlaws and rustlers from trying to exploit the image of young and old gringos, Mexicans, and Indians who have more cattle than they can handle.

It is a warm, sometimes humorous, sometimes heartbreaking story about a young man in the 1870s in the country where I grew up and hunted deer, antelope, doves, quail, ducks, and Indian artifacts for forty years. And where I looked for and found the southern New Mexico landmarks from the stories and tales I read about in books, and heard from ranchers, cowboys, and lawmen. I enjoyed mentally riding through that landscape and watching Rob Wilson and his friends building a cattle ranch in the Tularosa Basin while they learned a few of the hard lessons of the old West.

Printed in the United States
By Bookmasters